Active duty is no time for ,
themselves in truly close qu
to fraternize is hard to resist. Can two ambitious sailors follow orders
long enough to see if love is on the horizon when they're finally above
water?

Lieutenant Nic Riley is the only girl in a long-time Navy family, and she's determined to prove she's just as seaworthy as her brothers. When she aces training for submarine duty, it calls for a celebration—and one incredibly hot guy is happy to party with her all night long. But when Nic boards the sub and finds herself face to face with her hunky fling, the idea of spending six months underwater takes on a whole new meaning . . .

Having a girl in every port was Lieutenant Kyle Hutchinson's style—until the explosive night he spent with Nic. Dating onboard is firmly off limits, but Kyle can't get her off his mind much less out of his vicinity—until a junior seaman's devastating stunt puts Nic's career in danger. Kyle won't let her take the heat alone, even when it means risking his own reputation, but fighting for a future together will be a whole new battle . . .

Books by Gail Chianese

The West Side Romance Series
Bachelorette for Sale
Boyfriend for Hire
Fiancé for Keeps

The Changing Tides Series
Love Runs Deep

Published by Kensington Publishing Corporation

Love Runs Deep
The Changing Tides Series

Gail Chianese

LYRICAL PRESS
Kensington Publishing Corp.
www.kensingtonbooks.com

First Electronic Edition:
eISBN-13: 978-1-5161-0029-3
eISBN-10: 1-5161-0029-8

First Print Edition:
ISBN-13: 978-1-5161-0030-9
ISBN-10: 1-5161-0030-1

Printed in the United States of America

For all the women who serve. You ladies ROCK!
And for my grandpa, the first sailor I ever loved and who introduced me
to the magical world of books.

Acknowledgements

Years ago Eloisa James asked me why wasn't I writing about the world I knew so well—Navy life—after all, I've lived it for years. I guess I was just waiting for the right story to come along, but I have to thank her for putting that thought in my head.

I also couldn't have written this without the help of CDR Shawn Huey who took the time to answer my questions on current life on a fast-attack submarine.

Many thanks go out the former crewmembers of the USS Parche SSN 683, the most decorated submarine in the US Navy for sharing their stories with me. But there's one sailor in particular that I owe more than thanks to and that's my amazing husband, CWO James Chianese (also of the fore mention USS Parche) who not only answered about a bazillion questions, but read the story for accuracy. Any "errors" are solely my fault or liberties my imagination has taken. I love you, honey. Thank you.

To my editor, Martin Biro, thank you for your patience, input, and support.

To my amazing writing chapter, Connecticut Romance Writers, I'd be lost without you; especially my MTB's!

And to you dear readers, thank you for spending your time with me. As always, I am honored and forever grateful.

Chapter One

Music pounded in her ears and chest. Smoke filled the air, stinging her eyes. The smell of sweat and stale beer tickled her noise and Lieutenant Lily "Nic" Riley couldn't be happier. After weeks of study in preparation for life on a submarine, she and her fellow female officers had not only survived fire training, but also the wet trainer. Having twenty thousand gallons of water pumped into a small, enclosed space and then sticking a hood over her face had been almost more than she could handle. In the end, she proved her father wrong; she could take it like a man.

"Let's pray we never have to go out the escape trunk in real life. Y'all, I almost lost it right there." Cherise Johnson's slow southern drawl dragged the sentence out.

"Really?" Lindsey Pratt looked from Cherise to Nic and back. "I thought it was killer fun. Sure beats tipping cows in Nowhereville, Kansas."

"I'm with Cherise, once was more than enough." Nic raised her glass. "A toast to us, the future rock stars of the Navy and for kicking butt during training."

The three tapped the rims of their glasses together before taking sips of their drinks, or in Lindsey's case, downing half the bottle. They made an interesting and contrasting trio. Cherise with her close-cropped curls, curve-hugging dress, stilettos, and don't-mess-with-me face. It wasn't that she wasn't nice; she simply kept people at a distance. Lindsey, who had burned her good girl clothes the minute she boarded the bus for boot camp, wore leggings, knee-high boots, and a slinky top that was only held up by her double D's. Her blond, unruly curls fit Linds's personality. Both friends made Nic's outfit look very girl next door. Even her waist-length brownish-black hair hung straight as a stick.

In normal life, chances were low the three of them would have crossed paths, but the Navy had a way of bringing people together, of creating bonds stronger than blood and flesh. While Nic and Cherise had served together aboard the *USS Ronald Reagan* a few years back, they didn't meet up with Linds, who was brand new to the Navy, until sub school.

They'd ditched the base as soon as liberty hit, heading north and away from fellow squids and prying eyes. Being the only Navy brat in the group, Nic was familiar with New England and picked Boston as their destination.

New York would have been fun, if it hadn't been Fleet Week. All she wanted was a weekend of fun where she could forget she was the Admiral's daughter.

"Just think, in five days we'll report to our first boats. One hundred and forty men and me. Sounds like heaven." Lindsey took another drink of her beer and looked around.

"Um, Lindsey, you know you can't date the men on your boat, right?" Cherise, ever the practical one, pointed out the bad news to their man-crazed friend. "Fraternization?"

"Nic, tell me she's joshing."

"Technically, it's only against the rules if he's either over you or under you," Nic replied.

"Well, those are my favorite positions." Lindsey winked. "But man, does that suck the fun out of the whole deal. Guess we better get our fill tonight to hold us over. And Lordy, we've got some mighty fine selections to choose from."

Nic let her gaze travel around the bar. She'd picked this place on the recommendation of a friend who had lived in the area specifically because said friend had promised it wasn't popular with the military crowd. The men-to-women ratio was in their favor. Not that she was looking to get laid like Lindsey, but it would be nice to let her hair down and have a little fun.

"Pick up a guy from a bar?" Cherise's stiff posture and snippy tone sent Lindsey sliding off her stool. "No way. I'll pass. My mom would roll in her grave—if she were dead. Plus, he could be a psychopath."

"Whatever." Lindsey went and stood at the bar, her back to her friends, head held high.

"Cherise, hon, don't you think that came out a little harsh?"

This was not what Nic wanted, to play the mediator, but she wanted to cut the tension and get back to relaxing. Once they reported aboard their respective boats it would be nothing but hard work and her focus would be strictly on business.

"Maybe, but that's all she talks about—men and sex. Some of us weren't raised that way."

"Neither was Linds. Her dad is a pastor and her boyfriend broke up with her right before she reported to sub school. Do me a favor?" She reached out and gave Cherise's arm a squeeze. "Go easy on her tonight."

Cherise nodded and Lindsey came bouncing back to the table with a fresh drink for each of them. "Nic, check your six. You've got an admirer."

Grabbing her phone, Nic slid off her stool and went around the table to stand in between her friends where she could get a good look. She held the phone up, reversed the camera, enlarged the screen and hit the button. While she was at it, she took a second picture, this time of the three of them. Going back to her seat, she brought up the first shot and checked out the guy in question. Good looking in a rakish-sort of way. Light eyes. Maybe blue, maybe gray? Hard to say from a picture. High, sharp cheekbones, a couple days' worth of growth along the jaw line and framing his mouth, which drew her attention to his very kissable lips. Fit, and with his messy, long chestnut brown hair there was no way he was military. Meaning he was a perfect choice.

Should she be interested.

Which she wasn't sure if she was or not.

Linds wasn't the only one who had wounds to lick, although Nic had dumped her own boyfriend, not the other way around. It had been over for a year, not weeks like her friend's relationship, and she couldn't say she'd been bitter about the break-up. More like relieved, which told her she hadn't been *in* love. Thank goodness since Mark had the emotional maturity of a thirteen-year-old and the staying power of cheap glue.

The whole thing did make her question her ability to feel deep emotions, because she always picked guys like him. Guys who seemed great at first, loved to have a good time, who everyone loved, made everyone laugh and yet, couldn't see past the end of the day to plan for tomorrow much less the future.

The music broke and deep, masculine laughter rumbled through the room, dragging every woman's attention in the place to the men at the pool table. Mr. Smooth's hand clamped down on his buddy's shoulder before stepping away to allow the man to take his shot.

He lifted his head as he brought the frosty beer to his mouth, eyes locked on to Nic and in that moment the world around her slowed. Her breath caught in the back of her throat and heat rushed her cheeks.

The corners of his mouth slipped upward right before he saluted her with his bottle and took a long pull, eyes never releasing her.

She broke first, turning back to her friends.

Linds grinned like a damn fool and Cherise sat with her mouth hanging open.

"What?" Nic didn't wait for them to answer. She took the last swallow of her Chambord and soda to moisten her desert-dry mouth and stalked off to the bathroom to splash cold water over the back of her wrists.

Holy guacamole. She needed more than cold water after that smoldering look; more like a time-out on an iceberg. Desire and embarrassment from the thoughts racing through her brain sent heat coursing through her body, turning her pale skin bright pink. Thank goodness for bar lighting. Since she didn't see any handy icebergs, she grabbed a paper towel, ran it under ice cold water and placed it on the back of her neck.

What the heck was up with her? It took more than a pretty face to turn her to mush. She needed a guy with a sense of humor, a personality, and brains, which is why even though she'd succumbed to Mark's soulful brown eyes, she'd hadn't *fallen*. Okay, she'd admit his rockin' hot bod had helped, but that was kind of expected when the guy's a Navy SEAL.

Still she knew better. After all, she also had two older, good-looking brothers and watched friend after friend fall for them, only to be crushed when Liam and Reece looked the other way.

As her body temp cooled down, Nic shoved thoughts of the past and the future away. Deep contemplation of her future or past wasn't for tonight. Nothing could be done about the one and the other wasn't here yet. Nope, tonight was all about fun, hanging with her girls, and living in the moment.

Making her way back to the table, she let her gaze linger on the men around the pool table. Her 'friend' from earlier, for lack of a better word, currently had his backside to her as he bent over the table to take a shot. *Not bad.*

As if he felt her gaze on him, he looked over his shoulder. One corner of his mouth lifted in a caught-you smile. Then he turned away and took his shot, sending his ball into the opposite pocket. She left him to his game and joined her actual friends, who had played musical chairs, putting her in the perfect spot to see and be seen by him.

Both Lindsey and Cherise had grins a mile wide on their faces and there were three fresh drinks on the table. Looks like one of them had a goal to get drunk tonight.

"Uh, guys thanks for the drink, but I'm not sure I want another yet." Nic twirled the ice around in her glass. At least it'd give her something to focus on other than a certain guy.

"We didn't order them." Lindsey's smile twinkled with mischief.

"Nope," Cherise chimed in. "These are from your admirer. Not that you have to do anything about it, but it is nice to be noticed once in a while."

Nic looked to each of her friends, to her drink, and, finally, across the room. Mr. Smooth lifted his beer in a salute, which she acknowledged with a smile and a nod.

"Suppose we should go over and thank him," Lindsey mused out loud.

"It is the proper thing to do." Cherise's pinched face didn't match her words, probably worrying again that the men at the pool table were serial killers or something.

"I wonder if his friend could teach me how to play," Linds asked.

Right. The chances were high that Lindsey wasn't talking billiards. Whatever; the girl deserved a fun night out as much as the rest. Even if she'd been the type to judge, Nic was in no place to do so. Something about glass houses and throwing stones flitted around her brain.

She hesitated, not really in the mood, but knew Lindsey would nag about wasted opportunity and Cherise would fret about proper protocol until she gave in and talked to the guy. *Ugh.* The things she did for friends.

Nic took a couple of minutes to calm the bouncing bumble in her stomach before walking over. She stood next to a pillar by the pool table, out of range of getting poked with a cue stick. It was Mr. Smooth's turn to shoot, and he had his back to her where she quietly admired his form. Feeling a little stalkerish, she cleared her throat. Not once did he look over his shoulder at her. The guy had focus, that's for sure.

* * *

Kyle Hutchinson hadn't started the day with any plans other than getting the hell away from home as fast as a commercial jet could fly. Five days with his family was more than he could take. One minute more of listening to his dad rag on him about taking care of him and his mom or being there for his dumbass brothers and he'd explode. Regardless of what his old man said, he wasn't running away from his responsibilities.

Hadn't he taken leave and flown home the second he'd gotten word about his mom's heart attack? Didn't he send home money every month to make sure the rent got paid? Of course if the dipshit twins, Keith and Kenny, would get jobs, his mom could cut back her hours. Just because Kyle chose to show his support from afar, didn't make him a cold-hearted bastard.

He knew not to let the barbs sink in, that he should be more than used to the comments and verbal slashing, but ten hours later and his dad's parting words still stung like a fresh wound with saltwater rushing over the raw flesh.

So yeah, while he'd started the day out with very few plans, after the guys picked him up at the airport and suggested that they grab a couple of rooms and find a place with cheap drinks and a pool table, he jumped at the chance. He didn't have to report back into the command until Monday morning. They'd have very little downtime for the next six months once the boat got underway. They'd also have no female companionship either, but he wasn't looking to get laid. Not that he had anything against sex.

Then again, if opportunity knocked, it would be hard not to answer.

After all, this would be their last night out before getting underway in a couple of days and so far they didn't have any port calls scheduled. One hundred and eighty days of playing hide and seek with the enemy.

When his buddy, Bryant Gatlin, pointed out the women, Kyle had originally dismissed them, until *she* turned her head. He wouldn't describe her as pretty, at least not in the traditional sense. More like striking. Almond eyes, full lush lips, dark slashing brows that didn't fit with her slim face and creamy pale complexion. She was intriguing; some sort of mixed heritage that took the best of both parents and came out with the perfect package.

He could have gone on ignoring her too, except for that moment. If he hadn't looked up and caught the hungry yet wary look in her eyes, seen the flare of attraction when she met his gaze, he could have gone back to his game. Her instant dismissal piqued his curiosity. She dressed like she was heading out for a weekend picnic—flat shoes, short pants and T-shirt that hung loose on her frame, a sort of don't-see-me vibe, comfortable, casual but not the type to draw attention—rather than a woman on the prowl in a Boston bar. Maybe they had driven in from the Cape for a night of excitement? Yet, by the look of her two friends, who were dressed to impress, that didn't ring true for him. Curiosity got the best of him. He went against his better judgment and bought a round of drinks for the ladies hoping she'd come over to say thanks.

The three stopped short of getting in the way of his game and waited. He sunk the eight ball and held out a hand to his buddy, Mace Havers.

"Ladies, care to join us in a game? Mace, here, is on a losing streak and could use some help." Kyle pocketed the twenty that had been the wager between the two of them and held out the cue stick.

"Only if I wanted to make money by betting against myself, but thanks for the offer and the drink." Nic replied.

He liked her warm voice and the tilt of her head, confident with a touch of humor flashing in her eyes. This close up he could see she'd barely reach the middle of his chest putting her somewhere around five-four. The pièce de résistance was the sprinkling of freckles across her nose and over her cheeks.

He'd always been a sucker for freckles.

"Trust me, you can't be anywhere as bad as Mace." He offered up the cue to prove his faith.

She smiled and shook her head as she slid onto a nearby stool.

The petite blonde looked to Mace before answering. "I've played a little before. I'll partner with you."

"Count me out. I'm more of a darts girl," the tall black woman said.

"Well, looks like I'm stuck with Bryant as a partner." Kyle let out an exasperated sigh. "Guy can't shoot straight to save his life."

The third member of their party walked up in time to hear his comment. "Right, Hutch. Run with that, but we know the truth," Bryant said.

"He says that now, but I'm not the one who prematurely shot his last ball." Kyle winked at the woman before gesturing to Mace to go ahead and rack 'em.

"Whatever. I'll pass on this round. I'm going to see if I can get my ass kicked in darts too, just to round out the weekend humiliation," Bryant said.

Kyle's phone rang. He tossed Mace the stick and told them to start without him as he headed outside to take the call. He hit the Talk button.

"Mom, is everything okay?"

He listened to his mom ramble about how much she missed him already, how she wished he would come home to stay but knew his naval career was important to him.

"Don't let your father's words drive you away. You know he doesn't mean anything he says."

"Already forgotten and you're supposed to be resting. Not stressing about me. Thankfully it was only a mild attack this time. I'll call you when we return home, but if you need me before then, you've got the contact numbers. Love you, Mom."

As he headed back inside he put thoughts of his family out of his mind. He'd worry about his mom the whole underway, but he'd left both her and her doctor a list of names of people who could get a message to him in case of an emergency. It was the best he could do for now.

Mace and the blonde were laughing over something at the pool table, Bryant and the other woman were deep into a game of darts. Still perched on the barstool, sat... *Well damn.* He hadn't had a chance to get her name before he'd stepped out and now she wasn't alone. There went his plans for the night. Not that he'd planned to get laid, but given the option to hang with the guys or a beautiful woman, he'd taken option B every time.

Guess he'd read her wrong, because he'd sensed a reciprocated interest.

Based on the way the college boy was all up in her space and she didn't seem to be putting up a fight, he'd misjudged her interest.

Looks like it's just me and my pool stick tonight.

Not a big deal. He knew he wasn't God's gift to women—that would be Bryant—but he was usually good at reading body language and facial cues, especially from the opposite sex. He'd have to brush up on his skills, but for now it didn't really matter, as   he wasn't looking for a hook-up or a long-term deal. Kyle started to walk past. Then stopped when he noted her rigid posture, clenched jaw, and the defensive position of her hands.

"Come on baby, just one drink."

"Take off. I'm not interested." She punctuated each word before meeting Kyle's gaze.

"You need to loosen up. I got what you need right here." The college kid grabbed her hand and shoved it against his crotch.

She ripped her hand away and Kyle stepped up, pushing his way in between the two. "Beat it, pal. The lady said no."

The jerk took a step back and eyed Kyle from head to toe before crossing his arms in front of him and sneering. "Yeah, what are you? Her boyfriend or something?"

"We'll go with something like a guy who's had a hard week and wouldn't mind finding a release." Kyle stepped in closer, getting in the guy's face and invading his private space.

The guy looked him over again, then glanced over his shoulder before bringing his attention back to Kyle. "Hey, if uptight teases are your deal, she's all yours."

Kyle watched as the guy sauntered away and turned around only when the loudmouth had rejoined his buddies at the bar.

"Thanks for coming to my rescue," she said.

"I get the feeling he's the one who should say thanks."

Her smile kicked up a notch. "Really? Why is that?"

"You might be little, but I think you could have kicked his ass. Then what? The bartender would have had to toss you out and I'd never even get a chance to learn your name."

She cocked her head to the side, with a look that said she was debating her options. "I'm a little surprised actually."

"About?"

"Well, I didn't exactly fall into your arms after you bought me and my friends drinks."

"You weren't obligated to."

She swirled the ice around in her glass, studying it, searching for the right words, or deciding on her next move. He let her take her time, all the while fighting the urge to play connect the dots with her freckles.

Smoldering dark brown eyes with tiny flecks of gold, framed by short black lashes met his gaze. "Most guys who had been turned down would have left me on my own. So either you're a really nice guy or a serial killer luring me into a false sense of security."

"My grandmother would strike me down from the heavens above if I ignored a lady in need."

Her tongue swept across her full bottom lip in a nervous gesture before a small smile lifted the corners of her mouth. "Well, we wouldn't want that to happen. I'm Nic, and thank you again."

She held out her hand and when he took it in his, a sizzling spark of energy shot through him. He wondered what would happen if she were pressed against him from chest to thigh, skin to skin.

"Kyle, and you're welcome. What brings you ladies out tonight? Celebrating or getting away from the kids?"

She left her hand in his. "Celebrating a work accomplishment. What about you? Escaping the wife and rugrats?"

He noted her vague response and smiled. "Nope. Unattached. Flew in this evening from the West Coast and blowing off steam after a long, stressful week."

"Amen. Had one of those myself." She raised her glass to him. "Here's to a night of forgetting about the drudgery of work and having fun."

A woman after his own heart. He tipped his bottle to her glass and drank. After the week he had at home dealing with his family, he didn't want to think about work or anything. Shoot some pool, chill with his boys, and flirt with a pretty woman. Monday would come soon enough and with it, the demands and stress of being an officer on a submarine.

But what he wanted more than anything else right then was to feel this woman in his arms. The music switched to some slow, sultry old-school ballad.

"Care to dance?" He held out his hand and waited.

***

She didn't make him wait long. Placing her hand in his, she let him lead her to a dark corner on the dance floor. They moved in sync, her body snuggled up against him, causing her heart to stumble and trip over itself as every nerve in her body lit up with excitement.

It was one dance, so why not, she'd thought. She'd had no idea the minute he took her in his arms her body would come alive and her brain would start to shut down.

He was big, almost a foot taller than her, and solid muscle as she found out when her hands slid up his chest to land on top of strong shoulders. His hands moved too, from her hips to the small of her back, and down to mold to the curve of her butt.

Somewhere in the back of her mind a little voice told her she should make him move his hands. Another voice, louder and with a mischievous laugh said to live a little, have some fun.

His breath—shallow, slow, and warm—tickled the hollow below her ear. He pulled her closer, his hands still cupping her rear and his erection pressed against her. She may have let out a little moan, or that may have been Kyle. Her brain had ceased thinking straight, it was impossible to do more than feel and oh, did it feel wonderful. Clearly she'd lost her mind, but she didn't care. This man made her feel wicked and wanted.

Years of self-control and being the good girl slid away like ice cream melting on a hot summer day. Under her palms hard muscle flexed as his hands took a leisurely stroll up and down her backside. When he said her name and dipped his head, she angled hers to meet him halfway.

The kiss caressed her mouth, leaving her wanting more. Then he swept his tongue across and past her parted lips. He tasted of warm beer and dark desires and sent her head spinning. Never before had one man affected her as intensely or in such a short time. As everything inside of her turned to molten heat, she threw caution to the wind and did something she said she'd never do again.

"Do you want to get out of here?" she whispered.

Chapter Two

Another reason Nic and her friends had chosen the bar: it was next door to their hotel. Not that she had envisioned making a mad dash from one to the other, barely taking the time to tell them where she was going with a guy she'd just met. No, that was lunacy, and if the trip to his room had taken any longer, she might have come to her senses.

As it was, when Kyle pinned her to the wall inside his room, his mouth devouring hers, all common sense went out the window. Emotions and hormones took control. She tugged his shirt out from his Levi's, not taking time to unbutton, simply slipped her hands up and inside to trace all those wonderfully sculpted muscles. Kyle's hands explored as his head dipped down to play with the soft, sensitive area at the base of her throat. Little shivers of pleasure danced across her skin, igniting small fires along their pathway.

With a hunger like she'd never known before, she stripped away his shirt, as he pulled hers over her head. He was beautiful, chiseled and tan with a light dusting of dark hair on his chest. Abs ripped to perfection and if she weren't standing there in person, she would have said only Photoshop could have created them. Her breath caught in the back of her throat, followed by a moan as he ran his thumb in circles around her nipple.

Briefly, she had contemplated saying stop, running back to her friends, or to her room alone, where she would have lain awake all night with her mind racing and her body thrumming with unfulfilled desire. It'd been a long time since she'd given into passion and she was tired of playing it safe.

Kyle's other hand slipped her bra strap off her shoulder as his mouth trailed little kisses in its path. Just when she was about to beg for more, he dropped to his knees. Whereas the sweep of his thumb was gentle and slow, the onslaught from his mouth was intense, fast, and furious. He latched on to her breast with a deep pull, then ran his tongue back and forth over the wet cotton material.

Why didn't she choose the lace and silk set she'd bought last month? The thought didn't last long as Kyle's teeth teased the sensitive bud, sending shivers straight down her back. She dragged her fingers through his hair, urging him with whimpers of pleasure.

While his mouth worked its magic first on one breast and then the other, his hands slid down her ribcage. He hooked his thumbs into the waistband of her capris and slipped them off of her.

She reached for his zipper, but he pulled out of her reach, stood and carried her over to the little desk. The cool of the wood hitting her bare, warm butt had her sitting up straight. With a quick tug, he brought her to the edge and spread her legs apart.

It was clear by her position what was on his mind. Still, when he swooped in and kissed her, she gasped. He worked his way down, taking a leisurely exploration down her body, only stopping long enough to check out the tattoo on her side. He didn't comment and she didn't explain the caged bird or the meaning behind it. Maybe he got it on his own. Most didn't.

Sitting, naked on the edge of the desk, one wouldn't think she could get more exposed. But she could. There were secrets deep down, along with hopes and dreams and while she had no problem sharing her body with Kyle, she had no plans to share more.

This was simply a night of hot, meaningless sex.

As his finger slipped inside her, all other thoughts vanished. All except thoughts of him and the night ahead. He knelt before her, gazing at her like a prized gift that he'd savor every minute playing with. Fine with her, if he'd hurry up. With every stroke of his finger she came closer to exploding. His head dipped and he swept his very clever tongue across her nub. She cried out and grasped the edge of the desk to keep from sliding off. Each lash of his tongue was sweet torment and left her panting and begging for more. The grazing of his teeth was more than she could take and shattered her into a million spent pieces.

She threw her head back, the rapid rise and fall of her chest making it impossible to talk. Kyle kissed his way back up her core, stopping to pay homage to each breast.

"Ready for round two?" he asked as he nibbled his way up to her earlobe.

Round two? She was still trying to catch her breath and bring the room back into focus, but somehow she nodded or made some kind of affirmative noise and found herself being lifted again, this time to land on the soft mattress.

It didn't take long to get his jeans off. Thankfully, somewhere along the line, he'd removed his shoes. She ran her fingertips down from his chest, across his torso and over every indent in his abs. "Are you a professional bodybuilder or something? These could only come from hours in a gym or the depths of my imagination."

"I'll go with or something. Uh, I guess we should have the talk before it goes any further," his voice came out husky and raw with need.

"I haven't been with anyone in over a year, I'm clean and on the pill."

"The same here."

"Really," the edges of her mouth lifted as she fought the laugh back.

"Well, two out of three and I have condoms."

He reached over, grabbed his discarded jeans and came out with a handful of Trojans.

"Looks like we're ready for round two." She sat up on her knees and crawled across the king-sized bed. Snatching one of the foil packets out of his hand, she gave him a gentle push and sent him to land on his back.

She took the lead, and what followed was mind-blowing. Even with her ex, Mark, whom she'd been with for a couple of years, she'd never felt this way before. Burning hot, like a volcano building to an eruption and more. Somehow she felt … cherished. With every stroke, caress and kiss, the pressure built as Kyle alternated between fast and hard to soft and slow. His hands explored, tweaking her nipples, sliding down her ribs to knead her hips and cup the curve of her butt, to back up and tracing the tattoo on her side sending shivers all over.

And when he took her over the edge again, he swapped positions and built the fire back up. Murmurs, pleas and moans from both of them filled the air. Uncontrollable and insatiable passion consumed them, demanding more as the night wore on. Worshipping her with his mouth, his tongue, his hands, she strained to bring him as much pleasure as he delivered. With every surge of his hips she slipped a little closer until together they both collapsed in spent pleasure.

Exhausted, she didn't argue or pull away to leave when Kyle wrapped her in his arms and snuggled up behind her. While her body wanted rest her mind whirled around her actions. It was unarguably the best night of sex she'd ever experienced. Sadly there'd be no repeat performances as she was scheduled to fly out in five days for Georgia where she'd report to her new duty station, the USS Alaska.

Nic quietly gathered her clothes and dressed as streaks of red and gray slashed across the sky. She should have left hours ago. Cherise and Lindsey.... Well, Cherise would be worried sick about her. Probably thinking she'd been strangled and chopped up into little tiny bits, based on her warning as Nic had left the bar. And she would have left, if lying in Kyle's arms hadn't felt so right, all warm and safe and wanted. The total opposite of being with her ex, who used to give a quick kiss before rolling over with his back to her.

So she had stayed, had even toyed with the fantasy of waking with Kyle in the morning and him asking her to spend the day with him, which was ludicrous. Her life was taking her to Georgia and he had said he'd just flown in from the West Coast. Being a Navy brat and active duty, she knew long distance relationships never survived.

She thought about waking him to say goodbye or to at least leave a note, but what would she say? Thanks for the great sex? No, it was best to leave it as it was and what it would be, a fun memory. With one last look at Kyle's sleeping form she slipped out the door.

* * *

Kyle rolled over at the soft click of the hotel door closing. It took a few seconds for his brain to register the origin of the sound and the fact that he was alone in bed. Without thinking he jumped up and tugged open the door to an empty hallway, which, given his state of undress, was probably a good thing. He closed the door and gave the room a quick inspection.

No note.

Damn.

He'd gone to sleep, dreaming of the woman in his arms and fantasizing about how he'd wake her up with another round of sex. Kissing those soft lips, running his hands over her smooth skin as her long, silky hair cascaded over him.

After, they'd call up for breakfast in his room and while they waited they could indulge in a hot shower where he'd talk her into spending the morning with him until they had to check-out and go their separate ways. For a while he toyed with the idea of their one night turning into something more, but what was the point? In less than a week, he'd be gone and no woman wanted to wait months for a guy she just met.

Besides, as much as he liked her and enjoyed their time together he didn't see her as the type to fit in with his life or family. She screamed of tradition, two point five kids in matching outfits, Sunday dinners with the in-laws, vacations on the Cape, and deep roots. They hadn't talked family, but he wouldn't be surprised to find she lived in one of Boston's Back Bay Victorian brownstones or some high-rise facing Central Park in Manhattan.

She came from a class too many levels above his origins. Not that his parents embarrassed him. They worked hard and did the best they could with the obstacles life had thrown them. The dipshit twins were another thing, not to mention the extended family, all prime candidates for a daytime talk show.

No, Nic wouldn't fit in. She had an air of sophistication about her. She belonged in a country club and he belonged in a dive bar.

She'd be a fantasy he'd reflect back on during those long, lonely watches. It was a shame the fantasy had to end so soon.

A soft tap on the door had him grinning as he grabbed the sheet and headed for the door. "Forget something?" he asked.

The ugly mugs of Mace and Bryant peered back. "What?" Kyle snarled.

"Expecting someone else?" Mace pushed the door open and he and Bryant walked in.

"Yeah, room service. You two look like shit. Are you just now rolling in?"

"Unlike some, I went to bed alone." Mace propped himself against the desk and Kyle had to turn away to block out the memories of the night before.

"You're looking well rested for a guy who left with a babe. What happened? Did you crash and burn?" Bryant leaned against the wall near the bathroom, a cocksure grin on his face.

"I don't kiss and tell." Kyle stared at the alarm clock on the nightstand in disbelief. It had to be wrong. "What time is it anyway?"

"Six a.m., buddy, and you need to get dressed." Mace stood and stuffed his hands in his pockets.

Kyle dropped back on the bed and closed his eyes. "Go away. I don't want breakfast."

"That's good. The XO called a wardroom meeting at 0830," said Bryant.

Kyle shot up to a sitting position and swung his legs over to plant his feet on the carpeted floor. "On a Sunday? This can't be a good sign."

Mace tossed him his jeans before shoving his hand back in his pocket to jiggle the car keys. "If it hasn't been one thing, it's been another with this upcoming deployment. Makes me question why the hell I stay in."

"Because you'd miss us," said Bryant.

"Not as much as I miss my wife. Meet you downstairs in fifteen, Hutch," Mace said.

Grabbing clean clothes from his bag, Kyle hit the rain locker. Yeah, the Navy life wasn't for everyone. Even for the best of couples it was a trial, which was why he should let Nic go and enjoy the memory.

Chapter Three

Nic dropped into the chair opposite her girls Wednesday night with a heavy sigh. Excitement and nerves bounced around inside of her. The class officer had just handed her a primo opportunity. While she was stoked about the idea, it meant staying in Groton instead of heading to King's Bay, Georgia with her friends.

"What's with the look of despair?" Lindsey asked.

"Did you get into another fight with your dad?" Cherise gave her a sympathetic look, as neither of her parents had been on board with her joining the military either.

"No, I haven't talked to my dad in over a week." Nic tapped her heavy boots on the linoleum floor of the lounge. "Actually, there's been a change in my orders."

"Oh Sugar, your dad didn't get you kicked out of the sub force, did he?" Cherise asked as she sat up straight, her jaw clenching.

"No, I'm pretty sure he had nothing to do with this. I'm not going to Georgia. One of the supply officers here in Groton had a serious accident this past week and now his boat is in need of a replacement."

"But I thought the boats here aren't set up for coed crews?" Lindsey voice was filled with concern and confusion. Not that Nic could blame her.

"They aren't, except this is urgent as they're deploying in less than a week and I'm the best option they have. I'm not sure how they're going to make it work. That'll be the XO's problem. I'm just glad my parents are on vacation, because if I'm bunking with two guys, my mom will flip."

"What about your brothers?" Cherise gasped.

Nic rolled her eyes and let out a deep sigh. "Oh, fudge. Let's not even go there. I'm just glad we're getting underway so quickly. Sometimes, Liam and Reece can be the worst. By the time they find out, there will be nothing they can do like give me a hard time or call our parents or the detailer and finagle some new deal to have me sent elsewhere."

"Well, if you don't want the orders I'll take them. I have no problem with a coed stateroom and no interfering family to worry about." Lindsey gave her a salacious grin, her eyes lit up with hope.

Nic laughed and Cherise let out a long, drawn-out sigh.

"Somehow I think the XO will figure out a way to avoid coed berthing. The thing is, while I'm excited, I'm also scared. We're only the second wave of women on Tridents, but I'll be the first on a fast-attack and I'll be alone. Not to mention we're not talking about being underway for eighty-five days. We're talking one hundred and eighty. What if I can't hack it?"

Cherise waved her concern away. "Please, if any of us can, Sugar, it's you. You've been Navy your whole life. I'm gonna miss you, girl, but you'll do right by all of us."

"Thanks, but it also leaves you a roommate short."

"We'll manage," Lindsey cut in. "And look on the bright side—since you're staying here, you can hook up again with Mr. Hot-One-Night-Stand and turn it into a smoldering hot love affair."

Nic looked to Cherise, who simply shrugged her shoulders and smiled. Lindsey's optimistic and outgoing personality was one of the reasons they'd hit it off so well. Her daring, I'll-try-anything attitude was another and something Nic had looked forward to being around. With Lindsey there was never a dull moment, of which she'd had too many of in her life this past year. Nic had turned from a fun, spur-of-the-moment person to the Mayor of Dullsville.

"Except that," she said and held up her fingers and ticked off her points, "One, I'm leaving in a few days for six months. Two, he said he's from the West Coast and three, we didn't exchange contact information." They hadn't even exchanged last names, which told her he clearly wasn't interested in more than the one night.

Linds let out a little groan. "I can't help you there either, because the minute I found out his buddy, Mace, was married, I backed away like the man had the plague."

A second later, Lindsey's face lit up and she turned to Cherise. "Hey, you and Bryant hit it off really well. Did you get his number?"

Before she could answer, a group of young sailors, all in the eighteen to twenty age bracket, walked by and their conversation had all three women clenching their jaws.

"I agree with my dad. Women on subs are nothing but trouble," one guy said.

"Next they'll want to play professional football," another said.

"Hey, I've got no problem with them being on board, especially that hot blonde. She has needs too."

The men walked out of range and the three of them sat quietly. Change didn't always come easy and they knew getting into this that they'd come up against some old-fashioned frames of mind, but hearing it out loud hit home hard.

"I'd like to be a fly on the wall when their COB hears those comments. The Chief of the Boat is going to rip them apart, put them back together and do it all over again," said Nic.

The first time Nic had ever seen her dad, who was now a vice admiral, rip into a young sailor she'd been shocked. Up until then, she had thought he'd been hard on her and her brothers at home. Compared to his men, they had it easy. There was no place in the military for disrespect and unruly conduct and she had a feeling the young NUBs would find that out the hard way.

"They're young. They'll learn," said Cherise.

"Yeah, but it's not just the young guys who feel that way. I overheard a couple of the wives talking at the NEX the other day when I was shopping. They're worried we're going to sleep with their husbands," said Lindsey.

"Have they ever been on a sub? Where would we get horizontal?" Cherise threw up her hands and let out a snort of disgust. "Our racks are more like open-sided coffins and we sleep snuggled up next to torpedo tubes. That doesn't scream romance."

Lindsey shifted her gaze to the group of guys across the room. "Seriously, I may joke about it with the two of you, but if I could control myself in Nowhereville, Kansas, where there actually *was* space to get horizontal with another person, then I think I can control myself on a sub. Besides the only two places with privacy and enough room to get down and dirty with another would be the XO or CO's staterooms. No thanks."

"Don't want to live on the edge, Linds?" Nic teased her friend.

"Honey, that's not the edge. That's dancing with the devil."

"Agreed. My dad would have flipped had someone ever used his stateroom for a tryst. The surface community isn't a whole lot better. Women have just been part of it long enough that the scuttle has died down."

Nic knew though, that a cheater would always find a way to cheat. Blame the long separations, long hours, kids, insecurity, or whatever. They were nothing but stories to clear the conscience.

Jumping up from her seat, Nic said, "Enough of this depressing talk. Today we graduated and tomorrow is the start of something new and fabulous for all of us. Let's get out of these uniforms and go out to celebrate. I vote for Italian."

The other two agreed and they headed out of the student lounge.

"Hey, Cherise, you never answered whether you had Bryant's number or not." Lindsey reminded them as they headed to the car.

She hesitated in answering, looking at her phone and then to Nic. "I do."

"Great. Hook a sister up and get Nic that guy's number."

"I'll give him a call if you want, Nic, but first there's something about Kyle you should know."

Nic held up her hand and stopped her as she unlocked the car doors. Did she want to know this something? Did she even want to get in touch with him? The night was great and the sex was amazing, but some niggling doubt held her back. Some fear that if she really got to know him, he'd be like all the others or a total jerk. She batted the idea back and forth, while the other two stood waiting.

"Tell me one thing first," Nic said. "He's not married is he?"

"Nope," Cherise answered.

"Not wanted by the police or an ex-con?"

"Highly doubtful." At Nic's pained expressed, Cherise laughed. "It's not like I asked. Okay, I did ask if he was a serial killer or rapist, but I was only joking. Sort of."

Well, okay, that was good news. So what was so vital that her friend felt she needed to know before getting her the number? Obviously it was something that would make Nic think twice or Cherise wouldn't have brought it up.

"You know, don't tell me and don't get me his number. If it's meant to be, the fates will bring us back together. If not, I get a happy memory to cherish."

* * *

All hell had been breaking loose for the past five days and Kyle couldn't wait to get underway and have life resume its normal flow. Tempers were running on high, which was par for the course. The married guys were bitching about leaving their families, all the while fighting with their wives. The single guys were itching to get the hell out of Dodge and see some place new. Not that Kyle blamed them. "It's not just a job, it's an adventure" was still one of the first things out of a recruiter's mouth.

They'd had equipment break down, supplies not show up, a few reported as unauthorized absent, and of course, a couple of fistfights. Nothing new there or in the neverending lineup of meetings he had to attend.

He'd just finished up a meeting with his own guys, giving them instructions on what he wanted done by the time he got back. Now he was at another meeting, this time in the wardroom with all the officers, the Chief of the Boat, and their Leading Yeoman. Kyle grabbed a cup of stale coffee and dropped down next to Mace and Bryant.

The Commanding Officer, Aaron Holloway stood. He was short, built to mow down linebackers and wore a perpetual frown. Every set of eyes focused on him and the room went as silent as a church during prayers. By the look on the old man's face, shit was about to hit the fan.

"I know the last few days have been stressful on everyone and I want to thank all of you for handling the bumps we've encountered with efficiency and professionalism. The crew has done a great job getting the boat ready even with tensions running high. We're all anxious to go and dreading to leave our loved ones behind at the same time. I know I don't have to emphasize the importance of our mission or the danger to you."

He stopped speaking to take a sip of his coffee, while making eye contact with each and every one of them over the rim of his cup. The speech was old news to Kyle, as was the deployment, only this time he had his mom to worry about and Nic to fantasize over.

"I want the crew off the boat at sixteen hundred hours today and tomorrow. Let's get these men home to their families at a decent hour and maybe we'll have a week or two without their pissing and moaning. That goes for me too."

They'd be making port calls in Scotland and Spain en route to their destination to gather intelligence on the enemy; no date set. The CO rambled on about the mission, stressing to the men to take advantage of family grams and to not share boat movement or port calls on social media, e-mail or over cell phones. He then went on to check in with each department head.

"We have one last order of business before you can get back to work. As you all know, Lieutenant West was in a serious accident last week. He's been upgraded to stable and the docs believe he'll be released in the next couple of days to rehab. The spouses group has pulled together and has been and will continue to be a big help to Cecilia West and the kids while he makes his recovery. With that said, we're short a supply officer. Or were until this morning."

The CO paused and set down his mug, but didn't release it.

Kyle tilted his head toward Mace. "What's up with the Captain? He doesn't usually stand during these things," he whispered.

"No clue. He's been in rare form all day."

The CO looked up and met Kyle's gaze. With hands relaxed on his hips, Commander Holloway glanced at all of the men before continuing.

"There weren't a lot of options on such short notice, but PERS did present me with an interesting option. One that will put the *California* in the history books. We're stealing one of the Trident's female officers."

The room broke out into cheers. There was nothing a fast-attack crew liked more than to stick it to a Trident sub. The CO broke out into a smile and let his guys get their good-natured comments out before continuing.

He used his hands to quiet the room back down. "Okay, settle down. Obviously, with such short notice, we've got some shifting to do to accommodate everyone. Gatlin, you're in with Hutchinson and Havers."

Bryant groaned. "They snore."

"That's what earplugs are for," one of the junior officers teased.

"Master Chief Ronquillo will work out a schedule for the aft head for showers. I want it stressed to each and every man under you that when the "Women Only" sign is up, they respect it. I will not have this boat be the center of a scandal because some young pup got a wild hair. Am I understood?"

"Yes, sir," came from all in the room.

"Some of you may recognize the name, Lieutenant Lily Riley. For those of you who don't, she's the daughter of Vice Admiral Riley. The last thing I need is SUBLANT breathing down my neck."

Instead of more applause or cheering, the CO's announcement was met with pure silence. They had stolen the Golden Goose, at least according to Kyle's buddy Tom, the weapons officer on the *USS Alaska*. As far as Kyle was concerned the Tridents could have her. Having the only daughter of the man who ran the entire Atlantic submarine force on board was asking for a headache. Sure, if the mission went well and baby girl reported back to Daddy good things, then no problem. They might even get an extra medal out of it. If things didn't go so well?

The Commanding Officer could kiss his career goodbye, and so could every other officer and the Chief of the Boat.

The rest of the wardroom broke into various small conversations while the CO and COB consulted on the schedule.

Bryant leaned over to look at him and Mace. "Either of you ever met the Rileys?"

Kyle shook his head and looked at Mace.

"Served with Liam, the oldest of the three kids. Decent guy. Big guy. Should have played linebacker. I think he's out west, Bangor or San Diego. Never met the others, but Liam mentioned her a few times."

"Yeah, what did he say?" Kyle asked, wondering if they were going to have to live with a prima donna or what.

"Let me put it this way—I pity the fool that messes with his sister."

Which told Kyle squat about the woman herself, only that she was protected by her family.

"Lieutenant Hutchinson, I'm assigning you as Riley's sponsor. Make sure she gets settled in. Between you and the COB, I expect her to feel like one of the crew. Get her through her quals. You know the drill."

"Yes, sir." As her sponsor she'd practically be in his back pocket until she got settled in. He really hoped she was a fast learner.

The XO, Christopher Ward, who was the exact opposite of the CO, stepped through the door and every eye turned in his direction. Kyle's heart slammed against his rib cage twice and then failed to start again as he looked at the woman peeking around the man. A petite woman, with dark, almond-shaped eyes, a scattering of freckles and silky hair that he'd been dreaming of for days.

"Sir, gentlemen. Our new supply officer, Lieutenant Lily Riley."

Her eyes locked on to Kyle's. Images of her screaming his name pierced his brain.

It's going to be a long six months, he thought.

Chapter Four

The walls were closing in on her. Claustrophobia hadn't been an issue on the carriers where she could escape outside to feel the wind on her face and breathe in the fresh sea air. Which was a little hard to do on a submerged submarine. Since coming aboard she'd been fighting the desire to run, to find an escape into the open. Instead she worked on pushing back the darkness edging her vision and focused on the breathing techniques her therapist had taught her years ago. In the small, cramped pantry-slash-office it took everything she had in her not to bolt.

As the supply officer, the galley fell under her and she wanted to get a feel for the routine and the chemistry of the cooks on duty and let them get a chance to know her. Not something she could do while working in her stateroom.

Not that anyone had talked to her yet. A few 'morning, ma'ams', a nod of the head and lots of grumbling by the head mess chief had met her entrance into the galley after breakfast as she set up to work. She didn't think she'd been taking up a lot of space, but as the Chief reached over her head for another can, she couldn't help but feel in the way.

She shut down her computer, stood and secured the pull-down desk, as the mess chief looked on with a frustrated grimace.

"Chief Boone, I'd like to go over the galley schedule and procedures with you," she said.

He glanced over his shoulder into the busy kitchen area before responding. "Of course."

"Perhaps tomorrow or the next day, when you've got a moment? I imagine the first day out is a little hectic."

The tight line of his mouth and the hard clamp of his jaw relaxed. A smidge.

"Tomorrow would be fine, ma'am. If you don't mind waiting until after dinner? The first couple of days are a little hectic. Plus, I've got a few newbies in the galley I'd rather not leave."

"That's fine, Chief Boone. From what I've seen this morning you run a tight shift. Very impressive."

"Thank you, ma'am." He stepped back, shifting the giant can of beans to his other hand.

"I'm going to get out of your way so you can get lunch done. I'll be in my stateroom if you need me." She gave him a curt nod and got out of his way. The pressure on her chest eased with the first step out of the small room.

The boat was a hive of activity, with sailors hustling from one station to another, those not on duty joking with others in the mess hall and a few sleeping. One young sailor approached from the opposite direction caused the two of them to shift sideways in order to pass. He scooted by, mumbling 'ma'am' and she noted his flushed cheeks. It was going to be a long six months if these boys couldn't handle brushing up against her without getting embarrassed.

As the boat made its way down the Thames River, through the Long Island Sound and out into the Atlantic for destinations far from home, Nic scanned the menu and inventory her mess chief had sent over. The menu was fine, but if it had been her, she would have ordered more chocolate ice cream. Thank goodness she'd brought her own stash of chocolate. It was shaping up to be one of those kinds of days already.

Her mom had called bright and early to say how excited she was to see her baby girl. The disappointment in her voice when she heard Nic's orders had changed overrode the words of encouragement. After thirty-five years of military life, not much surprised her mom, especially changes in orders. As the saying went, until it happens, everything was chipped in Jell-O. And of course, there was the slight layering of guilt about how the boys would be home and her dad's birthday party wouldn't be the same without Nic there too.

Then there was the lack of a call from her dad.

She'd miss hearing his gruff voice, the lame jokes and even his not-so-subtle hints that he was ready for her to settle down and make him a grandpa. Most of her friends had to contend with their moms nagging for grandbabies. Not Nic. Truth was, the man most men in the Navy feared was really a big softie and loved nothing more than his family. Which was why when he fully backed women in the service and on submarines, he didn't endorse her serving. He wanted her home, safe, married, and in a job where she didn't have to face a lifelong fear.

But it wasn't her parental issues that had her jonesing for chocolate all day. Nope, that honor went solely to *Lieutenant* Kyle Hutchinson.

The man her commanding officer had paired her up with.

The man she needed to stay far, far away from.

She couldn't believe Cherise hadn't warned her. Yeah, sure, Nic told her not to tell the big bad whatever. But there are special circumstances when the person with the secret should know to override the person in the dark's wishes. Walking into the wardroom and locking eyes with the man she'd done the horizontal tango with?

Talk about beyond awkward, especially when you were the center of attention and your face was the color of a cooked lobster.

Whatever. They were adults. They had engaged in consensual sex. No promises were made. No lies exchanged. No hurt feelings. They could do their jobs without the past getting in the way. Besides, he had his job and she had hers, plus a boat to learn and qualifications to cross off her list. Subs were not known for excessive amounts of personal space or time and the chances of them being alone were slim to none.

The 1MC crackled overhead and the announcement came to rig the ship for angles and dangles. Nic secured her computer to the Velcro strip on the desk. Next she cleared everything from her desk and stuck the papers she'd been working on in the cubby. Moving around her stateroom-slash-office she made sure the drawers and doors were all secured and wouldn't open during the maneuvers. A small thrill coursed through her as she gave the room one last look. This was definitely a maneuver a surface ship couldn't pull off. At least, not on purpose.

"Settling in, *Lily*?" His deep, commanding voice sent her nerves scurrying all over the place.

With a casualness she didn't feel, Nic turned around and faced Kyle. "Please don't call me Lily. That's not my name." She'd forgotten how his gunmetal gray eyes could look deep into your soul. At least, that's how it felt when he looked at her.

"Are you sure? It's the name on your orders."

She blew out a breath and counted to ten. "If you must know, not that's it's any of your business, my full name is Lily Nicole Riley but no one outside of my family calls me Lily."

His eyes searched her, his jaw clenched and unclenched as he stood there watching her. *What do you see?* she wanted to ask. Did he see the scared newbie? Or did he see the pampered princess so many thought she was? Or did he see the woman who drove him crazy days ago?

She really didn't know which one she'd prefer the answer to be. After a few minutes he shifted and relaxed, letting whatever question was on his mind go.

"I didn't see you at lunch. Everything okay?"

His gaze travelled up and down her body and she wanted to laugh. No one looked sexy in the dark blue, baggy coveralls they wore onboard the boat fondly known as "poopy suits." Although the audible sigh, which was more of an exasperated exhale made her think she wasn't the only one remembering last weekend.

To put distance between them, even if it was only metaphorical, she crossed her arms. "I've been trying to catch up."

Something in her voice, possibly the hesitation or maybe the stain heating up her face caught his attention. Kyle leaned against the doorway, his eyes scrunched up as he studied her. She studied him back. He'd gotten a haircut, leaving barely more than peach fuzz where he once had silky, out-of-regs-length hair.

"Are you sure that's all?" He glanced around the tight space before meeting her gaze. "You know if you didn't miss meals or worked in the shack you'd probably meet the crew faster."

Yeah, been there, done that, felt like a freak in a show.

"Chief Boone made it clear I was in his way in the shack."

Kyle's rich, deep rumble of a laugh rolled over her. "He probably thought you were trying to steal his better-than-sex peanut butter pie. Still, it's your department. You could have stayed."

Someone yelled "coming through" and Kyle stepped further into her space to clear the passageway. Her already small stateroom shrunk with every step he took.

"Maybe tomorrow I'll assert my authority. Right now the crew needs time to adjust to a woman onboard," she said.

"It doesn't have anything to do with your gender."

"Then what is it? The only ones who've even spoken to me are you, the XO, CO, and the COB. To everyone else I'm invisible or persona non grata."

"It's your dad."

Not a huge shock there. Every command she'd been at, her father's reputation hung over her head casting her into the shadows. If she'd slept her way to the top, she'd have had a better chance of being treated like an equal. Not that Lieutenant was even close to the top. After five years, she still had that new kid on the block smell. She'd made rank through hard work and time, just like any other sailor and just like before she'd have to prove herself.

For a while there had been a small kernel of hope that this time it would be different. Within the close confines of the boat, where people literally bumped shoulders and more just to pass and lived on top of each other, friendships formed that crossed boundaries. But apparently, not for her.

She leaned against the bulkhead, mimicking his stance. "So what's the general consensus? My dad called in a favor? Or, I know. I'm here as SUBLANT's spy to report back all the wrongdoing going on to him?"

"They're afraid of pissing you off and killing their careers."

"But not you?"

"Not really. After all, he puts his pants on like the rest of us, one leg at a time. He's not God, he's not infallible and I'm betting he didn't get where he is today by crossing the line."

"Ah, I see you've met him."

"No, I've not met any of the infamous Rileys. Except you." His slate gray eyes darkened, a small smile twisted up the corners of his lips.

"Yeah, well don't judge them based on me. I'm much shorter than the rest."

Just then the ship dove and Nic lunged forward right into Kyle's arms. He held on to her while she got her balance and rode the downward descent. He leaned backward as she leaned forward, their eyes locked. The heat from his hands radiated through her coveralls, leaving scorch marks on her skin. In Boston he smelled wholly male and clean. Now amine overrode everything else. She'd forgotten how quick the chemical for purifying the air penetrated your every pore and every fiber of your clothing.

"Sorry, should have been paying attention," she stammered as she tried to ignore his very talented lips in front of her.

"I don't mind." His words were dark, delicious, and tugged at a place deep inside. He'd said the same thing to her last weekend when she'd... well, that thought was better left undone.

She dared to look up to meet his teasing gaze and tried not to smile back at his half-grin and mischievous eyes.

Tried.

Keyword.

She should step back, out of his hold, but her feet didn't seem to listen. Instead she ignored her common sense and held on tight as they plunged. Lost in the depths of his gray eyes she knew this was a bad idea and needed to say something, to clear the air and put them on the right track. First she needed to create some space. As the boat righted and then prepared for the climb back to the surface, she took a small step backwards.

"About last weekend…" She started as she searched for the words.

"What about it?"

"I know it's hard to believe, but that wasn't me. I mean, obviously it was me, and not my evil twin, but it's not my normal thing. I don't go around having one-night stands. Not that I have a problem with people who do—"

"Meaning me?" Now he stepped back, arms crossed in front of him.

She had to catch her balance as the boat started its ascent at that moment. "No, that's not what I meant. If you do, well that's your business, not mine and obviously we can't do it again."

He grinned. "Did you want to?"

"Yes. No." She blew out a deep puff of air and grabbed hold of the closet handle as the boat surfaced and leveled out. "I might have at one point, but that was before I saw you sitting in the wardroom."

He stepped closer, backing her up against the edge of her rack. "We wouldn't be breaking any rules."

"Technically, no. Neither of us is over or under the other."

"Which is a shame, as I really enjoyed you under me, and especially over me."

"Stop it, Kyle." With a shake of her head and an exasperated laugh, Nic sidestepped out from in between him and the bed. "You know what I mean—it wouldn't be good morale and conduct. We need to forget about that night. Just because we're on the same boat shouldn't be a problem either. You have your job and I have mine. We can easily stay out of each other's way."

Like that was really possible inside a tin can.

"You're forgetting one thing. The Captain assigned me as your sponsor. It's my job to see that your needs are met."

Before she could respond one of the young Petty Officers stuck his head in the doorway. "Sorry, ma'am, sir. The Chief wants to know if you want any changes made to the menu?"

She stepped away from Kyle, her full focus on the young sailor who couldn't be a day over eighteen. "No, tell the Chief they are all excellent choices."

"Yes, ma'am." He nodded to both and disappeared down the passageway.

"So, where were we?" Kyle's slate gray eyes met her as she turned around. "That's right. Meeting your needs."

"Umm." Heat crept up her neck and spread across her cheeks. She licked her bottom lip, before sucking it in as she searched her brain for her words. At the moment, well the moment Kyle mentioned meeting her needs, her brain melted. "Well, here's the thing. I'm a big girl and I can take care of my own needs."

"I bet you can. Although, I've heard it's more fun with a friend."

A knock on the open door had both of them stepping back.

"Sorry to interrupt."

"Hey, Doc. No worries. I was just reminding Riley that she doesn't want to miss meals, especially right now while we still have fresh stock on board. Plus, all work and no play makes for a long underway. Everything in moderation. Isn't that what you always tell us?" Kyle tapped the newcomer on the shoulder and walked away.

According to the insignia on the poopy suit, the new guy was the ship's corpsman, or as they are fondly known on a sub "Doc." He was tall, lanky, and with a boyish smile that instantly put you at ease. Good quality in a medical professional.

Nic shoved the encounter with Kyle and his generous offer to the back of her mind where she could take it out later when she was alone to analyze. "Hi ..." she held her hand out to the chief.

"Chief Corbett, but everyone just calls me Doc."

"Nice to meet you. What can I do for you?"

He shook her hand and stepped back, giving her space in the tiny room. "Nothing special. Wanted to introduce myself, let you know if you need anything, just ask."

"Appreciate it." She fiddled with the handle on the desk door, wondering if there was more to his visit than a simple hello.

"You know, I served with Reece. A couple of times."

Great. Big brother had a watchdog on board. Just what she didn't need, one more person looking out for her.

"Lucky you," she said with a grin.

He laughed. "Yeah, he can be a little intense at times, but he's a good leader. The men like him."

She sat on the edge of the bunk and pointed to the chair. Something told her she was in for a story. "So you're the one with the Dremel?"

Corbett laughed again as he scrubbed his hand across his jaw. "Well, in all fairness..."

He launched into the story she'd first heard last Christmas. Seems her big brother—the one that pulled her hair, chased her with snakes, and talked her into more trouble than she could remember—had his toenail set on fire. Well, not exactly flames leaping in the air, but there was smoke.

She let Doc tell his side, but her mind was elsewhere. With every beat of approaching feet down the passageway she'd catch herself looking toward the open door and every time it wasn't Kyle, her shoulders sagged just a little. The next six months were going to be sheer torture, especially when he looked at her with those gray eyes like he could eat her up. Yeah, it'd be torture. Even more than waiting for Nathan Daniels to ask her to senior prom.

If she'd learned anything in life, it was if you wanted to play with the boys, you had to pull up your big girl panties and tough it out, which is exactly what she planned to do. The night with Kyle had been hot and amazing and memorable. But there was no way she was going to jeopardize her career for a roll in the sheets.

No matter how great.

Growing up, becoming a naval officer was all she ever dreamed of, which shouldn't have been a huge surprise given her family's history. No one batted an eye when her oldest brother Liam went to the Naval Academy after high school or when Reece, the precious middle child, followed. If they thought Nic would be left behind, then they'd all suffered from mass delusion.

The boys had shook their heads and laughed at her announcement, not really shocked. Her dad had sat her down with a list of pros and cons of joining and then suggested a number of suitable careers she could pursue that wouldn't put her in danger. When that didn't work, he brought up the claustrophobia. She had lied, told him she hadn't had a panic attack in years; beside she'd be in the surface force. Her mom told her she should listen to her father.

Like that was going to happen.

If her brothers could hack it, so could she. They were Navy brats; they could hang with the best. She hadn't lived in no less than three countries and five other duty stations by the time she'd graduated from high school without learning how to overcome, improvise and adapt. Irrational phobias and female emotions—as her dad put it—wouldn't hold her back.

Now if only she could prove to him that she was right. Sleeping with Kyle while they served on the same sub? That was just giving the old man all the evidence he needed to say, "Told you so." Something she'd made a lifetime habit of not doing. As a matter of fact, she'd show him how wrong he'd been. Not only would she earn her Dolphins, the pin showing

32   *Gail Chianese*

she'd qualified as a submariner, she'd do it in less time than it took for the great and mighty Patrick Sean Michael Riley to earn his.

Doc stood, bringing her attention back to the present. "I hope you don't mind, but Reece mentioned your problem with tight spaces to me. Subs seem a strange choice, but I'm sure you have your reasons. If the confinement starts to get to you, come find me. I might have a few suggestions to help. Speaking of suggestions, the WEPS has a point. You shouldn't miss meals, especially while we still have real food in stock. Trust me, it doesn't take this crew long to go through the good stuff. Especially ice cream."

Unclenching her jaw, Nic dropped into the chair. Slowly she went through the motions of setting her desk back up, the whole time trying to wrap her brain around Reece ratting her out. How had he even known about the change in orders? It'd only been a couple of days. The length of her brother's reach didn't surprise her, his break in her confidence did. They simply did not share each other's secrets. Not even as kids.

He'd been the one person who knew the truth, knew the panic attacks still snuck up on her under stress. He was only one she had trusted with her secret. Obviously she chose poorly.

Clicking open the electronic reminder app on her computer, she made two notes: to procure more ice cream on the first port call; and to bop her brother upside the head next time she saw him.

* * *

Kyle yanked his chair out of the corner of the stateroom and shoved it up to his workspace. Firing up the computer he went straight to e-mail. The boat would go dark soon and he wanted to check on his mom before then, because once they shut down e-mail he'd only get happy news via family grams until they hit their first port call. As he suspected there was a message waiting for him from his mom. He read the short note, swore, and read it again.

The dipshit twins were at it again. Whatever it was, he knew the situation wouldn't turn out well and his mom suspected the same thing. Now, not only did he have to worry about his idiot brothers landing in jail or worse, he had to worry about his parents.

Searching his memory he tried to place who the 'rough' looking guy could be that had visited his parents looking for his brothers. His mom hadn't said she was scared, but she wouldn't have mentioned the guy if he hadn't set off all kinds of warning signs. The description alone put him on alert—big, muscular, dirty, torn clothes, and a scar down one arm. In fact, his mom, in her typical fashion of always trying to find the good in a person tried to brush off her concerns saying, "He was probably shy. The poor boy looked everywhere, but at me."

Shy, his ass. The dude, no doubt, had been casing the place—memorizing everything about the house: the location of the windows, doors, where the cars were parked, the lack of a dog, and the distance to the nearest neighbor's house. If they'd been in port, Kyle would have put in another emergency leave chit and jumped on the first plane home.

Stuck in the middle of the ocean, his options were limited. Basically unless one of his parents was fighting for their life, he was stuck on the tin pig. Without proof they were in danger the local authorities were out. Asking his brothers to curtail their nefarious ways would get him squat. The only option he could think of didn't fill him with a lot of hope.

He shot off an e-mail to his only somewhat reliable cousin asking him to find the twins, get them out of whatever trouble they were in, and help keep an eye on his parents. Kyle hit Send and said a prayer. Stevie was a good guy, loved his family, and—if he were sober—would do what he could to help out.

It was the "if" part that bothered Kyle. He stood, shoved his chair out of the way and paced the short distance to his doorway. Placing his hands on the frame he leaned forward and stretched out his tense shoulder muscles. When that didn't work he pushed off the hatchway and paced back and forth in the small space.

This was going to be one hell of an underway, he thought.

Distraction was the last thing any sailor needed during a patrol. He needed to be sharp, with his head in the game. They had a mission to complete and while being on a sub wasn't the same as being in the sandbox, the boat held its own risks, its own dangers.

Lives were on the line.

He didn't need to be worrying about his mom, but that was the hand life had dealt him. For as long as Kyle could remember his mom had worked too hard, never stopping. Up before the rest of the family, to bed after everyone else. Cooking, cleaning, checking homework, mending clothes—always something else for her to do and of course, trying to keep the twins out of trouble. She worked at a local drycleaner. Long hours over hot presses or bent over a sewing machine making alterations. She never stopped.

The old man, while hard on Kyle, didn't slack either. He worked at one of the local produce farms. Out of the house as the sun rose, in the fields all day, and then he'd come home to fix whatever needed fixing at home. It seemed like something was always broken. Maybe the old man drank a little too much, and passed out in his recliner without helping with the dishes, or yelled at the twins and Kyle too much.

What could he do? Kyle tried not to let bitterness eat away at him. Life had dealt his parents a crappy hand.

It was hard.

Especially when his dad blamed him for that crappy life, which was unfair.

No one made his parents have unprotected sex at sixteen.

No one made them get married and quit school.

Especially not his maternal grandparents.

If not for Nana and Pops, Kyle never would have gone to college, he never would have gone into the military, and he'd probably be behind bars. If only they were still alive, he could have reached out to them for help. As it was, he'd have to pray Stevie pulled himself out of the bottle long enough to read his e-mail.

Until they pulled into their first port, Kyle would have to shove his family problems to the back of his mind and concentrate on work.

If only it were that easy to put one Lily Nicole Riley out of his mind. It'd been hard enough the week before they left. Having her underfoot? Damn near impossible.

Images of Nic flashed through his brain: her pink cheeks when he teased her, the way she bit her lower lip when she was lost in thought, and her sprawled naked across his hotel bed, demanding more as he drove into her.

"Damn," he muttered, dropping his head against the top rack he'd claimed. It was going to be a very long and trying deployment.

"What's with the drama king pose?" Bryant asked as he walked into their shared stateroom and opened his locker.

"Nothing," Kyle grumbled before turning around to eye his so-called buddy.

Bryant ignored him as he opened a cabinet to pull out a binder. "Right. Just my luck you and Mace PMSing at the same time."

"Screw you, Gatlin." Kyle grabbed the chair he'd shoved across the room and dragged it over to the desk. "Go find someone else to bug. I've got work to do."

"What's with Miss Mary Sunshine?" Mace asked from the doorway.

"Nothing." Kyle didn't bother looking at either. He wasn't in the mood to deal.

"My money says a certain supply officer's got him twisted up," Bryant replied.

Kyle turned at his comment and gave his best scowl. "You didn't seem surprised to see Nic in the wardroom. Unlike the rest of us."

Bryant looked from him to Mace and back, scrubbing at the back of his neck. "Cherise told me."

"You didn't think to mention it before the meeting?"

"Didn't get a chance."

Mace snorted and shook his head.

"Right. No time. None during the ride into work or when we were walking to the boat or waiting on the skipper to start?" Kyle waited, fighting the urge to tell off Bryant.

They'd been friends for a couple of years. Been on numerous underways, worked long hours, and exchanged life stories. He couldn't believe after all that, the guy left him hanging.

"Guess it slipped my mind at the time." Bryant tossed the binder on his rack. "Look, I didn't think it was a big deal. You haven't said a word about her since we left the hotel last weekend."

"Can you get more clueless, Gatlin? The guy's been mooning over her all week long." Mace pushed off the doorframe and faced Kyle. "You willing to flush your naval career down the crapper, Hutch?"

"No." He didn't need Mace to point out getting involved with Nic while underway was a one-way ticket back to Hicksville and his family. There wasn't a woman on the planet worth throwing away everything he'd worked the past ten years for since he graduated from high school and escaped from home. Not even one with big brown almond shaped eyes, or porcelain skin, or who felt like she'd been made to fit up against him.

"Keep saying that to yourself. This life is hell on relationships."

"Amber still giving you a hard time?" Kyle asked.

"By a hard time do you mean refusing to come home so we can work on our marriage? Yeah and every time I call, her mom starts ranting in the background calling me every name you can think of and accusing me of all sorts of things."

"That's harsh, man. She knew when you two hooked up what she was getting into. I mean you told her, right?" Bryant came from a long line of sailors; his mom could be the poster wife for the Navy. To him, there was no other life. Kyle on the other hand came from a small farming town where none of his family understood his desire to go to sea, locked in a submerged tin can with over a hundred other guys and not see daylight for weeks at a time.

"Hearing about something is one thing, experiencing it is another. She did fine the first couple of years while I was on shore duty. Home every night, weekends off. The last two years have been hard. She doesn't want a part-time husband, especially one where she can't plan anything because schedules change frequently."

"Still pissed about missing your anniversary, huh?" Kyle asked.

"Ya think?" Mace blew out a huff of air and looked upward. "And this time, I'm missing her birthday."

"They're just dates on a calendar. Miss an anniversary? Big deal. Celebrate three years plus fifteen days or whatever when you get home. That's what my parents always did." Bryant walked up to Mace and clamped his hand on the other guy's shoulder. "I've got to get back up to the Nav Center. Hang in there, buddy. She'll come to her senses."

Mace raised his brow at Kyle as he stepped fully into the room and sat at the other desk. "Clueless."

"He means well, but yeah. The guy's got a babe in every port and no clue what it takes to make it for the long haul." Kyle closed out of the e-mail program and brought up his tactical weapons report. Time to update the skipper on the status of how many torpedoes, tomahawks and small ammunitions they carried.

"The thing is, Amber's got a point. How do we make our marriage work when I'm never home?"

Kyle turned around to face Mace, noted the pained look on his friend's face and dreaded what was coming next. He'd seen the look before. Watched as others made the decision Mace was up against.

"Are you getting out?" Kyle asked.

"Thinking about it. Amber means too much to me to lose her. If working some nine-to-five, boring-ass desk job is what I have to do to keep her, I'll do it."

"You're six months from shore duty and more than halfway to retirement. You've got one, maybe two more rotations of sea duty and you're willing to throw away everything you've been working toward?"

Mace tapped his fingers on the desktop and met his gaze. "Yeah. I am."

Kyle closed his mouth. Would he ever meet a woman worth giving up all his dreams? With his luck, he'd already met her, didn't recognize her for who she truly was, and let her walk out of his life.

"What would you do?"

Mace grimaced. "Her dad owns his own insurance agency and has invited me to work for him."

"Insurance?" Pure torture. The guy would go nuts within a year's time, Kyle silently bet. Mace hated paperwork. Hell, who didn't? Kyle had spent enough time during every deployment and patrol over the last three years listening to his friend bitch about reports. Now he wanted to do paperwork for a living? No way.

Forget a year. Within six months Mace would be back and Amber would be a bitter memory.

"I wish you luck, my friend."

"Thanks. I better get this fucking drill set report done. Tomorrow we play war games."

For Kyle, there's no way he'd swap his life in the Navy for sitting behind a desk. He couldn't live without the smell of sea air, amine, standing topside and seeing nothing but miles and miles of blue all around him. Nothing against civilian life, but they were doing something important here.

He never knew what each mission would bring. Punching holes in the ocean, sitting off the coast of enemy territory showing force or waiting for the orders to seek and destroy. He'd sailed under the North Pole—and popped up through the ice much to a polar bear's surprise, gone around through the Panama Canal, played hide and seek with Russian subs, and backed down a terrorist leader's threat with just their presence.

They protected America's freedom at all costs.

Living at the tip of the spear one day and the next sitting in some office far from the action? He couldn't do it and doubted his friend would find any satisfaction there either.

As if to prove his thoughts right, Mace sat drumming his fingers on the desk, staring at him.

"What?" Kyle asked.

"How goes it with Riley?" Mace broke through his thoughts with the one subject he'd rather forget.

"She's settling in despite feeling like the odd man out."

"Explains not seeing her at lunch. You gonna let her miss dinner too?"

"Nope. Right after I finish this report, I'm dragging her out of her stateroom. It's time for a tour of the boat and a lesson on Subs 101."

"Keep your hands to yourself, WEPS, unless you want to join me in the insurance world."

Chapter Five

Kyle stopped next to Nic's open stateroom. As usual she was at her desk working, but right then she had her eyes closed with a cup of something steaming underneath her nose. He hated to end her peaceful moment, but they had work to do.

"Coffee break?" He stepped fully into the room as her eyes popped open and the liquid sloshed over the edge and splattered on her poopy suit.

She scooted back, away from the computer, setting the cup down to wipe at the wet spot. "More like I better eat before I kill someone, because I skipped breakfast and lunch today."

"You looked like you were lost in thought." He sat on the edge of her rack and took in the contents of her so-called lunch. Rice cakes? *Gah.* Tasteless cardboard circles if you asked him.

"Trying to solve a mystery."

"Maybe I can help, if you tell me about it."

"Got any idea who would fill my room with condom balloons?"

"Well, I think it's safe to rule out the skipper and XO." Kyle rubbed his chin with the palm of his hand trying to hide the smile. "It wasn't me, so that leaves about a hundred and thirty-six suspects."

"That's okay. I'll figure it out and when I do, I hope they remember revenge is a dish best served cold." She chuckled and shook her head.

"Is everything else okay?" Bright spots of pink stained her cheeks, but he didn't see any dark circles under her eyes, which was a good sign that she was adjusting to the eighteen-hour days.

"Everything is fine." She closed the laptop and focused those dark, almond shaped eyes on him. "Just trying to play catch-up on paperwork and quals."

"Speaking of, I hear you've already got Sub Force History and the Ventilation System signed off on your card. Not bad, especially for being on board for a week."

"I've got a goal." She smiled and everything inside him lit up.

"So I've heard. Beating SUBLANT's record of earning his dolphins in four months. Aggressive. I like it. If you're going to succeed, we better get started on your next checkmark." He stood up and waited at the doorway for her to secure the room before leading her down the passageway.

She tagged along after him. "What system are you going to teach me?"

He ducked through the hatch and headed up the stairs. "Not me. The Chief of the Watch. It's time you learned the trim and drain and to keep this pig stable and not sink her to the bottom of the ocean."

"Oh."

Was that a hint of disappointment in her voice? He'd been keeping his distance, letting her get her bearings without him and the memory of their night together crowding her space. According to Mace and Bryant, the crew was still a little unsure how to behave around her, not sure if she'd get offended by their jokes or give back as good as they gave. In time, she'd learn the ropes, learn to tell when someone was yanking her chain and most importantly, that they were a family down here.

Once they returned home, the married guys would return to their wives and kids. The single guys would hang out in the barracks or they'd converge at someone's house for a barbecue before hitting the bars in the hopes of getting lucky. Underway or at home, if you found one submariner, you found more.

Another thing she'd learn is that life underway got monotonous and a bunch of bored men quickly turned into adolescents. Someone was always razzing someone else or playing practical jokes. It was only a matter of time before Nic was the next target.

They entered the Control Room and Kyle nodded to Mace before leading Nic over to a short, balding man with a paunchy belly. "Chief Knowles, she's all yours."

He passed Nic off and went to stand at the Conn where he could keep an eye on everything in the control room: the planesman, helmsman, dive officer —basically the guys driving the boat—all the while keeping an eye on Knowles and Nic and doing his own job.

Knowles instructed Nic to take a seat on the NUB bench and Kyle suppressed a smile. Leave it to a Chief to put an Officer in their place. To Nic's credit she sat without a word, eyes scanning the BCP—Ballast Control Panel—pen and notebook ready. Knowles gave her a quick rundown of the system, how they bring seawater in to submerge, move it from one end to the other to the keep the boat steady and release it back to the sea when they want to surface.

It sounded simply enough and it was, it was the knowing how many gallons to bring on board, how to disperse it and how fast to empty the tanks that was the tricky part. Too much too soon and you'd sink her like a rock. Empty the tanks too fast and you chance hitting a ship on the surface that you missed on SONAR.

"Sir." One of his men approached and stood stiff as a board.

"Relax, Petty Officer Stone. This is a control room, not a parade grounds and the captain is in his stateroom." The guy went from attention to parade rest. Major suck-up. The helmsman nodded to the planesman and snickered. "What can I do for you, Stone?"

"Sir, Chief Long asked me to give these to you." He stuck out a stack of papers. Great. More reports. One of those things the recruiter forgot to mention. Kyle distinctly remembered 'Join the Navy, see the world, go on an adventure.' Nothing about spending over half your time filling out freaking reports. He held his hand out and waited for Stone to pass them over. And waited. And waited some more.

He gave the sheets of paper a little tug. The young man's eyes shifted quickly to meet Kyle's gaze, let go and returned his attention to a point beyond Kyle's right shoulder. He didn't need to turn around to know what the guy was staring at— or rather who he was salivating over. Kyle didn't consider himself a violent man. Sure he'd been in his share of fights before, but none for the fun of it. Not like his dipshit brothers. Right then, it took everything he had had in him not to punch the guy in front of him in the face.

Reining in the urge that would land him in front of the captain he glanced at the all-important papers. Standard evaluations. Nothing that needed his immediate attention.

"Was there anything else, Petty Officer Stone?" Kyle cocked a brow and cleared his throat as the other man, barely more than a kid really, continued to ignore him to watch Nic.

"Um, no sir."

"Good." He shoved the papers against Stone's chest. "Leave these in my stateroom. Lieutenant Havers should be in there and you can give them to him. Then you can join the crew in field day, starting with the heads."

The control room went silent as Stone exited so it wasn't hard to catch his 'asshole' comment. Every hair on the back of Kyle's neck stood up and the skin prickled. He didn't need to turn around to know she had her gaze trained on him. He crossed his arms and focused on the screens in front of him, doing his job, which is what he'd done with Stone. Yeah, sticking the kid on cleaning duty was harsh, but Kyle had a point to make. Down here Nic wasn't a woman, she was a submariner and as such she was to be treated like everyone else on board.

No exceptions.

Not by the crew.

Not by him.

"Okay, think you've got it now?" Chief Knowles asked.

Out of the corner of his eye he saw Nic wipe her palms down her thighs and nod, as her eyes scanned the BCP.

"Seems pretty straight forward."

Kyle let Knowles' instructions fade and his mind drift. He needed to keep his focus where it belonged and that wasn't Nic Riley. This would be his last run before he transferred to Hawaii and shore duty—something he was sorely looking forward to. A little sun, a little sand, a whole lot of surf 'n turf and babes in bikinis on vacations with no expectations but a good time.

He had goals and they didn't include getting tied down. Next year he planned on putting on Lieutenant Commander. Give him another four years after that and he'd be putting silver oak leaves on his collar and captaining his own sub. When he crossed the twenty-year mark he'd either be sporting Captain's birds or moving on to his next career. Either way, he'd show his old man that he had what it took to do something with his life, to make something of himself besides a farmer living paycheck to paycheck.

"What?" Nic's squeaked broke through his thoughts.

Kyle turned to her and Knowles.

"I can't sign off on your qual card until I know for sure you've got a full understanding of the BCP. And you can't move on to dive officer until that's done."

"I know, it's just… I…" She turned to Kyle. "He only just showed me, um… don't I have any time to study my notes first before I'm tested?" Even in the dim lighting of the control room he could see the pink stains on her cheeks. Was she afraid she'd fail? Didn't seem like her.

"Sure you can take your time. Most don't punch all the buttons for six, twelve months. SUBLANT's record is like the golden ring and most don't even come close to touching it."

There it was, the fire inside her.

He knew the minute his words hit their mark, saw the spark of determination light up in her eyes, the change in her stance that went from scared and uncertain to kick-ass mode. The many sides of Nic Riley: conservative, wild, insecure, confident, funny, serious. Who was she really when no one else was around? When the shades were pulled and the doors were locked, who was the woman no one saw?

Did she play her music loud and sing off-key? Throw things when she got mad? Soak in bubble baths? Leave a path when she got undressed?

Think of him and want to break all the rules?

Dangerous questions given their situation.

He turned away when Nic started re-explaining the system to Knowles. She'd do fine and it wouldn't surprise him when she beat her dad's record. It had taken Kyle six months to punch all the buttons, then again, he didn't have the same motivation lighting his fire.

As he listened to Nic, Kyle saw the other men in the room nod. Did she know they wanted her to succeed as much as she did? It didn't mean they'd grant her any special treatment. Before long he imagined she'd be the butt of a practical joke or two. He'd already heard the crew giving her crap about the soft serve machine breaking down. None of it meant they didn't like or accept her. It was the way of life on the boat, how they all survived eighteen-hour days, no sunlight, the monotony, and being away from their families.

Kyle kept his eyes glued to the dive monitor as the boat went deeper. Nic's soft voice swept over him in the dark Control Room bringing back memories best not revisited at the moment. The next six months couldn't go fast enough.

Out of the corner of his eye he saw Nic's arm shoot out right about the time someone walked into her path.

The XO jumped back, but not fast enough.

"Fuck, that's hot!" A wet stain spread across the middle of his chest, as coffee dripped off his hand and onto the floor.

Nic shot him a worried look.

"Sir." Nic stepped forward. "I'm so sorry."

"Not your fault, Lieutenant. Any idiot who walks around with an open cup of coffee deserves to get scalded. Carry on. A word, Hutch."

He stepped over as far out of hearing range as one could get on a submarine.

"How's she settling in?"

"Good, sir."

"Everything okay, between you two?'

"Sir?"

"Just something I overheard. I'm sure it was nothing and I don't need to remind you how small a submarine is. That there are no secrets and that I expect my officers to conduct themselves appropriately at all time."

"No, sir. You don't." *Shit.* Had he heard about the night in Boston? From whom?

"Good. At thirteen hundred I want you to run the drill. The *Virginia* will be ready."

"Sir." Kyle nodded and stepped aside to let the XO go. *Exactly what had he overheard?* Neither he nor Nic had stepped over any lines since she'd reported on board. Well, there was that initial conversation in her room. Still no one had overheard except maybe Doc and he wouldn't have repeated any of it. The man wore a perpetual cone of silence.

* * *

Great, just great. They'd been underway for a little more than a week and she'd already screwed up. Sure the XO said not to worry about her spilling scalding hot coffee down his front, but then he'd called Kyle over to the side and spoke to him in private. It might seem egotistical to think it was all about her. Really it was logic, as Kyle was her sponsor. The XO kept looking her way while talking to Kyle in hushed tones and after he left the control room, Kyle acted like she wasn't even there.

It made sense she'd been the topic of conversation and not in a good way.

Plus, she'd been called to the CO's office.

All she wanted was to fit in with everyone else and show she could hack it with the boys, not stand out as a screw-up who couldn't play with their toys. Suddenly she felt five years old again, trying to keep up with her brothers, Liam and Reece. It didn't make sense either because Kyle said everyone made mistakes. Although she'd bet few had roasted their executive officers.

She could hear muted voices behind the CO's closed door upon her arrival. Cringing, she leaned against the bulkhead and waited. Every now and then she could make out a word, like blatant disregard and dereliction of duties from the CO. Whoever was on the receiving end kept their responses short and low. She could only hope it wasn't Kyle or someone that fell under her command.

Had someone gotten food poisoning? Or what if they were short on supplies? Not that it would be her fault, as she didn't do the actual cooking and everything had been ordered before she reported in.

Still: her people, her mess to fix. Or as the saying went, her flying monkeys, her circus to run.

Her gaze darted toward the door and back as two sailors came down the passageway. Their eyes got round and big and they shot her an apologetic nod before scurrying away, probably hoping to keep out of the crosshairs. Given you could hear the CO as he told whomever that he didn't give a rat's ass whose fault the fuck up had been, to just fix it, she couldn't blame the guys. If she had a choice, she'd come back later.

The door swung open and a red-faced petty officer stepped out.

"Ma'am." He stepped around her and she let out a breath.

"Commander Holloway, you wanted to see me?"

"Lieutenant Riley, come in and close the door."

Shit. Based on his last closed door conversation, what little hope Nic had that this was just a quick welcome aboard or "Hey, can you get us a copy of *U571*" chat rapidly slipped away. She did as he said and turned back to him, wiping her palms down the back of her poopy suit where the CO couldn't see how nervous she was.

She hoped.

He got up, pushed a chair her way and stepped over to his coffee maker. He lifted a mug and she shook her head. She'd already made the XO spill hot coffee down the front of him; she really didn't need to spill it on the CO or worse, because with the way her nerves were bouncing all over the place there was no way the liquid would stay down.

"Sit down and relax. I promise, I only eat one sailor a day." He dropped back in his chair and inhaled the aroma from his mug. "You'll find out I have two vices. This," he held up the cup, and root beer floats. How are things going? Settling in?"

The men sidestepped her like she had leprosy, her chief cook scowled every time she stepped foot into the galley, she'd screwed up in front of the crew, and she'd been having steamy sex dreams about the weapons officer.

"Everything's going great, sir. No complaints."

A corner of his mouth lifted before he took a sip of his coffee. "I read your file. Top of your class. No reprimands. Excellent evals, which isn't surprising. Considering you could have picked any rating, why supply?"

The smile came easy, but wasn't one filled with joy. "To keep my family happy, sir. They would much rather see me working in the civilian sector than be put in harm's way. I picked a specialty that could easily convert to either the private workforce or government contractors or so I told my parents, but the truth is I've known for years women would be brought on submarines and I knew this was one of the first specialties they'd fill."

"Why subs?" He leaned back with one ankle resting on his knee.

"I could ask you the same, sir." She dropped into the second chair and grasped her hands in front of her to keep from twisting them. "Lots of reason, I guess. It's a family thing. Did you know my grandfather served with Rickover? My dad, my brothers, it's all I've ever known. There's nothing wrong with the surface community, but it's just not us. Is it?"

"No, it's not."

"I've missed the closeness of the sub force these past couple of years. Don't get me wrong. I've been with some great commands and the people in them, all top-notch sailors. Being on a sub, as a woman, it's a challenge, but it's more than that. We're making history. I like knowing I'm helping to change the future, plus what we do here on the boat... It may not be the front line, but we make a difference, sir."

"That we do. The COB has said you're off to a good start on your qualifications, Lieutenant. I do have some concerns on your goals though."

"You think I'm rushing through them, especially after this morning?"

"Are you?"

She thought about his question, her uncertainty about being tested so quickly, and then shook her head.

"No, I don't think I am. I wouldn't purposely put the crew or the boat at risk for my own ego, sir. No goal is worth a person's life. In hindsight, I realize, taking some time, even an hour or two to study my notes would have been the wiser move. I got lucky, but the situation could have played out differently. I endangered not only the boat, but also the whole crew. It won't happen again, sir."

"Good. Just for the record, Chief Knowles wouldn't have let it get that far. I don't have a problem with sailors setting challenging goals for themselves. In fact, I'm all for having something to aim for, if it's for the right reasons. I know what it's like to walk in someone else footsteps, someone big and bright. You wouldn't be the first person to serve onboard who comes from a military family or the first person to try to prove themselves to dad, grandpa, or Uncle Bob."

She nodded in silence.

A sense of déjà vu hit her. How many teachers said those same words to her? How many times had she been compared to her brothers? More than could remember and not for the first time she wondered how much simpler life would be if she'd been an only child or even better, because she really did love the jugheads, if she'd been first born. Then they could be compared to her. Yes, it was petty, but she was only human.

"I don't mind having one of my sailors beat SUBLANT, but not at the cost of my boat."

"It won't happen again, sir."

"Good. The XO briefed you on the nature and importance of our mission when you reported on board?"

She nodded. They'd be gathering intelligence in unstable waters that could aid in the war on terror. Her dad was probably popping Tums like candy.

"We'll make two port calls before then, Scotland and Spain. Be sure to take in the sights, get some fresh air and replenish any supplies we need. I don't want to have to turn the boat around because we ran out of eggs, if you get my meaning?"

She had a feeling his version of eggs weren't the kind you ate. "Yes, sir."

"Good. Welcome aboard, Lieutenant and if you have questions or concerns my door is always open, but I'm sure the WEPS is taking good care of you."

Not as much as her fantasies would like. "He is, sir."

She got up to go and he held up a hand. "One other thing. That other vice I mentioned. My root beer floats?"

"Sir?" She hesitated, wondering if he expected to have one delivered daily.

"I prefer them with soft serve ice cream. Kind of hard to do when the machine is broken. Get it fixed."

"Yes, sir."

Chapter Six

Life had fallen into a quiet routine since the scalding of the XO with daily drills, reports, movies on the mess deck, and practical jokes being dished out on all levels as the boat made its way across the Atlantic. They'd been underway for two and half weeks and would pull into Faslane, Scotland in a couple of days. As a kid her family had lived in Italy and England and had taken multiple trips throughout the UK. It was one of her favorite places and she'd been looking forward to the stop, albeit a short one.

Too bad she wouldn't be allowed to escape for a couple hours of alone time. A quick one-hour ride on the train and she could be in Glasgow with shops, restaurants and people who didn't know she was the big boss's daughter. The atmosphere on the boat had warmed up around her from ice cold to lukewarm. Occasionally someone besides Kyle and Mace included her in their conversation. Someone—identity still unknown—had even played a prank on her. Of course if they thought finding a plastic snake in her bed would make her scream they'd picked the wrong girl. She was Liam and Reece's little sister, after all.

It gave her hope that she was starting to fit in, maybe enough that someone would invite her along on liberty. Because while in port it was the buddy system or you didn't leave the boat.

She shoved what was starting to sound like the beginnings of a self-induced pity party in her head away and focused on the order forms in front of her. Top priority was getting the darn soft serve machine fixed, again, so she could get the crew to stop their whining. But first up was nailing today's security drill.

The 1MC crackled to life, "Security violation in the SONAR room." The general alarm sounded and she scrambled to secure her stateroom.

"Security violation in SONAR room. Petty Officer James has knocked out Petty Officer Banks."

Feet pounded down the passageway as the crew made their way either to the mess deck or to the armory. Nic joined the mass en route to the mess deck, squeezing past sailors headed in the opposite direction. For once, none paid any attention to her as they brushed up against her chest. She was just another crewmember.

By the time she arrived, a whiteboard had already been set up and Chief Boone stood next to it, marker in hand and nodded to her. Nic wasted no time. She let out a whistle that cut the din in the room to silence in seconds.

"Okay, you heard the Chief of the Watch. Our job is to find James. When you find him, call for security. We don't know if he's armed, but he's already taken out one person. Stay with your partner and watch each others' six. You two, Brooks and Stone, search the torpedo room. Smitty, you, Peterson, Roberts, and Wu take the crew's quarters."

On and on she went, assigning pairs to the maneuvering room, control, officers' quarters and so on until every department and nook and cranny of the boat was covered. They would start at the bow and work their way to the stern. When one team finished an area they'd fall in with the team behind them and do a second sweep. There was no way James could escape. Her team had one hour to find him.

She would not fail again.

As the minutes ticked down and each crew called in their area, she marked it off and directed them to a new location. Sometimes she sent them back to sweep an area another team had cleared. For one, you never knew if James was working alone or if the crewmembers missed a hiding spot. She didn't sweat it. She had this. It was child's play.

Literally.

When they were kids and their mom would go off to do one her charity events and leave her dad in charge, he'd keep them busy with war games. Probably training for her brothers disguised as play. She always got to be the intruder, or spy, as she liked to think of herself, because she was the smallest and could hide in more places. Not to mention, she had patience. Minutes, hours could pass and she'd sit there quietly waiting for Liam or Reece to find her without making a peep. If one of the boys had been hiding, they would have been moaning and groaning after two minutes.

"Smitty cleared the maneuvering room, ma'am." Chief Boone marked it off on the whiteboard.

They were almost done—where could James be? She scratched her neck as she pictured the boat in her mind, trying to think of all the little nooks and crannies.

"Send the first two teams back through the crew's quarters and tell them not to be afraid to the check the Captain's stateroom."

"Yes, ma'am." He turned and relayed the information to her teams.

A quick glance at the wall clock had her cringing. Time was running out. She pulled up a mental image of Petty Officer James: five-ten or eleven, medium build, decent shoulder width. Ruled out some places like lockers, but it left plenty of others.

"Any sign of James yet?"

Her stomach bounced and did a few somersaults at the sound of Kyle's deep voice. Heat stole across her cheeks when he turned his gaze from the board to her.

There was simply something uniquely sexy and soulful about his eyes. One minute laughing with you and the next stripping you bare, exposing all of your secrets and making you beg for more. When he looked at her like he did then, like he did at the bar, as if he could see past the surface. See all the imperfections and still thought she was amazing and beautiful.

He tempted her with that look. Tempted her to break the rules. Tempted her to put it all on the line—her career and her heart—and find out if it was worth the risk.

Thank goodness for a strong will power.

"Time's running out, Nic. Have you found James yet?" Kyle repeated.

"No. The crew is almost done searching and they've come up empty. No one has seen him." She glanced at the clock again, less than fifteen minutes until her deadline. Couldn't Kyle go back to where ever? Didn't he know he messed with her brain when he was around? "Shouldn't you be guarding the torpedoes or something?

The corners of his mouth lifted. "I came to see if you needed any help."

"No. No, Chief Boone and I have it under control. You can run along to your duty station."

His cocked brow matched his tilted smile and both said he didn't buy it for one minute. Maybe it was because while he'd been standing there three more of her teams had called in the all clear with no results.

"Fine. What do you suggest?"

She hated to ask, had wanted to prove to herself, the crew, to the Captain, and yes, to Kyle, that she could do this. Especially after the coffee fiasco that the crew still razzed her about every chance they got.

He stepped further into the mess deck and scanned the board. "Did you check the trash disposal room?" At her scrunched up face, he laughed. "Sounds disgusting but there's a lot of guys who pick it because of that very fact."

"Sir, Stone cleared the room," Chief Boone responded.

"Well, he has to be here. We're on a sub, in the middle of the Atlantic, a couple of hundred feet below the surface. It's not like he stepped out for a smoke." Nic thought back to when she'd play the games with her brothers. If it were her, where would she hide? She pulled up the mental diagram of the boat and checked off locations. He attacked Banks in SONAR, so the logical choice would have been either the crew's quarters or the torpedo room.

Kyle would have found him if he'd been in hidden among the weapons. Her next choice would have been the CO or XO's staterooms, but those were cleared too. So, where did the wily petty officer go? A light bulb clicked. But, of course.

"Chief, WEPS, we need to search the galley."

It made sense. Hide right beneath their noses. Boone headed to the walk-in freezer, and Nic really, hoped James hadn't picked there to hide. That would be taking the game to the extreme. She and Kyle headed to her least favorite spot—the pantry.

She slid the door open and sure enough, there was Petty Officer James munching down on a bag of chocolate chips with a grin a mile wide on his face.

"Call it in, WEPS and get security down here."

As the armed guards zipped tied James and hauled him off to the CO to finish out the drill, Nic looked at the clock and sighed with relief. They had one minute to go.

* * *

Day eighteen of captivity. Taco Tuesday. The same as always. Week in, week out. The only difference this round was the distraction known as Nic Riley and today she'd shown she was more than just an admiral's daughter.

Sexy, charming, intelligent, and beautiful—not words he usually thought of to describe a shipmate. Sure, Mace and Bryant were good-looking guys. At least that was the rumor. But sitting in the wardroom watching Nic smile, cheeks stained pink, eyes shining bright, biting down on that lush lower lip of hers while giving credit to her team as the other officers congratulated her on a job well done, floored him. Not all would be so humble. For a minute there, he didn't think she would either, especially when he'd offered to help and she'd brushed him off.

He got that she had a need. No, make that a burning desire to prove herself to everyone around her and to her family. The *I* mentality might work in certain jobs, more so in the civilian world, very few in the military. Not that he'd really done anything. It'd still been her idea that led to James's hiding spot, but she gave just the smallest bit and let him help. Which was a step forward. He'd learned a few things about Nic since they'd deployed: she was ambitious, competitive, and didn't like to fail and when she did, she took it hard.

She'd thrown herself into learning the ship's systems. If she wasn't on watch, she was holed up in her stateroom or the wardroom studying. No one could fault her dedication, but a body could go a little stir crazy with all work and no play, which is why he planned to show her the sights when they pulled into port. When he'd mentioned his plans to Mace and Bryant they'd insisted on coming along, stating Scotland could be the undoing of his career.

"He told you to check the TDU? Man, you'd have to be a kid to hide in there," one of the other officers commented from the far end of the table.

"Yeah, never believe Hutch. He'll lead you astray," Bryant said.

Thanks buddy, Kyle thought. He kicked back in his chair as Bryant focused on Nic, a total one-eighty from how he'd been since they'd lifted anchor. What was his friend up to now?

"So Nic," said Bryant, "A couple of us are going to catch the train and take a couple of days to explore Glasglow. Want to join up with us? I know this great pub where the owner serves the smoothest whiskey and mouthwatering meat pies."

What the hell? Bryant pre-empted him? He knew Kyle's plans and there was no way Kyle was buying his friend was trying to save him from getting in trouble. Bryant was a dog when it came to women. No scratch that. Dogs had more loyalty. Kyle knew damn well Gatlin had been involved, more than once, with women he'd worked with while on shore commands. Now he was going after Nic.

It took everything Kyle had to stay seated. Granted he had no claim on her and if she'd made the moves on his friend, he'd… Okay, he'd still be pissed, but Bryant had been there when they'd met, he knew why Kyle couldn't or wouldn't pursue a relationship with Nic.

It was a dick move. You didn't poach from your friends.

"Wouldn't happen to be the Hound and the Hare, would it?" Nic replied in response to Bryant's question about the pub.

"As a matter of fact, it is," Bryant replied.

"Then count me in. I can never pass up Maggie's cooking." Forget nuclear power. Her smile could have fueled the sub for weeks.

The fact she knew of the pub came as no surprise. Every port had that place, the one who catered to the service. Here it was Maggie's, Bar 57 in La Maddalena and the Horse and Cow in Guam. Some family-run, some classy, some raunchy. All a haven in a foreign land where they were made to feel at home.

The others talked about plans while in port. Some had shopping to do for wives, kids, girlfriends, or families. Others planned on indulging in the local delicacies. A few first-timers planned short excursions. Forty-eight hours didn't give them much time. Mostly enough to blow off steam, get some fresh air, or get into trouble. Unable to watch Bryant flirt with Nic any longer Kyle pushed away from the table and excused himself.

"Where you off to, Hutch?" Mace asked.

Kyle shot a glance across the table toward Bryant. "Unlike what some think, this isn't a pleasure cruise. Got work to do."

His body ached when Nic's gaze lifted to meet his, when she aimed her smile at him. It wasn't flirtatious or filled with promises or even one that hinted at their secret past. There were times he'd swear the whole night in Boston had been a figment of his imagination, because Nic treated him no differently than she treated anyone else on board: with casual friendliness and respect. He tried to forget, but the better he got to know her, the harder it became.

Maybe in Faslane he'd grab one of the other guys and they'd head off in a different direction. Go look for Nessie. Fish. Take a dunk in a cold loch. Anything to put some space between him and Nic. While he'd never break the rules or protocol on board the boat, port calls were a different beast and three-minute cold showers just weren't cutting it anymore.

Once they got back to base he'd be transferring and the temptation would be removed. Find a nice, uncomplicated woman who didn't put demands on him while he focused on his career. Until then he'd limit his time around Nic, because clearly even in a room filled with people he wasn't safe from his libido or lust or whatever was ruling his emotions. If anything, it was worse. Watching his buddy hit on her, his blood had boiled and he'd had to fight an urge not to go all caveman.

Yeah, he needed to keep his distance there. The last thing he needed in his life was drama. He had enough of that back home between his mom's health issues and the dipshit twins' shenanigans.

A couple of his guys, Petty Officers Wu and Brooks, headed toward him, deep in conversation, laughing.

"Good work on the search today," Kyle said.

"Thank you, sir," they both replied, still chuckling.

He eyed them back and forth. Sometimes it was best not to ask and he'd probably regret doing so. "Do I want to know what's so funny?"

The two looked at each other and burst out in full on belly laughter. Wu had tears streaming down his face as he tried to catch his breath. He shook his head, one arm wrapped around his gut and pointed to Brooks.

Kyle turned his attention to his other guy, expecting the joke of the century at that point.

Brooks took a deep breath, slapped Wu on the back and grinned like an idiot. After a few seconds he got his laughter under control. "We froze the COB's underwear. Every pair. We snuck them back in right before he returned from the shower. Didn't know he knew so many swear words in Tagalog."

Kyle rubbed the back of his neck. "Ah, that explains his earlier comment."

"What was it?" Wu, sober now, looked worried.

"Said he was going to string someone's balls up in the goat locker. Got the impression he thought it was one of the other chiefs." A chuckle of his own escaped as he imagined Ronquillo's reaction to the situation.

"You're not going to tell him it was us, are you, sir?" Wu shot a look to his buddy, all the color drained from his face.

Couldn't blame the guy; the COB had the ability to make their life a living hell for the next couple of months.

"Nah. Ronquillo has played his fair share of jokes on others. About time he was the butt of one. A word to the wise. Keep this to yourself for now."

Both men hustled away and Kyle continued down the passageway to the torpedo room. He didn't really think the COB would retaliate, but he might stick the two of them on watch while in port or assign them extra field duty scrubbing the heads.

"That's a pretty steep price. Smitty said he got it for a steal."

The comment caused Kyle to pause outside the entrance to the torpedo room.

"Now what?" he muttered to himself.

Both of the men inside had their backs toward him and every instinct he had told him whatever negotiation was going down wasn't going to make him a happy camper.

"Yeah, but he only got a short clip. I'm offering you the full uncut deal and if you like what you see, I can get you more."

What the hell was Stone involved in? Bootleg videos? Crap, the skipper would have a field day. If there was one thing the old man didn't tolerate, that was breaking the law. He expected good morale and conduct from all of his men one hundred percent of the time and when you let him down... Well, the CO had no problem going old school. He didn't tiptoe around and worry about PC bullshit. He saved the political correctness for when they were on land and dealing with the bureaucrats, with his sailors he was one hundred percent Navy.

"Stone, what are you up to?"

At the sound of Kyle's voice, both men spun around to face him. Stone stuck both his hands in the pockets of his poopy suit.

"Sir, Petty Officer Roberts and I were going over the maintenance reports, sir."

What a lying suck up, Kyle thought. He hadn't liked Stone from the minute he'd reported on board. Oily was the word that came to mind. Young and dumb were two others.

"What's in your pocket, Petty Officer Stone?" Kyle stood feet shoulder width apart, arms crossed over his chest blocking the exit.

Stone's eyes stared him down. He swallowed once, twice, then blinked. "Nothing, sir."

Kyle said nothing in response, glanced down, and back up, then held his hand out, palm up. Stone shifted from one foot to the other. Roberts hadn't said a word, but he nudged Stone with his elbow and gave a slight nod toward Kyle. Good, at least one of them was thinking.

"It's just my phone, sir." Stone pulled his cell out and handed it to Kyle.

Kyle hit the button on the side, saw the locked screen and handed it back. Without saying a word, Stone unlocked the screen and gave the phone back.

"You know smart phones aren't allowed in here. That alone could get you written up, taken to Captain's mast."

"Sir, I wasn't filming the boat. I'd never do that."

"Then tell me what were you showing Roberts." Kyle continued to thumb through the different screens and apps.

"Tell him, Stone or I will." Roberts' tone was sharp. His cheeks were flushed and his eyes flared with anger. Kyle knew the signs and ordered Roberts to stand over on the other side of the room while he spoke with Stone. He really didn't need a fight to break out on top of whatever this was.

Once Roberts was a safe distance away, Kyle turned back to Stone, his finger over the gallery app. "Last chance, Stone to come clean on your own." Stone shot a look toward Roberts and then focused on Kyle again. Once again he stared straight-ahead, not blinking, mouth drawn tight. "Sir, it's a long deployment. I downloaded a few adult vids and I was offering to share them with Roberts."

Out of the corner of his eye, Kyle caught Roberts' body freeze, heard the quick intake of breath and noted the lack of exhaling.

"For a price?" Kyle asked.

"Well, yeah," Stone replied. "You know how it is, sir. We don't make squat as an E-4. Got car payments to make, bills to pay, a girl back home who expects me to bring home presents from our port calls. Guys got make some extra scratch."

He knew the pay sucked at Stone's rate, but he also knew the guy didn't have to pay for housing or food and he drove a car that even Kyle couldn't afford and he'd been in for a hell of a lot longer than Stone. Kyle also didn't throw his money away at the local strip club, which is probably where Stone got the video.

Still smartphones weren't allowed in here for a reason and he just didn't trust this guy. Every instinct Kyle had told him Stone lied through his teeth, not to mention the dead giveaways between him and Roberts. Something was on the phone that was going to get both men busted.

Kyle hit play on the file marked 'video one'.

It opened with a woman in the shower. What do you know, the little shit told the truth. Kyle was about to hit the off button when the woman turned around, as she ran her soapy hands down her wet body he zeroed in on her face and saw red.

Nic.

Kyle grabbed Stone by the lapels of his poopy suit so fast the guy started sputtering as he slammed him against the bulkhead.

"You fucking piece of shit!"

"Sir." Roberts grabbed his arm, got into his face. "You don't want to do this. He's not worth it."

He locked eyes with Roberts. He wanted to tell him how wrong he was, how it would be worth whatever punishment the Navy sent his way to teach the scum in front of him a lesson, but his mouth couldn't form the words. Stone had violated Nic, had broken the trust of one of their own, and Kyle was going to see that he paid.

"What the hell, Hutch?" Bryant's voice cut through the red haze in his brain as his hands and Mace's pulled him back, but Kyle didn't let go.

"I don't know how," he said through gritted teeth, "but he's got a video of Nic... Lieutenant Riley in the shower and he's selling it to crewmembers."

Out of the corner of his eye, he caught Mace's jaw drop, heard the whoosh of air expel as if someone had gut checked him.

"Are you sure?" Mace asked.

"Yeah. I caught him in the act."

"No, are you sure it's her?" Bryant clarified.

Stone started shaking his head. "I swear, man. It's not Lieutenant Riley. I downloaded that video off the net weeks before we left. Not my fault the chick looks like her. The WEPS is mistaken."

"Hutch?" Mace looked him square on.

Kyle turned to meet his friend's questioning gaze. "I saw the video, enough to know it was filmed in a submarine shower and the woman's face was that of Lieutenant Nic Riley. Vice Admiral Riley's daughter." He threw that last part on while looking at Stone and Roberts.

"SUBLANT?" Roberts stepped back, ran his hands over his head and held them at the back of his head. "Shit, Stone you are one dumb motherfu... I knew she was some bigwig's daughter, but I hadn't really paid any attention to who."

"Hutch." Mace brought his attention back to him. "Look, I believe you and I know you must feel right now."

"No, you really don't."

He wanted to rip Stone's head off. Shove him in the torpedo tube and shoot him out to sea. He was a lowlife sexual predator and some slick dick of a defense lawyer would probably get him off with a slap of the wrist.

Every time Kyle tried to let go, his fingers clutched the material tighter. This scum had seen Nic naked, had violated her trust and privacy. He couldn't even imagine what Nic's reaction would be, or how she would feel, but Kyle was willing to risk the consequences to see that Stone met with justice.

Mace got in his face.

"Look. I get it. You want to pound his face into the bulkhead. You want to teach him a lesson and I'm not going to disagree and say he doesn't deserve it either. But you do this, and I let you, we'll both end up in the brig next to him."

Slowly Kyle released his hold on Stone. Mace had a point. Getting himself in trouble wouldn't help Nic. He needed to pull it together and play it by the book so that not only Stone, but also every idiot who saw the video would pay for their betrayal.

Chapter Seven

"Sit," the XO ordered. His normal easygoing manner sounded more like the captain's gruff I'm-too-tired-for-this-bullshit tone. "If this isn't a cluster fuck, I don't know what is." He dropped into the chair opposite of Kyle and blew out a breath.

"You know I've seen some messed up stuff in my time. Sailors sleeping with shipmates' wives, stealing, smuggling contraband on board, drugs. I've heard pretty much every excuse there is for the stupid shit people do." The XO—Chris—slouched back in his chair, crossed his feet and got comfy. "Did I ever tell you about the idiot who swallowed a joint? Someone put it out in his beer bottle. Said he couldn't spit the beer out. He was driving his car and it was raining. Stupid. This though... it's beyond stupid."

Kyle let out a small chuckle. At least the stupid guy didn't hurt anyone else. This? Recording someone without their knowledge wasn't showing a lack of brain cells, it showed a lack of a moral compass. If he didn't laugh at the one guy to let off some steam he'd probably stalk out of the XO's stateroom, find Petty Officer Scumbucket and beat the shit out of him. The really funny part? Never before had Kyle been the type to get into fights. Something about Nic brought out the caveman in him.

"Did Stone confess?" Kyle asked.

"Not at first. I talked to Roberts and then Smitty before him. Roberts hadn't seen the video before today. Smitty told him about it, but didn't show it to him. I guess that's something. Roberts didn't put it together and realize it was Riley. He's only seen her a few times coming and going to chow. Smitty knew. He tried to deny it, but that guy can't lie to save his life."

They sat in silence for a few minutes while his words circulated through Kyle's brain. Smitty and Roberts surprised him. Both were good guys, excellent sailors and had come across as having working brains.

"Who else has it or has seen it?"

"According to Stone, once the captain got him to talk, only the three of them, but I don't buy it. I think he had help. He admits he sold the video to Smitty and planned to sell it to others. The captain has already signed off on the written warrant and the COB and Havers are conducting a berth-by-berth search. Everyone's electronics will be checked—enlisted, chief, officer. No exceptions."

"You've seen it?" The XO nodded. "Obviously, Ronquillo and Havers so they'd know what to look for, plus me and the captain—"

"No. The skipper refused. Said if legal required him to view it, he would and not until then."

Kyle slammed his palm down on the XO's desk, jumped up and walked around to stand behind the chair. "Sorry, sir. That still makes at least seven of the crew who've viewed the video or at least part of it. Seven shipmates Lieutenant Riley will have to face knowing they've seen her during a very private moment. She's not going to take it well and I can't say I blame her."

The XO leaned forward, rested his elbows on his knees and let his hands hang in a loose grasp in front of him. "She's not the only one. There's her father... and you."

"Me?" Kyle rocked back on his heels. *Crap.* It was true that he and Nic had a past, but he'd feel this way if it had happened to any woman.

"During Stone's interview he accused you of assaulting him after seeing the video. Said you acted like a jealous husband, not a shipmate."

"Stone's an idiot and doesn't know the first thing about loyalty, friendship, or what it means to be part of a crew. Not to mention how to be a real man."

The XO stood and walked over to him. With a hand clamped on his shoulder he looked him in the eye. "Hutch, you and I've served for the last three years together. What's said here, right now, is just between us."

Kyle nodded in agreement. The two of them had shared a few beers along the way, during port calls, over discussions about family and what comes after the Navy. He was more than just Kyle's boss. He was a true friend.

"Stone's a lowlife. We could shoot him out the torpedo tube and I wouldn't have a problem with it. In his heart, the captain probably feels the same way. I'm not thinking too highly of Smitty either. Oh, I don't begrudge the man for wanting a little adult entertainment, but when he saw the subject of that video he should have hightailed it to my office. Keeping his mouth shut, or rather being Stone's mouthpiece? He's no better, but we've got to do this by the books. Are you getting my drift?"

Kyle dropped his chin into his chest and looked back up. "Yeah, I get it Chris. Don't go beating the crap out of either guy."

"Trust me. They will see the inside of a jail cell. SUBLANT will make sure of that. I need you to let the COB and Havers handle this, stay away from the investigation, and I know she's going to need a friend right now, but watch yourself with Riley."

Holy shit. Somehow he knew. Probably freaking Bryant.

"What are you saying, sir?" Kyle took a step away, put the distance back in their relationship.

"Let's not give Stone or his defense any ammunition to back up any more of his claims. Keep everything on the up and up. No lingering looks at chow time. No private discussions in her stateroom. No getting pissy when some other guy talks to her and no slamming any more crewmembers against the bulkhead."

"Understood, sir." Kyle turned to leave hesitating at the door. "Does she know yet?"

Chris blew out a breath and Kyle saw him drop back in his chair out of the corner of his eye. "The captain's in with her now. Felt the news needed to come from him"

Without another word Kyle left and headed down the passage to his quarters, by way of the crew's bunks. He didn't plan to get involved, just see how things were progressing. He spotted Mace with a laptop, while the COB was going through a locker.

"I'm heading to the rack for some shut eye," Kyle told him. "You need to check my laptop, you know the password."

"Already done." Mace didn't look up from the screen.

Kyle stood waiting. The COB kept his head behind the metal door, presumably still digging through the crewmembers' stuff, but there was no way it took that long to search the small space. He was giving Mace time to fill Kyle in.

Mace shut down the laptop and returned it to the bunk. "You know I can't tell you anything."

"And yet you will anyway, so just tell me now."

Mace didn't look at him; he kept his focus on the clipboard in his hand. "You're determined to see my ass in a sling, aren't you? Fine. The COB searched the officers' quarters and came up with nothing. I took the goat locker, same thing. We'll be down here for a while. So far, we've found the video on one other smart phone. No," he said as Kyle opened his mouth. "I won't tell you whose. Go. Get some sleep. You're on duty in a few hours."

With that Mace turned his back on him and joined the COB at the other end of the berthing area.

Damn.

Eight crewmembers had seen Nic in the shower. Seen her naked and he couldn't even go to her and make sure she was all right.

* * *

Nic sat curled into a corner of her bed, gaze darting from one corner to the next around her room. She hadn't slept last night after the CO destroyed her world. Instead she'd searched every nook, cranny, and compartment, checking for recording devices. Twice. They'd said the video was only of her in the shower, but who was to say there wasn't more they hadn't found?

Every time she'd closed her eyes and tried to sleep she'd open them again and search around the room, sure she'd heard a noise or saw a flash of light behind her closed lids. Around zero four hundred she'd given up the ruse, got dressed and slipped into the galley to make hot tea and grab something to eat before the crew showed up for chow. Both the drink and the muffin sat untouched on her desk, as did the burger and fries Chief Boone had sent down when she didn't show at lunchtime.

About an hour ago the CO had stopped by to give her an update. Mace and the COB had completed their search, only finding the video in one other person's possession. Petty Officer Tarasov had been Stone's accomplice, his lookout man, letting him know when the coast was clear to film and when Nic headed to the shower. He was also a logistics specialists and one of her men.

Per regs the CO had filed the SITREP—situation report—and they'd been ordered back to Groton. Another boat was being sent to complete their mission. By now the full crew knew what had happened. Knew it was her fault they wouldn't be making port in Scotland. She really hoped none of their wives or girlfriends had spent the money to meet them.

Some of them, at least eight by her count, knew what she looked like naked. Who else had seen the video?

Unless someone confessed or were ratted out, she'd never really know.

Fighting back tears, she uncurled and swung her legs over the edge of the bed as someone knocked on her door. Normally she kept it open during her wake hours, not wanting to close herself off from the crew.

But not today. Today, drifting alone on the high sea in a lifeboat sounded better than facing the crew.

The knock on the door came again. "Nic, you awake?"

Kyle. Could she face him? He'd seen it. She'd made the Captain tell her who exactly had viewed the video and why. He also told her Kyle came close to crossing a line in her defense.

She climbed off the bed and tried to smooth out the jumpsuit before quickly pulling her hair back into a ponytail and re-wrapping it into a knot.

"Come in."

The door opened and he filled the entry without stepping into the room.

"Hey, how are you holding up?" His voice was soft, soothing and way too serious.

"Peachy keen, jelly bean."

He rubbed the stubble along his jawline, looking like she'd thrown him a curveball. Maybe so, but how else did he expect her to answer his question? Cry on his shoulder? Confess she was too embarrassed to leave her room, to face the crew?

He glanced at her desk and then his cool slate gray eyes met hers.

"Guess I'd be peachy keen too if I were getting room service. Didn't know that was available these days on the boat. Wonder what's next. Laundry service?"

"If you wanted the easy life you should have joined the Air Force."

"Maybe a state of the art gym or game room? Or private ba—" He shook his head. "Sorry."

"Just say it, Kyle. It's the giant pink elephant in the room. And from what I hear you have no reason to apologize. Actually, I should be thanking you."

Kyle looked over his shoulder and back at her. "Stone was my guy. I should have kept a better eye on him."

"Tarasov was mine, so if were playing the blame game, we're both guilty then."

"Nic..." He looked back over his shoulder.

"You know you can close the door. I'm not going to yell for help or anything."

"Actually, no I can't. XO's orders. Stone's making some noise. Look, I know none of us can really understand how this affects you. You know, get what's going on in your head, but if you need to talk…"

She held up her hand to stop him. "I appreciate the offer and you stopping by, but you're right. You don't get it, none of you do and the last thing I need is the crew's pity on top of everything else."

Something cold and hot flashed in his eyes before he stepped fully into her room and shut the door. She lifted a questioning brow that he ignored.

"You think the crew pities you?" he said.

"Don't you? I'm not one of them anymore. I'm not a Naval officer serving by their side. I was violated. In their eyes, in yours, I'm a victim."

He stalked across the small room until he stood toe-to-toe with her. "Don't tell me how I see you, especially when you're wrong."

"Tell me." Her voice had dropped to a whisper, her mouth as dry as the Mojave, and her heart pounding in her ears. She'd kept her distance from him, but with him standing so close and once again defending her she was transported back to that bar in Boston and reminded again of the chemistry between them. Except now it was so much more because she knew the man behind the sexy smile and mischievous eyes.

"You're an amazing person, Nic."

She looked up to find those smoldering eyes with ridiculously long lashes looking down at her. He didn't touch, didn't move back. Every square inch of her body burned with the heat from his.

"You're intelligent, ambitious, and kind. You're also strong and resilient and I don't believe for one minute you're going to let those jerks get the better of you."

Words got stuck in her throat, blocked as she fought to keep her emotions in check and not cry all over his coveralls. She couldn't look at him, or she'd lose the internal battle, because while he thought she was all of those things, basically a warrior, she was only human. Finally she managed to say, "You have a lot of faith in me."

Gently he lifted her chin until their eyes met. "You're the only woman in a crew of one-hundred and forty. In the past few weeks you've qualified for a third of the systems on the boat. You've taken all the ribbing in stride up until now. You'll get through this, Nic."

"I feel so alone."

He stepped back, his jaw dropped, hands held out. "What am I? The Ghost of Boyfriends Past?"

She dropped back to sit on the edge of her rack and buried her face in her hands. If only, she thought. It'd be so nice to wake and find this had all been a dream.

"I'm pretty sure one night, no matter how great, doesn't qualify you for the term of boyfriend. However…" She held up her hands in surrender. "I get what you're saying."

He held a hand out. "I'll be with you every step. Okay?"

She gave him a shaky nod.

"What do you say we get some chow? Based on what you didn't eat, you've got to be starving."

"Yeah, food would be good. First I need to hit the head, if you could do me a favor?"

"Sure. Name it."

She wiped her sweat-slicked palms down her sides. "I know it's stupid, but can you stand guard for me?"

A few minutes later, with Kyle at her side, Nic entered the wardroom as the rest of the officers were grabbing dinner. Conversations continued as they filled their plates with steak, mashed potatoes, gravy and salad—comfort foods—and joined the others at the long table. No one mentioned Stone or the incident directly. A few talked about how they'd surprise their wives and kids with the unexpected return. The chatter flowed around her, not really ignoring her, yet not really including her.

She pushed the steak around on her plate. Shoved a spoonful of potatoes and gravy in her mouth when Kyle looked down at her plate and then met her gaze. They tasted like glue and lodged in her throat making it impossible to swallow. Half a cup of hot tea and several hard swallows later and the lump of goo made its way down.

She looked up to find the CO watching her. He smiled. It didn't reach his eyes. Her gaze bounced around the other members at the table, everyone seemed to be watching her, their smiles too bright, the conversation too mundane, too normal. She should have stayed in her room. Snuck down between dinner and midrats and grabbed leftovers. Then everyone could relax.

Especially poor Mace. She'd purposely sat on the other end of the table from him to save him any embarrassment. Every now and then she could feel someone watching her. Was it him? Was he picturing her naked right then? Oh God, who else? Even if they didn't see the video, were they thinking about it? Wishing they had seen it? If it had just been Kyle she could handle it, after all, he'd already seen her in the buff, with her consent, but this…

The more the thoughts crowded her brain the harder it got to breathe as if a giant's hand were squeezing her lungs. Sweat trickled down her back.

White spots danced before her eyes as black fog crept in. She had to get out of there before she passed out in front of everyone.

If she ran out, that'd just up the pity factor. There was one sure way to get her excused and get their minds off of her. As much as she hated to play the girl card... Desperate times and all that.

As she stood and pushed back her chair, all eyes turned toward her.

"If you'll excuse me, I'm not feeling so well." She saw it, the instant pity so she laid her palm across her abdomen. "Cramps."

Fifteen sets of eyes suddenly found something more interesting to look upon. She escaped while she could because the blackness at the edge of her vision still threatened and the giant hadn't released his hold on her lungs.

Chapter Eight

For the past six days Nic had spent most of her time in her room, not really hiding out, but still avoiding people. She couldn't meet anyone's gaze without wondering what they were thinking and if they'd seen *it*.

Thankfully it was almost over, at least, this portion of the nightmare. In a few minutes they'd be pulling back into port and she could escape what had become her personal prison cell. Most of her stuff was already packed. She'd changed from the shapeless poopy suit into her aquaflage—NWU, a Navy working uniform which looked like blue camouflage, that they wore while in port—and grabbed for her jeans, shoving them into her duffle with extra force.

Freaking Stone and his buddies. They'd screwed everything up. And for what?

As far as porn went it was pretty tame, even boring.

Thank goodness he hadn't caught her on one of the days she'd been fantasizing about a certain weapons officer. During one of her late night trips to the galley, as she'd taken to skipping most meals, she'd overheard a couple of the men saying she was overreacting to the whole thing. Given the content was three-minutes of her shampooing, soaping up and rinsing off, she could see how they might think that. However, it wasn't what she was doing in the shower that made the video wrong.

Stone invaded her privacy. Spied on her. Stolen away her sense of security and broken her trust with the crew.

She didn't understand it. Did he really think he'd make money off of it? Or did he do it to prove that women didn't belong on subs? There were still some old school holdouts; those who believed women had their place, like the kitchen and bedroom, but not in uniform.

Whatever the reasoning behind his actions, it was time to put it behind her and move forward. He'd taken up enough of her headspace. These last few days… if it hadn't been for Kyle. She'd still be curled up in the corner of her rack. He'd been her rock, her pillar of strength, and most importantly, her friend.

"Hey there." Kyle's warm voice cascaded over her, bringing a smile to her face.

She turned around to greet him. Like her, he'd swapped out his coveralls for the working uniform, but where it swallowed her up, the material hugged his body. "How are you doing today?"

He'd asked the same question every day for the past week and where once she'd worried about them crossing a line and breaking rules, now she worried that he'd moved her into the friend zone.

"Good. Done packing and looking forward to seeing some blue skies and breathing fresh air. How about you? Got any big plans since we're home?"

"Pick up my roommate's cat from the kennel, order some pizza, and chill in front of the TV. Thought you'd want to know security is here and they're taking the guys to the base brig now. Captain's told them to give you a day before questioning you."

"Oh, that's good. Good." The strength in her legs left her and she sunk down on the edge of the rack. "What about you? You'll need to give a statement, right? I mean you're the one who discovered… who found them out."

The giant was back, squeezing on her lungs and the boat started rocking back and forth. Which was not a normal thing on a submarine. For a second the lights went out and when they came back on Kyle was kneeling in front of her.

"Put your head between your knees and breathe," he said.

"I'm okay."

"You don't look okay. You passed out and you're as pale as a ghost." He rubbed his strong, warm hand over her back as she focused on breathing.

"That's just my Irish showing through." She sat back up. "Really, I'm okay now. I guess I just didn't think about having to talk to anyone else about this situation once we got back. That I could pretend like it never happened and go on with my life. Then it hit me. I'll have to talk to the squadron investigators, lawyers, reporters, and oh God, my family."

He lifted her chin to make her look at him. "It'll be okay. I told you, I'll be with you every step of the way."

"You say that now. You haven't met my dad or my brothers."

He grinned. "I'm not worried. Remember, I'm the hero of this story."

She laughed as she looked into his eyes that were a stormy gray today. "That you are, Kyle Hutchinson, and I don't know what I would have done without you throughout this mess. Once again, you were my champion. Thank you."

"You would have been just fine, Nic."

His voice was low and husky. Over the past month his hair had grown back in and it was still damp from the shower and she could smell the fresh scent of his soap. He leaned in closer, stopping shy of touching her.

"The skipper gave everyone forty-eight hours of liberty. I was thinking I might escape for a few days. Wouldn't happen to have any recommendations would you?" She was thinking abandoned island, just the two of them.

"I know this great little place in Boston. Right next door is this bar where you can shoot pool or lose yourself on the dance floor. Not very popular with the Navy crowd." He was so close she could almost taste his minty toothpaste on the air.

"Yeah? Too bad all my girlfriends are busy right now."

"Yeah, too bad." His hands slipped up and around to the back of her head, drawing her to him. His lips skimmed over hers. She reached out to grab on to something, anything to steady her and curled her fingers around the lapels of his shirt. The temperature in the room kicked up a couple of degrees.

"Kyle, we shouldn't."

He nibbled along her jawline until he reached her ear. "Okay, we'll go to the Cape instead."

Liquid heat pooled in the center of her body and he ran his tongue in slow circles in the sensitive hollow below her ear, making his way to her collarbone. "Kyle."

He framed her face, his gaze steady on hers. "I've missed you, Nic. Missed this. I'm transferring soon, so it won't matter. We'll go away for a couple of days, no one will know."

Before she could respond, he stole her breath away with a soul-searing kiss that left her hearing bells.

They broke apart as the 1MC came on. "SUBLANT on board."

"Oh shit," Nic jumped up, knocking Kyle over. "My father's here."

Quickly she smoothed the sides of her hair, trying to tuck any strays that Kyle's hands pulled free back into their bun. She threw the last remaining personal items into her duffle and closed it before realizing Kyle was still standing in her room.

"What are you doing?" She pushed him toward the door, or rather tried. "You've got to leave before he sees you in here."

"Nic, we're not doing anything wrong."

She crossed her arms, cocked her head and said nothing.

"Now. And I'm not afraid of your dad." He wrapped a loose strand around his finger and pulled her toward him. "Relax. He'll see the CO first. You've even got time to escape if you want to avoid seeing him, which sounds like a great idea. Let's drop your stuff off, pick up the cat, and go back to my place. We'll have pizza delivered and let it go cold while we make up for the past couple of weeks."

She was so very tempted to say yes. The idea of losing herself in Kyle's arms for a few hours sounded like heaven. But first she had to face her dad. The men and women who worked for Vice Admiral Patrick Riley might fear the man, but underneath his gruff and tough exterior laid the heart of a teddy bear.

"Maybe later. I need to get a room at the BOQ and well, if my dad's here, there's a good chance my mom is too. They might have family plans for tonight."

Like lecturing her about getting out of the Navy. She also needed to apologize to her dad for dragging them into this mess and publicity nightmare. Not that she pictured the story on CNN or the front page of every major newspaper in the country. In reality the civilian world would probably go along with their blissful lives and never know this kind of thing happened. No, it wasn't John and Jane Smith of Middletown, America she worried about. It was the high and mighty at the Capitol.

"Give me your phone." Kyle held out his hand, waiting.

She did as he demanded and a few minutes later he handed it back.

"Now you have the number and address. If you want to escape, I'll be there." He turned to go right as the door opened.

A giant bear of a man with strawberry blond hair and piercing blue eyes filled the doorframe. Out of the corner of her eye she could see Kyle snap to attention.

Yeah, he's not afraid of my dad at all, Nic thought.

She joined Kyle, showing proper respect for her dad's rank, but she took her time doing so.

"At ease, officers." The deep baritone of her dad's voice lifted the corners of her mouth. Not a lot. Not enough for most to notice, but Patrick Riley did. He cocked that left brow of his like he always did when something caught his eye. "Lieutenant Hutchinson, I understand we owe you a debt of gratitude."

"Just doing my job, sir." Kyle's spine was a straight as a ruler.

Her dad waited a beat, never breaking eye contact with Kyle. "I'd like to talk to you for a minute. Wait for me in the wardroom while I speak with Lieutenant Riley in private. Dismissed Lieutenant Hutchinson."

Kyle glanced her way once on his way out the door, not a word said, his mouth a grim line. Nic waited until her dad dismissed the XO as well and then rolled her eyes at him.

"Seriously, Pops. Do you have to be the hard ass all the time? Kyle— Lieutenant Hutchinson—isn't the bad guy here."

"What was he doing in your room?" He stood feet shoulder width apart, fingers splayed on his hips, eyes glaring somewhere between teddy bear and polar bear.

"Letting me know the scum buckets behind what I expect is the reason for your visit today are on their way to the base brig." The humiliation hit her square on and she fought to hold the tears back.

The man who thrived on being called an alpha-asshole by the fleet opened his arms and she flew into them, just like she did when she was little. She let the tears she'd been holding back all week flow, not caring that his summer whites were getting wet. No one would chastise him. Not caring about her so-called adult independence or need to prove she could play with the boys. Sometimes a girl just needed her dad.

He rocked her back and forth, smoothing her hair and murmuring soft words. When her eyes dried up, she stood on her tiptoes and kissed her dad on his cheek before stepping back to sit on the edge of her rack.

Her dad pulled out the chair and sat. It was a normal size office chair, but he made it look like it belonged in a classroom.

"Feeling better, Lily-Pad?"

"I hate that name," she sniffled.

"I know."

Suddenly she felt a little more like herself than she had all week. It could be that with her dad by her side, she knew nobody would fuck with her. She was safe.

"I've missed you, Pops." She found a Kleenex stuffed into the side of her sea bag and blew her nose. "I'm sorry."

"Not your fault you missed my birthday party, Lily-Pad. Orders come first. Although, I'll tell you your mom went out of her way on this one. It was one for the record books." At the mention of her mom, his eyes got a misty twinkle and his mouth automatically slid into a smile. His fidgety hands gave away the calm he was trying to portray.

"That's not what I was referring to, but you knew that. And I am sorry I missed the party too. Admiral, why are you here?" She held up her hands to hold off his reply just yet. "Please tell me it's personal or a coincidence."

"It's business and personal. I had a retirement ceremony yesterday to attend and I stayed over to see my girl. Is that a crime?"

She sat back and studied him. Patrick Sean Michael Riley had been blessed at birth and could tell a tale with the best of the Irish and make you believe every word of it was real. His eyes sparked with mischief, but then they usually did. His cheeks were ruddy because he'd spent more than five minutes in the sun recently. His body appeared relaxed, as if they were kicked back at home in the living room. So why did she have a sinking suspicion he was here as more than just her dad?

"Pops," she reached out to grab his hand. "I know you have the power in your little finger to send those men to the brig for a very long time. As much as a part of me wants that... I can't let you. It would undermine everything I've worked for and cause a bigger scandal than this already is. You have to step back and stay out of this."

"Lieutenant, I do not need you or anyone else to tell me how to do my job. Not as a naval officer or a father. Understood?" He lashed out in love and she suspected her mom had already had this conversation with him, so Nic didn't take offense to his gruff tone.

"Understood."

He stood and pulled her up to tuck under his side. "Your mom's worried about you. Wants you to take some leave time and come home for a couple of weeks so she can fuss over you."

She poked him in the ribs. "Mom's worried, huh? Tell her I'm ... okay." She couldn't tell them how she really was: scared, angry, ashamed. "It's been a rough week. I need to talk to the CO, the squadron or group, and I guess the lawyers before I can do anything. We'll see how it goes. Tell mom I'll call in a couple of days and maybe I can get away for a long weekend."

He gave her another hug and then held her out to look at her. He gave her a little nod and smiled. "I have this friend who's looking to hire—"

"No, thank you," she said. "For now."

It was the start of an old argument, one she didn't have the energy, patience, or strength to fight. Plus, the man's friend list ran a mile long. If it came down to that, if the fear that had been her constant companion all week won and she resigned... No, she shoved that thought away and smiled at her dad.

"When do you head home?" she asked.

"First thing in the morning." He pointed a finger at her. "Dinner tonight, six sharp, at Olio. Now, I'm going to talk to Hutchinson and he better have a good reason for being in your room."

She rolled her eyes at him and smiled. It wouldn't have done any good to try to talk him out of grilling Kyle. Her dad didn't miss much and the more effort she made to deter him, the more determined he'd be to question the poor guy. Instead she grabbed her sea bag, hefted it over her shoulder and headed out. If she left right then, she'd have time to check into the bachelor officer quarters—BOQ—get settled into her room and maybe even dress up. Look like Lily, the frilly girl her parents had wanted instead of Nic, the girl who liked to get dirty and keep up with the boys.

As she made her way up to the foreword hatch voices fell and gazes shifted away. Not really surprising considering she hadn't spent much time out and around the crew during the cruise home. She stopped short behind a wide set of shoulders that were well above her head.

The line stood still. Not the norm for a return home. She peered around the guy in front of her to see what caused the hold-up. Her sea bag slipped from her hand and landed with a thunk on the steel floor. The grumbling from the men at the ladder ceased as they all turned to stare. She was met with a mix of emotions: animosity from Stone and Tarasov, remorse from Roberts and Smitty, and frustration from the two masters-at-arms escorting the men off the boat.

The guy in front of her shifted as he turned to block the others view of her.

"I thought you'd already left with the prisoners. Is there a problem, Chief Faraday?" It took every ounce of nerve she had to control the tremble in her voice.

"No, ma'am. Dealing with the usual paperwork shuffle. We'll step aside and let you depart." His striking hazel eyes, which were neither more blue nor green, held no trace of pity. Either he had an exceptional poker face or he didn't know what crime the men had committed.

Right. She could only get so lucky.

"You'll understand when I say I'd rather not have them at my back."

"Understood. Give us a minute and we'll have them up and out of here. Alright men, let's get a move on it."

Stone opened his mouth but before he could say anything Faraday got in his face. He had to be a good six or seven inches taller than his prisoner. "Petty Officer, unless you are directed to do so you will keep your trap shut and proceed foreword. Eyes on the man in front and you might want to watch your step. It's a little slippery topside."

At the man's not-so-veiled threat the other men made double time up the ladder, followed by Stone, who surprisingly did exactly as he'd been told. Chief Faraday gave Nic a curt nod and disappeared up the hatch.

* * *

Kyle poured kibble into the bowl for his roommate's cat and then popped the top on a Guinness. Precious wound around his ankles purring. Although a better name, which he used often was Princess PITA as she thought she was the first and he knew she was the second.

"Yeah, yeah. I missed you too. Now go eat."

He powered up his laptop to check e-mail. He'd tried calling his mom and cousin when he'd gotten in earlier, but neither had answered. No surprise there. His mom firmly believed cell phones were for emergency use only and Stevie had probably forgotten to charge his again. Shit happened when you spent the majority of your time drunk.

The PITA ignored her food and jumped into his lap within seconds of his butt hitting the couch. The first claw struck gold. "Hey," Kyle scolded. "What's the rule on fluffing?"

The cat gave him a beady-eyed stare of boredom and lay down to purr on his lap.

"That's better." He grabbed the laptop and set it on the arm of the couch where he could reach the keys over the fluffball. As the page populated he stole a glance at his phone. No blinking lights. He couldn't believe he was sitting around waiting for Nic to call or show like a love-struck teen. With her dad in town, they were probably having dinner, and it wasn't like she could ditch him for Kyle.

The admiral had been everything Kyle expected and more. When he ordered Kyle to wait in the wardroom, Kyle figured he'd be asked about the video. He didn't, but then again he'd read the SITREP from the CO and already knew the details. Kyle hadn't been expecting to be grilled about his relationship with Nic or offered a job on the admiral's staff. He wondered if the offer was to thank him or to keep him away from Nic.

Tempting.

The job, not staying away from Nic. Although working for her father would be more effective than a dunk in the deepest loch in the middle of the Scottish highlands in the dead of winter.

Handpicked for the admiral's staff? Not something most officers saw, especially as a lieutenant, and most career men only dreamed of. He'd be a fool to say no.

So why didn't he say yes?

Who told the admiral in charge of the Atlantic submarine force "I'll think about it"?

He did, because apparently his mama raised a fool.

How else do you describe someone turning down a job like that? The thing was, Kyle had been handed very little in his life. If he had it, it came through busting his ass and doing the job better than the next guy. Accepting the job didn't feel right, and he couldn't even believe the thought was running through his head, but if felt like he was being paid off for sleeping with Nic.

"Or bought off to stay away," he said to the cat.

He finally finished clearing his inbox of junk messages and came upon the one he wanted, the one from his cousin:

Yo dog. Twins owe Walt Woodrow $$$. Still digging.
Stevie

Thoughts of Nic and the job offered slipped away as the name from his own past came back to haunt him. Walt "Woody" Woodrow. Kyle didn't know he was back in town. The last word had been that Woody was serving time in the big house. Should have known he'd get out and come crawling home.

Snakes like him always came out unscathed and resurfaced when you least expected them.

Kyle hadn't seen the dude since they were in middle school. Woody had been a year ahead of him. One of the cool kids. They hung out for a bit. Swapped some BS stories, tested each other out. Then one night Woody fed Kyle a tale about how Old Man Tomlinson fired him for no reason at the mom and pop store Woody worked at. Together they broke in, busted up a bunch of merchandise, spray painted the usual crap that comes out of kids' mouths. Someone spotted them, called the cops and both got arrested.

That was the last time Kyle saw Woody. His friend already had a record, no family that gave a damn, and a judge that was tired of seeing his face in court.

Kyle's maternal grandfather showed up at the police station with Old Man Tomlinson. They'd struck a deal. If Kyle cleaned up the place, worked off the damage and kept out of trouble, Tomlinson wouldn't press charges.

That was the first break Kyle had ever been given and he didn't look that gift in the mouth and say no. It took him a year of free labor to pay for the damages, but at the end of that year Tomlinson offered him a job. He accepted, kept out of trouble and kept his second promise to his grandfather, that he'd get out of that nowhere town and go to college.

Now Woody was back and the twins didn't have their grandfather to bail them out like he did. They only had him—not that he'd been a great brother—and he was three thousand miles away.

He hit Reply and wrote back:

Cuz, find out how deep and dark. ~K

He closed out the program and shut down the computer. Not much else he could do for the night. A grumble from his stomach reminded him he hadn't bothered to eat.

"Sorry to disturb you, your highness." He lifted the cat and laid her on the couch.

The clock on the microwave read eight p.m. He got out the makings for Korean beef and noodles. "Looks like I've got lunch for tomorrow because I do believe the girl is blowing me off."

The cat had joined him in the kitchen, probably hoping for a treat. Kyle sliced the beef into thin strips and looked down to meet the cat's gaze. "Yeah, I know. You'll happily help me eat this, but no can do. Your human has you on a diet. See that note on the fridge? Those are strict instructions that I not give you any people food and only one cat treat a day. Sorry, Princess."

"Meow."

"I know. Cruel and unjust punishment." He washed his hands and reached into the cabinet next to the fridge to pull out the bag of cat treats. "Just one, got it?"

He tossed the fish-shaped cracker into the bowl and went back to work on his own food. On the way home he'd stopped off at the commissary and picked enough supplies for dinner and breakfast, confident Nic would take him up on his offer. He hadn't been the only one feeling the heat that afternoon.

Of course that was before her dad showed up.

Had they been anywhere else, he was pretty sure Nic wouldn't have tried to shove him out the door. Out of the corner of his eye, he had caught her reaction when her dad entered. It was slight, but the smirk was there, the one that told him Nic wasn't afraid of her dad, but she did respect him. Hard not to when the man played hard, yet fair.

Did he say something to Nic about the two of them? He seemed to take Kyle at his word that they simply formed a platonic friendship underway. Had he seen through the lie? Technically they hadn't done anything wrong.

The timing sucked.

But then when didn't it when you were in the Navy?

"What do you think, cat?" Kyle plated up his food and dropped onto the couch. "Think I should forget the girl and carry on or convince her it'll be worth the risk?"

"Meow." Princess PITA jumped up on the back of the couch next to him to purr in his ear.

"You're right, nine p.m. She's already made the call and I'll be out of here in five months anyway. Doesn't really matter. So what are we watching?" He picked up the remote ready to spend the night with just him, the Princess and whatever he could catch on demand.

It was better this way, he told himself. He didn't want to end up in a mess like Mace with a wife who didn't trust him and ran home to mom every time life didn't go the way she planned. Or like a few others he'd known whose wives found someone else to warm their beds the minute the boat pulled out or refused to transfer with them because their job came first.

Nope, better to be single, enjoy the ladies with no strings attached and no responsibilities. If he wanted the latter he'd just go home and deal with the twins in person. Speaking of, he made a mental note to call his mom in the morning and see if either dipshit one or dipshit two were around so he could find out just how big of a hole they'd dug this time.

Just as he settled on a movie and dug into his dinner the doorbell rang. He jumped up from the couch. "I had given up on you," he said as he opened the door.

"Really?" Mace said. "Did you tell him we were coming over?"

"Nope, which means it wasn't us he was expecting." Bryant sniffed the plate and liberated it from Kyle's hand.

"Ah hell, Hutch." Mace scowled and dropped into the lone chair. "I thought you weren't going to be stupid."

Chapter Nine

Tuesday afternoon, the day after they returned to port, Nic exited the galley and headed to the wardroom. Technically, lunch ended an hour ago, but Chief Boone took pity on her and not only made her a double BLT but slid a giant chocolate chip cookie on her tray as she was getting ready to walk out. Guess he'd seen the stress lines and figured she'd need a pick-me-up. Or maybe it was the dark circles under her eyes that gave her away. She had just sat down at the empty table when Kyle walked in, coffee cup in hand.

He took his time, filling his cup and picked up a cookie from the tray on the sideboard before sitting across from her. He looked down at her plate, then to the cookie in his hand, and then finally to meet her gaze.

"How come your cookie is bigger?" Kyle asked.

"Chief likes me better." She took a bit of her sandwich and pushed the pity thoughts away.

He took a deep breath.

"Smells like it just came out of the oven."

She bit off a piece and groaned. Warm chocolate melted on her tongue sending waves of pleasure through her. Screw the BLT, life was short, she was having dessert first. Kyle's eyes never left her mouth as she licked a crumb from the corner of her lips.

"Want some?" she asked.

Fire…such a dangerous and tempting element. It filled his eyes and her body and if she didn't quit, one or both of them would end up burned.

Kyle's gazed dropped one more time to her mouth before meeting her look. "Maybe another time. Why are you here anyway? The CO gave you time off."

The casual rejection stung, although it shouldn't have come as a surprise after she stood him up.

"Gave you time off too and you're here, probably for the same reason. Work to do. Supplies to offload, new supplies to order. Besides, I had to talk with the squadron guy whose heading up the investigation this morning and this afternoon I have an another appointment."

He reached out and squeezed her hand. "How did it go?"

Awful. Degrading. Nauseating. "Fine."

"I would have gone with you, if you'd called." His voice soothed and she blinked back the tears that wanted desperately to fall. As bad as the morning's interview had gone, she knew it was only going to get worse with each new person she had to face who knew about or had seen the video.

They sat in silence as she finished her sandwich and he drank his coffee. There was so much going on in her mind. Work: getting the boat's supplies restocked for port, reports, and all the usual tasks. The case: should she transfer, resign—her dad had suggested both— or stay and face the humiliation and fears. Then there was Kyle and this thing between them. What it was, she didn't even know. Did she throw caution to the wind, follow her heart (or was that another part of her anatomy talking?) and explore what promised to be a torrid affair? Or walk away now?

Walk...no run away, her internal guardian angel yelled. Yet there was another voice in her head, that little devil, who whispered that she should run *to* him.

"Kyle, I'm sorry."

"Because...?" The crooked smile gave her hope that she hadn't killed their friendship. "Boone likes you better?"

"That's to be expected after you dissed his lasagna underway. No, this is for not calling last night."

"No big." He shrugged and stole a piece of her cookie. "Your dad was in town. It's only natural he'd want to spend the time with you."

"More like play the guilt card to get me to come home and grill me about you."

He choked on his coffee, but didn't say anything until he'd gotten up to refill his mug and rest against the sideboard. She didn't miss that he'd intentionally put distance between them.

"Me?"

"Yep. You impressed him and I'll admit, that's a rare feat given the Admiral's cynical mind." She'd also been stunned when she found out

Kyle hadn't jumped at her dad's job offer. She started to tell him but when she looked back up, he'd glanced away.

If she wasn't mistaken he was blushing, but maybe the red in his cheeks was just from the steam of his coffee.

She walked over to the sideboard and took out a cup. As she went through the motions of making tea her body hummed with energy and awareness. Since they were in port they'd donned their aquaflage uniforms. They weren't sexy like dress blues or whites and did absolutely nothing for her barely-there curves, but on Kyle they made her heart speed up and her blood pound hard. He had rolled up the sleeves, exposing tanned arms, toned biceps and leaving just a tip of his tribal band tat showing.

He was temptation on a stick.

She turned and leaned against the sideboard next to him, exhaling a soft sigh.

"Did you think I'd use your misfortune to my advantage?" His voice was soft and filled with disappointment like he expected her to say yes. Had he guessed how many people had tried to use her family connections for their gain? She'd lost count.

"Not at all, but you have to admit most wouldn't have passed up on a golden opportunity."

"Yeah, well in case you haven't noticed... I'm not like most people. I'd prefer to make my way up the ladder on my own sweat and blood." He turned to her and tucked a stray strand back into the knot. "Did you want me to say yes?"

Taking her free hand in his, he traced an intricate knot in the center of her palm. He should stop. She should tell him to or pull her hand back. Anyone could walk in at any moment. It felt...sensual, mesmerizing, enticing.

"It might have simplified things if you had," she said.

"I'm not sure simple is how you'd describe dating someone who lives over three hundred miles away." He tugged her closer until his mouth was a whisper away. "Frustrating is the word you're looking for."

No more so than working together and seeing each other every day but not be allowed to touch him. "It's a good thing we're not dating then." She pushed him back with one finger that he captured and kissed.

"There's nothing in the rulebook that says we can't be friends. Hang out. Enjoy a beer. Catch a game. It's even encouraged among the members of the wardroom. Come over tonight."

Had the invitation come from any of the other guys she could have pictured hanging out, chilling in front of the TV, shooting the breeze or swapping sea stories around the fire pit. Just a couple of friends hanging out.

Not with Kyle.

Give the two of them a private room. A guarantee of no interruptions. She'd bet a month's pay they'd be undressed and in bed within ten minutes of shutting the front door.

The door to the wardroom swung open and Mace walked in.

"Am I interrupting?" he asked.

"No," Nic said.

"Yes," Kyle said.

"Good, I think," Mace grabbed a cup and filled it with coffee. "Thought you'd want to know, Hutch, they're ready to offload your toys now."

"I'll head up in a minute to oversee. Now take your coffee and leave."

"Mace, you don't have to go anywhere. I was just about to head out." Nic walked back and picked up her dirty dishes.

"I'm leaving, but not because of him. As soon as I finish up I'm out of here for the next two weeks," Mace replied.

"Where are you off to?" Kyle finished his own coffee and left the cup in the bin.

"To see Amber and if I can save my marriage." With that, Mace left them alone again.

If Nic needed a reminder as to why she should keep things on the platonic level with Kyle, Mace had just given her one. Navy life was hard on relationships. Hard enough when one participant was active duty, twice as hard when both parties had signed on the dotted line.

As she headed toward the door Kyle stopped her with a gentle touch on her arm.

"You never answered me about tonight."

"Appreciate the offer, but I've got that appointment with the lawyer this afternoon. Something tells me I won't be in a social mood after. Rain check?"

"I'll come with you," he offered.

It would be so easy to say yes, to let Kyle's strength hold her up through this ordeal, to let him be her rock. Too easy in fact. Easy to get used to and easy to blur the lines.

Before she could decline, his phone rang. He pulled out his cell and held up a finger, asking her to wait. "Mom?"

The morning had taken a lot out of her mentally and where she had hoped over the weekend her involvement in the case would be minimal and simply put behind her, she was afraid it wouldn't be that cut and dry. She'd know more after talking with the prosecuting attorney. Until then, until she knew how messed up her life was going to be and how long this would drag out, she didn't have the energy or time to deal with anything else.

Especially something that could wind up complicated.

As Kyle concentrated on his call, Nic slipped away.

* * *

Later that afternoon the CO caught Nic on her way to her appointment and ordered her to take ninety-six hours liberty. Which sounded great and all, except she didn't know anyone other than her shipmates, all of whom were at work. After a few hours of mindless TV and reading the same page over and over in her book, she hopped into her car and drove to Newport to play tourist. Wandering around The Marble House, The Breakers and The Elms left her cold and empty. The houses were grand and gorgeous, but didn't feel like they could ever be anyone's home. There had been a solarium at The Elms that she might have been tempted to relax in had she lived there. The rest of the place looked fragile and uncomfortable.

She'd spent a few hours after chilling on Narragansett Beach. Or rather trying to. It being summer time, the place was packed with couples and families with lots of kids running around and digging in the sun. Not that she had anything against people, but sitting there watching everyone else have fun, talk and share the day with others drove home how alone she was.

She'd call Lindsey or Cherise, but both were deployed.

Dinner had been something unremarkable at a fast-food restaurant on the way home, where no one looked twice at a lone diner.

Thursday her eyes popped open at zero-six-hundred because even though she was on forced liberty her body was on its normal schedule. She dressed and headed down to the galley for breakfast. French toast day. Thank the powers that be for small favors because she could use some feel-good carbs. She by-passed the coffee, grabbed some juice and headed toward the dining room. All eyes turned her way as she made her way to an empty table.

They'd been back in port long enough for word to spread and if she'd had any doubt that it would or did, she'd just gotten confirmation.

A few familiar faces passed by with morning greetings, but they didn't join her. They were enlisted and as such wouldn't sit with an officer, even if she were alone and dying inside for their company. The French toast turned out to be overcooked and tough. The bacon soggy and undercooked. The juice warm and sour.

Whatever. The scale probably would have jumped up five pounds anyway and then she'd have had to work twice as hard to lose it. She dumped the food and headed back to her room, avoiding eye contact. The book sat on her nightstand where she'd left it last night. Grabbing it, she dropped on to her bed and flipped the pages back and forth. Her mind whirled. Sitting around doing nothing when there was work to be done wasn't her style.

Call it Catholic guilt, but she wasn't Catholic.

More like Navy brat upbringing. Almost the same thing, just tougher.

They were brought up to get the job done first and then play. She tossed the book on the bed and jumped up. A quick inspection of her space scrapped the idea of cleaning her room. Less than a week's occupancy didn't create much of a mess. Playing tourist again held no appeal either. Unspent energy danced along her nerves like a thousand ants on the march to the ultimate picnic.

Another three days of this and she'd lose her freaking mind.

She stripped down and changed into workout gear. Shoved her clothes into a duffle bag and walked to the base gym. Since it was mid-morning and a weekday, only the two attendants and a couple of women and an octogenarian were there. The teen behind the counter checked her in, handed her a towel and promptly ignored her. Nic let the rudeness roll and headed for the treadmill. A good run was exactly what her body craved.

She picked a machine in the middle and started walking, increasing her speed until she hit a light jog. The older man took up the machine to her left, smiled and within a few minutes was walking faster than her.

"Nice day for a walk." He winked.

Nic smiled and picked up the pace.

The old guy chuckled and kept on at his own speed. If she were a betting person she'd bet the table he was a retired Chief Warrant Officer or a Commander. Clearly he'd put in his twenty or more to still have access to the base, but he didn't sound like a Chief—they tended to bark orders. A non-commanding officer would have minded their own business and kept quiet. Nope, the man next to her had style and knew how to motivate. She hoped to be like him one day. The kind of officer her crew looked up to and sought out for advice.

For the next twelve miles she ran to the beat of her feet pounding on the treadmill, purging the unspent energy and frustration from her body.

The machine came to a stop and Nic grabbed her towel to wipe off the sweat running down her face and neck. She turned around and came face-to-face with a man in his mid-thirties with a dark red line across his throat. He hadn't been there when she'd arrived or she hadn't noticed him before. Whichever, he made an impression now, eyes locked on hers. He held her gaze then let his drift down her body, lingering every few seconds before returning to meet her bored look.

Chills ran down her spine.

Did he know?

He wasn't from the boat. If nothing else, she would have remembered the scar because at first she'd thought it had been some weird tattoo. Now she could see the dead tissue running down the middle of the jagged line.

Had they missed a copy of the video? If they had it wouldn't take much for it to make in the hands of every sailor stationed in the area.

Don't be a ninny, she silently chided herself. Mace and the COB had been thorough in their search. Maybe the guy knew her brothers or her dad, had seen a family picture?

She brushed the feeling away. Not everyone on the base knew about her and she had to stop imagining the worst every time someone looked her way. Chances were he was just a guy checking out a girl, thinking he was cool and sexy when in reality he was just being a cliché.

Instead of falling prey to his game, she walked past him to the first machine and set the weight amount for her first set of reps. Finishing one machine she moved on to the next, losing herself in the count, in the burn coursing through her muscles. Maybe the CO had been right in making her take time off. Give her time to clear her head, let the boat settle down, and everyone get back to business. A couple of days in port with families, work, and normal life to occupy everyone's brain and they'd forget about why they were back home early.

At the end of her first circuit, she hopped on the elliptical, or the machine from Hades, as she liked to think of it. The women were spread out, a few on the stationary bikes and another two on the mats. Her admirer was on the free weights and her treadmill friend had left. Music pumped through the speakers spread throughout the room, but over head the silent TV screens were set to various programs, mainly games shows and news with closed caption running. She didn't pay much attention until she saw the women across from her on the bikes come to a stop while staring at the screen. One of the employees pointed to the screen and she caught the word Groton over the whirl of her machine.

Her gaze drifted to the TV in front of and she looked into her own eyes.

Oh God, this can't be happening.

Her steps came to a standstill as she read the words at the bottom of the screen.

Her name.

Her boat.

Her father's name

The whole sordid story spelled out for the world to know. One by one heads turned in her direction. In their eyes were pity, disappointment, disgust, and curiosity. Not that she blamed them. Grabbing her towel, she lifted her chin and walked out of the room with as much dignity as she could muster. It wasn't much, but she'd be damned before she'd let them see how shaken she was or worse...cry. As soon as she got in the locker room she leaned back against the closed door, took a few deep breaths. Her legs shook, her stomach rolled and she raced to the bathroom before she'd lost what little breakfast she'd eaten.

Well if she thought everything would die down and be back to normal in a couple of days, she'd better think again. Nic kicked her sneakers off into the locker and grabbed her go-bag with her toiletries and headed for the shower stall. No one else was in the room; still she waited until the curtain had been pulled close before pulling her T-shirt over her head. As she hung it on a hook a creak overhead had her looking up.

She stood for what seemed like forever listening. When no other sounds came she slipped her yoga pants off. Her hands hesitated at her hips, thumbs hooked into the waistband of her underwear. Was that the door opening? Silence greeted her. No footsteps or talking or any sign of life. Still, the hair on the back of her neck tingled. Her gaze darted all around the small cubicle looking for any opening no matter how small.

Labored breathing jerked her head up. She poked her head through the curtain.

"Hello? Is anyone there?"

Nothing. Her gaze landed on the mirror and she caught sight of her own reflections and that's when it hit her. The hard breathing... it was hers.

Quickly she pulled her workout clothes back on, ran to the locker, slipped her shoes on, grabbed her bag and left.

She sent one text message on the way to her room. By the time she made the fifteen-minute walk she had her answer.

Five hours later she boarded a plane to the one place she knew she could find peace and feel safe again...home.

* * *

There was nothing like a cold beer on a hot summer day while watching half a dozen babes in bikinis bounce around smacking a volleyball. Kyle took another long, slow pull of the brew and settled deeper in his beach chair. He'd have to remember to thank Bryant for dragging him out of the apartment to join the party.

As a sailor he could appreciate the meaning behind Independence Day, but on a personal level it'd never been that big of a deal to him. When you're a kid from a family that scrapes by from paycheck to paycheck things like fireworks and big parties didn't fit in the budget. Since joining the Navy it basically meant he'd have a hangover the next morning.

"Heads up." A blonde with legs that never stopped bounded over his way to grab the ball that barely missed his head. "You should come join us."

"Maybe later." He held up his bottle. "Wouldn't want it to go to waste."

She smiled, flipped her hair and sauntered back to the game. He took another drink of his cold beer and sighed. Can't say he'd ever done that before—turn down an invitation from a sure bet.

All around him were people. Some he knew, others he didn't. Families, couples, friends. People everywhere. So why did he feel like he was on a deserted island?

He'd always enjoyed the perks of solitary life. No responsibilities. No one to boss him around. No stress. Whatever he wanted, when he wanted, how he wanted. Except right then he found he didn't want to be alone. He wanted someone to laugh with like the CO and his wife who sat a couple of feet away, whispering to each other and enjoying a private joke. Even the guy getting buried alive in sand by his daughters looked to be having more fun than him.

Man, what was up with him? Rugrats? A wife? He glanced down at the bottle in his hand and read the alcohol content. Nope, not enough to get him drunk off half a bottle. Maybe it was hotter than he'd realized and the sun and heat had baked his brain.

"Hutch." Bryant waved to him, signaling to come join him and two lovely ladies in barely-there swimsuits. He pushed up out the chair, leaving the beer behind—the last thing he needed was more crazy thoughts—and reached for the cooler holding water. He'd taken no more than a few steps when his cell phone rang. Hoping Nic would call he pulled the phone out of his back pocket, but it wasn't her.

"Hi, Mom." He waved Bryant off.

"Kyle, I'm so tired. I just don't know what to do anymore." His mom's voice was soft and broken. She sighed deeply and then he heard the tears.

"Mom, talk to me. What's going on?" Kyle walked down the beach to get away from his co-workers and find a spot with less noise. Not easy on a holiday.

"It's Kenny. He's been arrested."

Shit, he should have guessed, but he'd been more worried about his parents' health and safety. He stopped at the water's edge and waited for the request. How much would his brother's stupidity cost him this time? If his savings account got any lower it'd be running on fumes.

"How much do you need to bail him out, Mom?"

"None. I didn't call for Kenny. He's made this mess now he'll have to face it. I'm not going to bail him out so he can sit at home until his court date just to go back to jail. It's Keith I'm worried about. For once the two of them weren't together so he's not in a cell with his brother."

"Mom, what was Kenny arrested for?"

"It might be easier to list what he wasn't charged with. All I can remember right now is possession of a controlled substance with intent to sell, carrying a concealed weapon without a permit, resisting arrest, and the car he was driving was stolen. I swear you'd think I had dropped that boy on his head as a baby."

What could he say? That he'd always thought she'd dropped both of his brothers on their heads when they were little? That it wasn't that bad? Because he had thought it and it really was bad, but she didn't need to hear either thoughts.

"What can I do to help?" The waves rushed at his feet, tugging him out to sea and at that moment he'd been tempted to let them wash him away. He was tired of dealing with his family's drama.

"Kyle, I hate to ask, but I'm afraid for Keith. This place is no good for him. It's no good for anyone. If it hadn't been for your grandfather, who's to say where you'd be right now? I'm betting not a college graduate and an officer in the Navy. Your brothers didn't have the benefit of his guidance. Instead they were stuck with two poor excuses for parents."

The beer he'd drunk earlier soured his stomach, which rolled as he listened to his mom. This was going somewhere and he was pretty fucking sure he wouldn't like the destination. He swallowed the sour taste. "Mom, what are you getting at?"

"Keith said he had nothing to do with this business Kenny is mixed up in and he didn't know what was in the duffle bag." She took a breath and stayed silent for a minute.

Right. Those two were Frick and Frack, two sides to a whole, and he'd never known them not to share with the other.

"I don't believe him," his mom's soft voice broke into his thoughts. "And if he stays here, he'll be next. I think they're working for that man who came to our door a couple of months ago. He needs to get away from the trash he's been running with or I'm afraid he'll end up not in jail, but dead."

Kyle waded out into the water to get further away from the people on the beach. This was not a conversation for public listening. He ran his free hand through his hair, stopping at the base of his skull to put pressure on the headache forming.

"Mom..." Out of the corner of his eye a father and son caught his attention. They were splashing each other, joking around, and wrestling in the water. Their dad had never played with them. He'd told them to do their chores, finish their homework, and to shut the hell up and let him sleep. Really what chance did the twins have? His mom was right, he'd had his grandfather, but he'd passed away before his brothers really needed him.

"Give me a couple of days, Mom. Let me make a few phone calls, talk to the command and figure something out. I don't even know how long I'll be in port."

Long after his mom thanked him and hung up he stayed put, knee deep in water, looking out across the horizon with no end in sight. What a day, first thinking crazy thoughts about kids and marriage and then practically agreeing to take in his trouble-finding kid brother. It was everything he'd joined the Navy to get away from.

"What the hell was in my beer?"

Chapter Ten

The eight days at home had flown by and Nic was back in Connecticut standing outside of Kyle's apartment building. When she'd checked back in that morning it didn't take long for word of his transfer to reach her or the theory that he'd been transferred because her dad blamed Kyle for the video incident. After all, it was his man who'd done the deed and he should have kept his guys in line.

She'd heard the same accusation from both of her brothers when they'd Skyped her at home.

If her dad did blame Kyle he never said anything to her about it. Then again, he'd been too busy introducing her to one friend after another, all of whom were hiring. Her mom didn't mention the 'incident' unless Nic brought it up first. Then she'd listen, give her hugs, and ask Nic what she wanted to do next. While her mom had been raised in a traditional home—they didn't talk about unpleasantness and the husband ruled—Nic knew all she had to do was say she wanted X and her mom would make it happen.

The time at home had allowed Nic to heal some, to put everything in perspective and find her inner strength. She'd returned to work ready to face the crew and get back to work. She hadn't expected to hear that Kyle was leaving or for the guilt that slammed into her like a freight train.

She gave a hard knock on the door, hoping to be heard over the loud music on the other side. The music stopped and she could hear Kyle's voice through the closed door.

"Yes, I know you're comfortable, but someone's at the door. I'll be right back and you can reclaim your place on my lap."

Aw, jeez, she should have called. Then again she hadn't expected him to move on so quickly, even if she had left without a word or even a text.

Heat crept up her neck and stole across her cheeks at the thought of what or who would greet her.

Cold air blasted her from the open door. Her gaze locked on to Kyle's bare, tan chest—one she'd dreamed of running her hands down for the past month—and then slid down to take in his low slung sweats.

"Nic." The smile lit up his eyes. "I didn't know you were back."

"Clearly."

"What's that mean?" The smile dropped in confusion.

"Nothing." She leaned in just a little trying to see past him. "I didn't mean to interrupt. We can talk Monday. I should have called first." She waved him off and turned to go.

"You're not interrupting anything." Kyle reached out and grabbed her hand. "Come in. It's good to see you."

"Are you sure? It sounded like you had company." She so did not want to face whoever he'd found to replace her.

He pulled her into the apartment, shut the door and dug his hands into her hair. The kiss that followed shook her world, leaving her unbalanced and breathless.

"I've missed you," he said.

Nic scanned the room, baffled by Kyle's greeting and the comment he'd made before opening the door until a giant white cat hopped down from the couch to twine herself around Kyle's feet.

She started laughing. How stupid could she have been? "Is that who I dislodged from your lap?"

"Heard that, did you? Yeah, meet Precious or as I refer to her Princess Pain in the Ass or PITA for short." Kyle bent and picked up the kitty, holding her close to his chest.

The cat purred in response.

"I owe you an apology. See, I thought you had company... of the female type." She twisted her hands together in front of her, nervous and unsure, and feeling a bit of a fool, but she wanted to be honest with him. "Can't say what was going through my mind was particularly nice and I should have known better. So, I'm sorry." She reached out to pet Precious who responded by swiping her claws at Nic.

Kyle scolded the cat and then set her down. "She gets grumpy when her naps are interrupted. Hang on a sec." He left her to do something around the corner.

Nic took that opportunity to take in her surroundings. The apartment was clean, but not sterile. He had a brown leather couch and chair placed in front of a flat screen TV, a framed photo of a submarine with the crew's signatures on it and a small bookcase loaded with paperbacks. The tantalizing aroma of melted cheese, onions and something spicy hit her right about the time she heard him swear.

"Everything okay in there?" she called.

"Yep, just burning my fingerprints off."

She should offer to help or to kiss his boo-boo or something, but if she started she was afraid they wouldn't stop and she really needed to talk with him. Needed to clear the air, to make sure he knew she didn't blame him before he left for parts unknown.

Which was another reason not to kiss him.

It was hard enough to date a man in the military, even harder when both parties were in the service. Throw in a couple hundred or thousand miles in between and it was a break-up waiting to happen.

"Whatever that is, it's smells amazing." She wandered in further to look at the photos on top of the bookshelf. She picked up a family picture—parents, a young man in uniform along with what looked like a younger brother and sister. She had a similar one taken on her graduation day from the Naval Academy, but this one wasn't of Kyle.

He came around the corner, sucking on the side of his thumb. "That's my roommate. Nice guy, nicer family and bad taste in pets. Precious belongs to him, although she's a slut for kibble and if you feed her, she'll love you. I prefer dogs."

"I could see you with a Papillon or maybe a Chinese Crested."

He blanched. "I was going to invite you to stay for dinner, until you insulted my manhood."

"My bad. You're right. Not your type of dog at all, too much work. But now that I give it some thought, I'd have to guess you're more of the teacup Poodle kind of guy." She might have to forfeit food, but the stunned look on his face was worth it. She sniffed the air again, her stomach rumbling with hunger. "What are you heating up? It smells really good."

He pulled her close and nipped at her lower lip.

"Come with me and I'll show you." His voice had gone low and husky and she wondered if he was still offering her dinner or they were skipping to dessert.

"You know my mom warned me about guys like you. I know all about the dark side. There are no cookies."

She shouldn't be teasing him or flirting but she found she couldn't help it. He made it so easy to relax and forget about everything else. They weren't two Naval officers at the same command. For the first time in weeks she didn't feel like a victim. Kyle didn't treat her like a victim and he sure as hell didn't look at her like a victim.

"Aw, not true, I do have peanut butter cookies and chicken enchilada casserole and I promise I'll keep my hands to myself, until you tell me otherwise."

Her mood deflated faster than a popped balloon and she had to force her smile to remain steady. Stupid fantasy. She should have known reality would rear its ugly head and ruin everything. But for a moment there, right when she arrived and Kyle had practically kissed her socks off... Yeah, it was every bit as good as she remembered.

Didn't matter. She hadn't come to start something she couldn't finish. Now, more than ever, she needed to keep her head down and focus on her career. Too many people were watching her, judging her actions. One wrong step and she wouldn't be the only one to pay for her foolish choices. An entire program's future hung in the balance and she didn't want to be known as the person who set women's rights in the Navy back a generation.

Overdramatic? Maybe, but her dad had warned her to watch her step.

"How was the trip home?" Kyle handed her a plate loaded with casserole and salad and nodded toward the counter for the dressing. At her stunned silence, he must have guessed what she was thinking. "Just 'cuz I'm a guy doesn't mean I don't eat my veggies."

Her mom had to blackmail her dad and brothers to eat salad. "The trip was okay." She waited for him to get his food and then followed him to the couch.

"Just okay?" He sat in the middle leaving her the choice of the end or the chair.

She took the end section next to him and filled him on the trip in as few words as she could. She didn't want to talk about her family or think about the job offers she'd received or her family's not-so-subtle clues that she should take them. "This is really good. Who taught you to cook?"

"It was this amazing lady named Betty Crocker. My mom worked, even after the dipshit twins were born when I was ten. My dad specialized in PB&J or cereal. So I had a choice, learn to cook, wait until eight at night to eat when my brothers were asleep or live on sandwiches and fruit rings."

"That was really sweet of you." When he shrugged it off, she reached out to touch his arm. He looked up to meet her gaze. "I'm sure your mom appreciated the help."

"Yeah."

There was something in that one word. It held hurt and disappointment and anger. Sensing they were heading down a dark alley, she searched for something to lighten the mood. "So you can cook and cats love you. You're a badass Naval officer. Anything else I should know?"

"I give a killer foot massage."

Oh, she was a goner for sure. "You've been holding out on me."

"Well, if I had given you one underway then I probably would have had to give foot massages to the rest of the wardroom and frankly, Bryant's feet stink. I wouldn't touch them with a twenty-foot pole after they've been soaked in a bubble bath."

She laughed. "Wow, that's bad."

"You're telling me. He was my roommate."

It was the opening she'd been waiting for, but she loathed to bring up the subject of his leaving. She'd miss him. Miss his easy friendship, his quick smile, how his eyes went from slate gray to the color of clouds before a downpour depending on his mood.

But mostly she'd miss the way she felt when he was around—alive and capable and one hundred percent female. He never doubted her ability to do her job. He'd offered to stand by her side, but not fight her battle for her. And when he looked at her... well. Let's just say, she didn't see him looking at any of the male officers in the same way.

She picked at what was left of the delicious food on her plate. What she had eaten sat like a ton of bricks on her stomach. Pressure built up behind her eyes, stinging as she fought to hold the sudden onslaught of tears back. So stupid. She wasn't the sentimental type. Over the years she'd lost track of the number of friends she'd said good-bye to, people whom she'd known longer and better than she knew Kyle. So why the idea of him leaving hit so hard she had no clue.

The only answer she could come up with was sleep deprivation and stress.

"Something wrong with your food?" He tucked a strand of hair behind her ear before running the pad of his thumb down her cheek.

"The food's delicious. I'm just full." She sat the plate on the coffee table before turning to him. "I hear you won't have to worry about sharing a room with Bryant soon. Is that true?"

"Damn." He sat his plate next to hers and leaned back against the couch. "I wanted to tell you the good news myself."

She sat back and studied his face and posture. While he seemed disappointed that someone stole his thunder, he wasn't scowling, there were no deep stress lines, his shoulders were relaxed, and the vibe coming off of him was good.

"You're not leaving because of what happened to me, are you?"

"What?" He seemed to have trouble concentrating on her words. His brows were drawn down like he was thinking, but his focus was on a strand of her hair he twirled between his fingers. "No. Why would you think that?"

"I'm not stupid or deaf. I've heard the comments."

He took her face in his hands, brushing his lips softly across her. "Nic, this wasn't your fault. You didn't ask for any of this to happen. You never acted inappropriately and I have nothing but respect for you. You've handled this whole situation better than anyone could ask of you."

She tried to look away, but he wouldn't let her break his gaze. "No, I haven't. I ran away and hid behind my parents, letting my dad's clout keep the haters at bay."

He caressed her cheek. "There's nothing wrong with turning to your family when things get tough. It's not a sign of weakness, Nic. Not everyone has that, that rock or safe haven they can run to. Be thankful for them, not ashamed." His voice turned rough and a little harsh at the end. It reminded her that they came from different worlds. From what little he'd told her, he was the one his family turned to. Which made her wonder, whom did Kyle Hutchinson turn to in his darkest hour?

"I am thankful for them, even when they drive me crazy, which is ninety percent of the time." She reached up and covered his hand with hers. "I'm also thankful for you and the rest of the crew. This can't be easy for any of you. Stone's little stunt taints us all. When I heard you were transferring, I was more concerned that you were being forced to because my dad blamed you for not controlling your men."

Kyle kissed her, first on the forehead, then on each cheek and finally on the mouth. He took his time. Each one a sweet gesture that touched Nic's heart but lacked the sexual heat of his earlier kisses.

"My little tigress. Were you ready to take on the vice admiral of the Atlantic Fleet for me?"

"Hell yeah. What happened wasn't anymore your fault than it was mine."

He pulled her onto his lap, captured his mouth with his and kissed her.

This was no sweet action of thanks or friendship. It was an all-out assault on her senses as he dug his hands into her hair and nibbled on her bottom lip until she opened her mouth to let a moan escape. Her hands slipped around his neck as his hard chest pressed into her aching breasts. She scooted closer and the heat between their bodies flared up. Dang, did the air conditioner go out?

He kissed her again before turning his attention to her neck. His hands skimmed down her back to cup her butt. He picked her up and repositioned her so that she straddled his lap bringing her in direct contact with his erection. He bent his head and kissed her collarbone as he slid her shirt up. Her whole body was on fire, every nerve end tingling with delight. She'd dreamed of this moment for weeks and couldn't believe she was about to stop him. Clearly she'd lost her mind.

"Kyle, stop."

He did as she asked, dropped her shirt, stopped kissing her and sat back. His eyes looked dazed and confused.

Right there with you, buddy.

"Sorry. Got carried away." His voice was rough with arousal and frustration.

She pushed herself back with her hands on his chest. "Please don't apologize. Considering it was consensual and the feeling was mutual, that's a pretty big compliment." *I'm just an idiot,* she thought.

"But…"

"Kyle, I know given how we met it's hard to believe, I'm not really a wham-bam-thank-you-ma'am kind of person and I don't want to start something we won't have time to finish."

"What if I said this didn't have to be a one-time thing?"

Her pulse stuttered as she contemplated his question. Tempting, but there were outside forces to take into consideration.

"Are you saying your transfer is local?" she asked.

"Yep. Going to Naval Submarine Support Facility, just a five-minute walk from the pier."

"And your transfer has nothing to do with me?" He'd never really confirmed when she'd asked before and the suddenness of the move nagged at her conscience.

"Well, no and yes. My mom called while you were away. One of my brothers got in a shit-ton of trouble. Bottom line, she asked me to take in Keith—my other brother—in the hopes that I can get him on the straight and narrow. I was due to transfer when we got back from the deployment anyway, so I put a call into the detailer and apparently all the stars were in alignment because he had a hotspot to fill and now I'm transferring." When she opened her mouth to ask him a question, he laid a finger across her lips. "I could have kept the orders to Hawaii, but you're here and I want to see where this goes."

Wow. No pressure.

Sure, she was flattered. He'd given up Hawaii for her. Hawaii…warm sandy beaches, year-round sunshine, and unbelievable sunsets to name a few perks. Not that Connecticut didn't have nice beaches too, but come February people in New England dreamed of being in Hawaii…not the other way around.

But there were those outside forces to think about and he'd just added another one—his brother.

He ran his finger up the line between her eyes. "You're thinking too hard. Tell me what's going on behind those beautiful eyes of yours."

"That we're setting ourselves up for failure. It's hard enough with both of us being active duty, throw in the investigation and now your brother. It sounds like a lot to deal with."

"So we'll deal with it." He laced his fingers with hers. "Keith doesn't need me to babysit him. He's twenty. He's going to want a job and friends of his own. As for the investigation, that's out of our hands now and on the group's shoulders."

Looking down at their clasped hands, she realized she didn't want to win this discussion. It felt right being with Kyle. She didn't know how long it would last, a week, a month, a year, or longer. She found she didn't care. Marriage wasn't something she was after, not that she had anything against it, and imagined someday she'd be ready to take that step. It had just never been a life goal. That didn't mean she wanted to hop from one guy to the next either. She liked relationships that lasted, liked the rush of a new attraction, but also the comfort that came with being with someone you knew.

She also liked the times when she was on her own. They gave her the opportunity to explore what was going on in her own head without the influence of hormones or another person, because both could really screw with a person's thoughts. Time on her own gave her the chance to grow and to experiment and to heal and be open for what life brought to her.

Like Kyle.

He'd been a pleasant surprise and she wasn't ready to let him go.

She worried her bottom lip, biting down on it as a thought crossed her mind. "Won't it seem odd? Us hooking up so soon after you leaving the boat?"

"Not really. We're both single. I was your sponsor, which meant we spent a lot of time together. We found out we liked each other. We waited until I transferred and then I asked you out." He brought their hands to his mouth and kissed hers.

It sounded like he'd put a lot of thought into the two of them while she'd been gone. All of her defenses came crashing down as she looked at this man before her, who put so many others before himself and took care of everyone else around him. He tried to ease her worries, yet he had his own problems to deal with, ones she had a feeling were going to wreak havoc with his well-ordered life, and he'd need a rock of his own to lean on.

"If you're not comfortable going public with our relationship for now, we can keep it under wraps. Or if you just want to be friends, we'll be friends. Either way, I'm here for you when and how you need me."

There was a loud, internal crash as the last defense she had went tumbling down. The man knew just what to say and when. She let go of his hands. He closed his eyes and his face went slack. She reached down to grab the hem of her T-shirt and pulled it over her head. His eyes were wide open as she dropped the shirt on the floor and reached behind her back to unclasp her bra and let it drop. For a split second his chest didn't move and she wondered if she had given him a heart attack, but then the corners of his lips lifted as his eyes locked on her breasts.

He ran his tongue across his bottom lip and she laughed.

"You know if you're still hungry I think there was mention of peanut butter cookies." She scraped her nails down his bare chest.

"Not what I'm hungry for. Now come here because I've taken so many cold showers I should get a second or third Blue Nose certificate." He leaned forward, caught her nipple with his soft lips and grazed it with his teeth before his tongue did a slow sweep around and over bringing it to tight bud.

"Yes," Nic moaned as she slid her hands to the back of his head pressing him closer.

He switched sides and her head dropped back as another moan escaped.

Uncontrollable sensations swept her away, replacing thought and logic with pure emotions and instinct. The time for talking had ended and the last thing she wanted to do was examine her emotions. Right then and there, she wanted to feel, to lose herself, to escape.

He released his hold on her nipple and trailed kisses up the long column of her neck, over silky soft skin. They'd come together so quickly their first time. He wanted to take his time tonight to give her hours of pleasure, to explore and learn and taste ever inch of her, to drive her as crazily out of control as she'd done to him.

He kissed the underside of her jaw, while his thumbs traced lazy circles around her beaded nipples until she moaned his name. It came out as a half-protest, half-plea.

He nipped her lower lip. "Tell me what you want," he demanded.

"More." She sat forward pushing her breast into his hand and nipped his mouth in return before turning it into a kiss that practically set the room on fire. His dick strained against the soft cotton of his sweat pants and Nic wiggled closer pulling a groan from him. A few more minutes of this and he'd wouldn't last.

Sliding his hands down he cupped her ass and pulled her in tight as he stood. Automatically she wrapped her legs around his waist and he carried her into the bedroom. Carefully he laid her on the bed and Nic reached out for the waistband of his sweats, but he grabbed her hand and stopped her.

"Ladies first."

He kissed her on the forehead, then each eye, and the corners of her mouth before laying claim to her full lips. What had started out as a need to satisfy a basic urge had turned into something more.

Something he couldn't explain, but that something had taken over and he knew this was more than just sex.

He should know; he'd been with enough women to know the difference. Not that he'd call himself a man whore. More like a connoisseur of the fairer sex. After all, what was there not to like about women and all their soft, wonderful curves, especially when they were pressed up against him?

But with Nic it was more than a physical reaction. If she had asked to keep their relationship in the friend zone he would have agreed. He'd miss this part, but he'd have made the sacrifice for her. She whispered his name and he gave thanks to the Fates for having mercy on him.

He continued his exploration of her body, taking his time, loving how she called out his name, pleading for him to end his torment. He pinched her nipples and she arched her back and called out "Yes." She was so responsive to his touch. His tongue circled her bellybutton and she squirmed. As his hands unbuttoned her jeans and slowly slid the zipper down, he trailed feather light kisses along her abdomen leading to her hipbone and she suppressed a laugh.

So his girl was ticklish? Good to know.

Hooking his thumbs into the loops on her pants he inched the jeans down, taking her silk panties with her. She lifted her butt to give him easier access and he pressed a kiss to her pelvic bone.

"Kyle, you're killing me here."

"We've got all night."

"No, you've got all night. I've got duty in a couple of hours."

"Damn."

He slid his finger between her slick folds and smiled. He stroked and caressed, gently circling her clit before slipping it deep inside of her as she moaned his name. His mouth joined in next. Slowly, his tongue circled and then flicked her clit before grazing his teeth across her. She cried out and raised her hips, pressing closer. He repeated the process, never stopping the slow and steady in and out rhythm of his fingers. With each stroke, each pass, her breathing sped up. Her fingernails dug into Kyle's shoulders as the climax hit her and she whispered his name.

Her hips dropped back to the bed and Kyle placed a kiss in the middle of her stomach as he reached over to the nightstand drawer to pull out a condom. While she caught her breath, he rolled it on. Nic lay sprawled across his bed, arms flung out, eyes closed, chest heaving with a serene smile. He kissed her again, this time on her right rib cage and then the left before planting one in between her beautiful breasts. Nic wrapped her arms around his head and held him.

"Wow. Thank you. That was amazing." She released her hold and let him look up at her. "Is it my turn to return the favor?"

"Nope, I'm not done with you yet."

She arched her brow and the smile grew.

He positioned himself over her, holding himself up on his elbows. Slowly he entered her and felt her muscles clamp tight.

"Omigawd, that feels incredible," she moaned.

"I haven't even started. I'm going to fuck you six ways to dawn tonight. Slow, fast, rough. Whatever it takes to hear you scream my name."

Her breath hitched. Her eyes widened and she gave him a little nod.

He inched his way in and then slowly withdrew, taking his cues from her body language and facial expressions. After a few minutes, she shifted, bringing him deeper.

That was the clue he'd been waiting for. He hooked her knee over his arm and brought it up to her chest, opening her wider, giving him deeper access and drove in hard. Bodies slapped against bodies. He pulled back and slammed in again and again until Nic was panting and begging, little broken pleas of "yes, more, please" tumbling from her lips.

"Fuck," he growled. He was so close to coming and there was no way he was going before she came again. He bent his head forward and grazed her nipple with his teeth before sucking it into his mouth.

The muscles around his dick contracted and Nic cried out his name as the orgasm hit her and she dug her short nails into his back.

He'd hate to have broken a promise and not have given her multiple orgasms. But then again, he'd promised her a record and two definitely wasn't it. He shifted and let go of her leg.

"Hold your leg for me."

As she did as instructed, he reached down, circled her clit with his thumb and then pinched it, all the while driving into her as fast and hard as he dared. This time when her contraction clamped down on him, he knew he couldn't hold out. He gave one last thrust and exploded. He held still as he called out her name before collapsing half on top of Nic. At least he'd had enough brain cells functioning to try not to squash her.

Nic wrapped her arms around him.

Together they lay, both breathing hard, neither making any attempt to move.

Not that he thought he could even if wanted to, and that was the thing, he really didn't want to move. He wanted to wrap Nic up in his arms and keep her there.

Maybe even forever.

Damn. Fuck. Double Damn.

He was in uncharted waters with no rescue in sight.

Chapter Eleven

The past couple of days had zipped by and he hadn't had more than a three-minute conversation with Nic. He couldn't remember what they'd talked about—something work related, as there had been eight other officers in the room with them—but he remembered the way she said his name and the way his dick sat up and paid attention. That had been yesterday, his last day on the boat. He'd spent all of today running around checking into his new command before making the quick drive to the Providence airport where he sat and waited for his brother's plane.

He kicked back at a table in the Starbucks café. It was situated in the middle of baggage claim, at the bottom of the stairs that every arriving passenger had to descend. Which meant he had zero chance of missing his baby brother.

The display screen on the column across from him announced Keith's flight had been delayed. No big. Hurry up and wait was standard operating procedure in the military. If you showed up on time and were seen right away…shit was about to get real. So he didn't mind the delay. Besides, it gave him time to enjoy his caramel macchiato in peace.

People came in waves down the stairs and escalators as flights landed. Grandparents, parents, kids, loved ones ran to greet each other with laughing smiles and welcoming hugs.

Yeah, he so didn't see that happening for him.

He'd probably get the finger.

According to their mom, baby bro only got on the plane when she'd pulled the bad heart card on him. For not being Catholic or Jewish, Bonnie Hutchinson had guilt down to an art form. Kyle had his doubts on how well this would work. He was practically a stranger to his brothers. They'd been eight when he'd left for college; from there he'd gone straight into the Navy with only a quick trip home once every couple of years. There was no reason why Keith would listen to a damn thing he said to him, except maybe he didn't want to end up in a cell next his twin. Kyle had agreed to do what he could to make sure that didn't happen because yeah, he carried his own guilt at not being there to help guide his brothers and keep them away from scum like Woody.

His phone pinged and he looked down and read the text from Mace:

What the heck? I return from leave and find out you transferred. What gives? Nic?

Family stuff, he texted back. *At PVD picking up baby bro now. Will fill you in tomorrow over a slice. How's Amber?*

Prego and grumpy.

Yours?

Honestly? Don't know. Fill you in at lunch. Hug the mini-me.

Yeah, right. Hug his brothers? Only if he wanted to get punched. He read the message again. Crap. He couldn't imagine having a pregnant wife, never mind not knowing if it was his or not.

Another wave of passengers swarmed the escalators and Kyle searched the crowd for a familiar face. According to the status screen, the flight had landed. He waited patiently as the crowd thinned to couples every minute or two, to a straggler here and there.

What the hell? Did he parachute out of the plane over Pennsylvania? Just as Kyle picked up his phone to call, his brother appeared. With a backpack slung over his shoulder, ratty jeans, a disheveled T-shirt and hair, along with an attitude that said screw you he sauntered over to Kyle. Keith stopped in front of him, removed the top from the bottle of soda he held and took a long gulp, then burped in Kyle's face.

Nice.

Why again did he agree to this?

Oh yeah, that guilt thing.

"Bags?" Kyle asked.

Keith held up his backpack and Kyle lifted his brow in question. Not much to live on, but then that didn't really surprise him. "Okay, let's go."

The walk to the car took all of four minutes and within ten they were on the interstate and on the way home. As soon as they'd gotten in the car Keith had slouched down in his seat, stuck in his earbuds, and closed his eyes.

Fine. He got it. The kid was pissed off at the world. No one asked him what he wanted to do, they'd just told him he to leave. At least Kyle had left of his own choosing, but he'd met plenty of kids over the years who'd ended up in the Navy because they'd had no other place to go, didn't want to live in their car/cardboard box or had gotten tired of doing so.

The drive home passed quickly, the route a straight shot down the interstate, and he nudged Keith awake before slipping out of his baby—a black Charger, fully loaded.

"Holy shit." Kyle said and turned to look back at his car.

Keith stood with his hand on the top of the car door, looking at him. "What?"

Shaking his head, Kyle turned around and strode for the apartment. Telling the kid it had just hit him that he'd have to loan his pride and joy to the last person, well, one of the top five people he least trusted on the planet, wasn't the best way to start things off. Kyle unlocked the door, pocketed the keys and caught the princess as she launched off the back of the chair into his arms.

Keith sneered at him. "A cat?"

"So?" Kyle walked into the kitchen and dumped a handful of kibble into her dish before depositing her on the floor. He grabbed a beer and flipped the cap into the trash.

Keith stood in the same place, a bored expression on his face with his backpack slung over his shoulder. Kyle pointed out where everything was, including Keith's room, but stopped him before he had a chance to escape.

"We need to talk." Kyle sat on the edge of the chair, hoping to diffuse the tension in the air. "Set some ground rules."

"I'm twenty."

"I know." Not that Keith's sneer or attitude backed his words. "I was there the day they brought you two home. Kind of hard to forget."

"Could have fooled me." Keith shifted from one foot to the next while he fiddled with the earbuds to his iPod.

"Who do you think changed your diapers? Taught you to read and ride a bike and hook a fish?" Kyle blew out a breath and counted to ten. "Look, I'm sorry."

"Whatever. Can I go to bed? My flight left at the ass crack of dawn."

"Keith." He put a hand out to stop him. "I should have come home more, should have called you and Kenny more… I should have been there for you. I'm sorry I wasn't, but I am now and if this is going to work you've got to follow my rules."

"Fine. Just tell me what they are." The kid flung the backpack on the couch and dropped down to the arm.

Princess PITA took that opportunity to jump up into Keith's lap. The kid looked down as the cat kneaded his legs before settling in. Interesting. She generally only deemed a human good enough to associate with after they'd fed her. For a minute, Kyle thought Keith would give her the old heave-ho, but instead his brother lightly ran his hand down the spoiled cat's back.

"Look, are you hungry? I could order a pizza." At the go-to-hell look he received, Kyle gave up trying to play host.

"It's simple. Stay out of trouble. I'm not your maid. Pick up after yourself."

"And?"

"If you have to borrow my car, you ask first and if you so much as even get a scratch on it, you better be bleeding and it better be the other guy's fault."

Keith's hand hesitated in petting the cat at the same time he snorted a laugh of disdain. "Nice to know you care. Don't worry about your precious car. I'd rather walk." The cat let out a roar of displeasure at being ignored. "Demanding, aren't you?"

At least they could agree on something, even if was a pain-in-the-ass cat.

Keith shoved his iPod into his pocket and continued with his feline worshipping duties. He refused to make eye contact. "This wasn't my idea, you know."

Kyle took a sip of the beer he'd been holding. It had started to grow warm but at least it wet his throat and gave him a few minutes to rein his temper in. As a Navy officer he dealt with kids like Keith, who felt like they were misunderstood, invisible, that no one listened to them, like they weren't important, all the time.

"Mom and I felt it best for you to get away, put some distance between you and the guy Kenny was working for."

A flash of heat passed over Keith's face. "I don't even know the guy."

"He knows you." Kyle focused on peeling the label from his bottle while watching his brother from the corner of his eye. "About a month ago, he came to the house looking for both of you."

Keith shrugged. "Small town. Not a lot twins."

He'd drop the subject for now. The kid didn't trust him, not that Kyle blamed him, as he didn't really trust Keith either. He had no idea what either of his brothers had been up to for years.

"The complex has a pool and a workout room. We're on the bus line and there's several beaches nearby. I'll arrange for some time off, take you up the local community college so you can check it out—"

"Whoa." Keith sat the cat down and stood up, arms crossed over his chest. "I'm not going back to school."

"What are you going to do?" He kept his tone light, steady all the while thinking his brother was a class-A idiot.

"I'll get a job."

"Doing what? Do you have any experience?"

"Some."

"Hamburger Hill is a five-minute walk. I'm sure you'll find something there."

Why couldn't either of the dipshit twins do anything the easy way? Tell them to go left, and they'd go right, insisting it was the best route. Tell them to learn from your mistakes and they repeat them. Everything had to be done the hard way. Couldn't they accept someone might know what's best for them?

Was he ever that pigheaded?

Probably.

"Whatever. I'll be out of your life soon." Keith pulled the iPod out of his pocket and stuck one of the buds in his ear.

Kyle reached out to grasp his shoulder but Keith shifted away. "I don't want you out of my life. You're family. You're welcome here for as long as you want and need."

He didn't know what he was expecting or what he'd really wanted from their conversation. Yeah, he knew the kid was mad and hurt, but deep down, maybe he'd hoped that the bond they'd had as kids would still be there. From the time the twins could crawl they'd followed him everywhere and they hadn't stopped until he'd left home. They'd even sneaked into his room and slept with him after a nightmare woke one of them or during a storm. Both had been terrified by the clash of thunder.

"I've got to work tomorrow, but after work I'll give you the grand tour. Show you the highlights of the area. Help you get your bearings."

Keith grabbed his backpack, hugging it to his chest like a lifeline. "Don't bother. I can find my own way."

Before he could say anything else a knock on the door interrupted them.

* * *

Nic took one look at the deep lines around Kyle's eyes and mouth and wondered if she shouldn't have come over or had at least called first.

"Hi, I figured with the trip to the airport and stuff, you wouldn't have a chance to think about dinner." She held up the boxes and handed them off to Kyle. "Everyone likes pizza, right?"

"Yeah. Of course. Thanks." He stepped aside for her to come in while he put the pies on the table. Standing at the hall entrance was a younger, lankier version of Kyle. Same scraggly chestnut brown hair and cloudy gray eyes. "Hi, you must be Keith."

The guy stared at her for a couple of minutes without responding and then pulled out his earbuds. He turned his attention to Kyle. "She your girl?"

Kyle stood next to her. A huff of frustration blew across her cheek. "I swear my mom taught him manners." He made the introductions and Keith nodded in her direction.

"She's hot." He stuck the earbud back in and headed down the hall. "Thanks for the pizza."

Nic turned to Kyle and smiled. "So I'm guessing he's the social butterfly in the family?"

Kyle wrapped his arms around her and pulled her in for a long, satisfactory kiss.

"More like a pain in the butt and he's part of a matched set. I can't believe he was rude to you. Me, yeah, I get that."

She ran her fingers through his hair, loving the feel and so glad he resisted letting the barber shop cut it in a high and tight like so many other sailors these days. "Don't worry about it. He's just doing what all younger siblings do and pressing your buttons. Trust me on this. Not that I'd ever torment my brothers." She rolled her eyes, gave him a quick nip on his bottom lip and stepped back.

"He's been pressing every button I have since he got off the plane."

"Give him time. He'll settle in. Look, I should go. Give you two time to catch up and settle in together. I just wanted to see you."

He pulled her back to him, nuzzling her neck as she tried to squirm out of his reach, laughing. "Stay. Grumpzilla won't be out of his room for hours. Eat pizza with me, tell me about your day, and then I can take you to bed and forget about mine."

"Food and sex. I'm starting to see a pattern here." She teased, tracing the ripples of his abs through his T-shirt.

"Not true. That first night there was no food involved at all." Kyle reached down and lifted her by her butt and plopped her down on the table next to the pizza boxes. "But I'm all for food and sex. We could even have food with sex. Strawberry jam isn't just for toast."

Nic choked on her laugh, pushing Kyle back, a quick look confirmed they were still alone. "Go get some plates."

By the time he returned from the kitchen with plates, napkins and two beers, Nic had gotten off the table and lifted the lid on both pizza boxes.

Kyle handed her a plate and took a deep breath. "It's like a gift from the gods."

"Do you want cheese or loaded?"

He leaned over to inspect the pizzas. "Are those mushrooms?" His voice was pure disgust and disbelief.

"Yes, and if you don't like them you can pick them off and put them on mine. It's also got sausage, pepperoni and black olives."

With a resigned sigh he let her give him a slice of each, and carried their beers to the couch where he waited for her to join him. They talked about non-important things as they ate. Nic stole the mushrooms from Kyle's pizza and a few pieces of sausage too. She filled him in on her non-exciting day of writing reports and reviewing inventory, sitting in on a couple of meetings—the usual. In turn he told her about the new command and how he was looking forward to the change.

"Have you heard anything new on the investigation? Are they ready to move forward with the charges yet?" They'd finished eating and Kyle wiped away a smear of pizza sauce from the corner of her mouth with his thumb.

"Last I heard the prosecution is building their case. Whatever that means. All of the men have been temporarily reassigned to the group, although they did offer to transfer me first. Gave me my pick of assignments. Have to admit, Naples was tempting, as was embassy duty in Australia." She shifted down so that she could lay her head back on the couch cushion and rest her feet on the edge of the trunk that served as a coffee table.

"Why would you turn either down?" Kyle ran his fingers up and down her arm, giving her goose bumps. "Both are prime billets."

It was a great question. When she was a teen, Naples had been Nic's home for three years. The city was magnificent, filled with a rich history, and the people—oh, how she loved the Italians! So warm and welcoming and then there was the food. Nothing beat homemade pasta that had been made that day with sauce that had simmered for hours, crafted by loving hands. If it weren't for all the walking one did in Naples, you'd gain a thousand pounds from the gelato alone. So why not return to the land she loved?

Or move on to the land down under where embassy duty would shoo her in for an early promotion?

Because she'd never been a quitter.

"I don't know if you can understand or not. Sometimes, I question my own logic on this subject. The day Stone shot that film he made me a victim. I know he didn't physically hurt me, but it doesn't change the fact that I was labeled that day. People look at me with pity in their eyes. I did nothing wrong, yet everyone expects me to run and hide. Probably because seeing me makes them uncomfortable and if I left they could forget the ugly reality of what happened."

"You don't make me uncomfortable."

"No, but you don't look at me that way either."

Kyle looked at her like a man looked at a woman. He looked at her like a friend looks at a friend. He looked at her like a person.

"Everyone expects me to leave. It's been strongly *suggested* by some that I should take a reassignment. Get a fresh start." She tilted her head up to get a better look at Kyle, to see if he really got what she was saying or not. "If I do, he wins. I stay the victim and no matter what the court does to him, he retains the power over my life he took that day. Does that make any sense?"

"Strangely enough, it does. He may not have physically touched you, but what he did was sexual harassment, Nic, at the very least. Guys like Stone are bullies of the worst kind. They have no balls to face their opponents. They hide in the shadows and attack in the dark, or from the safety of the Internet and in cases like this, use technology to terrorize."

She sat up and turned to him. "Exactly. Everyone expects me to be all shook up, and I am, but I'm not going to let anyone else dictate what I do with my life or how I live it." No matter how deep the urge to run was. "Today I talked with a counselor."

Kyle slid his arm around her shoulders and she snuggled in, resting her cheek against his chest.

"How'd that go?" His voice was quiet and soothing.

"Pretty good, actually. She really understood what I've been going through, not that she's been an unwilling porn star before. But the important thing is she understood the fear and anxiety I've developed when using public bathrooms. It was nice to just know I wasn't alone or being a drama queen. That what I was feeling was real and valid."

He kissed her forehead. "I didn't know," he whispered against her.

"No one did." She reached out and laced her fingers with his. "I didn't tell anyone, not even my family. I was ashamed. Afraid that what I was experiencing made me weak and not worthy of my position or it meant I didn't belong in the sub force. I mean, there are other women out there in the military who have experienced far worse, and they haven't tucked tail and ran."

"Nic." His voice brought her head up to meet his eyes. "You can't compare your ordeal and how you are dealing with it to anyone else's. Everyone handles trauma differently. There's no one right way."

She kissed him. Just a simple meeting of the lips to say thank you because what he'd said was one of the kindest things anyone could have said It also was so him, standing by her just like he said he'd do.

"I know that and the counselor helped me understand that I was putting too much pressure on myself, not giving myself anytime to process what happened. It'll take some time. I'm not going to walk into the base gym tomorrow and jump in the shower without feeling the heebie-jeebies. But in time I will take my life back. I won't let myself down, or my sisters-in-arms, or you."

"I'm pretty sure you could never let me down."

"Oh yeah? What if I said I had a headache tonight?"

Bailing and going home would be the right thing and the smart option. His brother was in the other room; they'd barely walked in the door from the airport when she'd showed up. And based on the tension in the place, they needed time to talk. But being alone in her room meant more time to think and for some reason her brain thought that instead of taking advantage of those moments to, oh say sleep or relax, it chose to replay the past couple of weeks over and over again.

Kyle traced his fingers from the top of her arm down to her side, skimming the side of her breast. "I have a surefire cure for headaches. Of course, it means you have to get naked first."

She laughed. "Oh really? Is this doctor approved?"

"Don't believe me? You can always ask Doc Corbett. He'll back me or you could test it out yourself." He blew warm breath down the side of her throat, a delicious sensation that was a direct contrast to the cool air of the apartment.

"What if this miracle cure doesn't work?" Her question came out low and little raspy, probably because the image of her sprawled out naked on Kyle's bed as he ministered to her body made it hard to swallow and breathe, much less talk.

"Then I'll give you two aspirins and haul my horny ass into a cold shower."

"Well," she shifted and swung her leg over him to straddle his lap. "Maybe we should give it a try and be thankful it's only a slight headache."

In one swift motion he scooped her up as he carried her off to the bedroom with his lips locked on to hers.

Chapter Twelve

Hurry up and wait. He should get the motto tattooed on his backside. Kyle glanced at his wristwatch and let out a bored sigh. The sailor across from him in the reception area of Navy Legal gave one of those yep-tell-me-about-it laughs and nodded. They'd both been sitting for the last half hour, whereas the one guy had been glued to his smartphone, Kyle had flipped through the Navy Times. *Why make an appointment if you were going to ignore it?* he wondered. Five more minutes, that's all he was waiting and if the damn defense attorney hadn't showed by then, Kyle was out of there. He had better things to do than to talk to Stone's lawyer.

Not bothering to check the time, Kyle stood and turned to the front desk with the baby Legalman who didn't look old enough to have been cut from his mom's apron strings.

"Tell Lieutenant Cruz if he still wants to talk to me, he can come to NSSF. I've got work to do—" Kyle started to say.

"Excuse me, Lieutenant Hutchinson?" The door to the right of him opened and a brunette of medium height addressed him. At his nod, she stepped back, expecting him to follow. "I'm sorry to have kept you waiting. The admiral's staff had me on the phone with an urgent matter."

Smart. She knew he couldn't argue with that excuse.

She led him to a cramped office that overlooked the parking lot, offered him coffee and apologized again for the wait and the mess before taking her seat behind the standard wooden office desk.

"Thank you for making time to talk with me. I'm Lieutenant Lupe Cruz," she said, "I've been appointed as Petty Officer Stone's defense attorney. This shouldn't take long. I just need to go over your statement again and have a few additional questions for you."

What was the point? She had everything he knew, had seen, right there on the paper in front of her. There was nothing new he could tell her, no forgotten memory that would absolve her asskite of a client from the crime he'd committed.

Once again, Kyle ran though the events of the day, from the minute he'd gotten up from the table in the wardroom, his conversation with Brooks and Wu, to the moment Mace and Bryant pulled him off of Stone. Same thing he told the XO, CO, the group investigators and the prosecuting attorney.

She looked up at him, eyes wide, pen poised over the tablet she'd been making notes on at the end. "You freely admit that you got physical with Stone?"

"Did you miss the part where your client videotaped a female officer in the shower and tried to brush it off as no big deal, just a way to make some scratch?" He was shocked at how calm he sounded. Inside he wanted to rail and yell and ask how she could defend scum like Stone.

"I'm just surprised you'd admit it, knowing you could get in trouble. Most people try to hide their mistakes." She scribbled something on her pad before looking back up.

"I own up when I screw up. Besides, Commander Holloway has already dealt with the situation." Basically a slap on the wrist, but she didn't need to know.

"Before this day, had Stone ever mentioned any money problems to you?"

"No."

"Did he mention problems with his girlfriend, that she thought she might be pregnant and wanted to get married?"

"No." Truthfully, he was surprised any woman would sleep with Stone.

"What's your relationship like with the rest of the men in your department, Lieutenant Hutchinson?" Once again, she paused in her note taking to glance up at him.

He gave her a slight smile. "Good. Friendly, respectful, but as you know there are boundaries. The guys talk around me. No one zips their lips the minute I walk in the door. Petty Officer Brooks is engaged to his high school sweetheart. It'll be a Christmas wedding. Her name is Ericka. Petty Officer Wu has two kids. Jayden is three and Emma is two and is already destined to be a heartbreaker. Oh, and his wife Jessica makes the best dim sum around. Do you want to hear about the rest?"

"No, I'm getting the picture." She set her pen down, brought her hand up to her face and rubbed at her temple with her index finger. "What's your boat's policy on smartphones?"

Was she kidding? "Same as everyone else's. You can take them on board, but you can't use the recording feature anywhere on the boat."

She held up a hand while she jotted down another note. What was she doing, writing a frigging book?

"Almost done, I promise. What is your relationship with Lieutenant Riley?"

This time she made sure to watch his every move.

Kyle had made sure not to flinch. But inside his heart slammed against his chest. The room turned a hazy red and the grip on his cover intensified until the pain in his fingers cut through the anger boiling his blood.

"We're shipmates."

"Is that all?" She sounded dubious.

"I was her sponsor when she was first reported onboard. Guess you could call us friends at this point. Same as with the rest of my fellow officers on the *California*."

"Uh-huh." More scribbling on the pad. "Interesting. Well, thank you, Lieutenant Hutchinson for coming in." She stood and extended her hand.

Kyle gave it a polite shake and reached for the door.

"Uh, how is Lieutenant Riley doing?" Cruz asked.

Kyle stood with his hand on the doorknob and looked over at the woman. "You would have to ask her. I haven't seen much of her since I transferred to NSSF, but then you know that already. I'm not sure what you're trying to get at, Lieutenant Cruz, but the simple truth is, nothing is going to change the fact that your client is as guilty as sin. Chalk this one up as a loss on your record and move on."

She came around her desk and got in his face. Arms crossed, nostrils flared. Good, she was mad. He could guarantee not nearly as pissed as he was.

"Like it or not, I have to defend Petty Officer Stone. It's my job. That doesn't mean I condone what he did or that I don't feel for Riley. It doesn't mean that I'm not sickened by the thought or repulsed by the fact that I have to sit in a room with him and listen to him spew his indignant bullshit. Just telling you this could get me in trouble."

"So why are you?"

"Maybe I want her to know she's not alone."

Later, the interview played out again and again in Kyle's head as he made his way to the bowling alley where he'd agreed to meet Mace for lunch. Something didn't feel right about the attorney's questions, but he couldn't put his finger on exactly what.

He swung in through the double doors and waved to Felix manning the rental desk to the left of him. The crack of balls hitting pins, followed by excited squeals made Kyle smile. It'd been a while since he and his friends had hit the lanes. Now that they were going to be back in port for a while, maybe he'd arrange for a lunchtime game, get Nic up and test out her skill in the alley. But today he had a different purpose—food and support—so he followed his nose, tracking the wonderful aroma of salt and fried foods.

Mace sat at a table in the back with a couple of baskets and two bottles of water in front of him. His shoulders were slumped forward and there were dark circles under his eyes and deep grooves lining his forehead.

Man, he'd aged a good ten years over the last couple of weeks..

Kyle nodded toward the food. "Eating for two, I see."

"You know I should say screw you and eat it all just because you're such a smart ass. You're late. I got tired of waiting so I ordered for both of us before I chewed someone's arm off. So shut up and eat before I change my mind."

Kyle hopped onto the stool and lifted the bun off his burger. "Aw, Mom you remembered mustard, hold the ketchup. You do love me."

"Fuck you, Hutch." The insult was followed by a laugh.

Neither talked while they devoured every bite, every fry and the pickles too.

Satisfied, Kyle took a really good look at his friend. He'd known Mace for most of his career and he'd never seen the guy so down. Together they had drunk more beer, ate more pizza, and charmed more ladies than he could count. Good times. Shooting pool, hanging out on beaches, traveling the world, and standing by each other's sides right up to when Mace had fallen head over ass in love with Amber. Kyle had been his best man. Since the wedding, they didn't spend as much time after work together, but that was expected and he didn't begrudge his buddy for wanting to get home to his bride. The two were crazy about each other.

How in the hell had that all gone to shit?

"So, congratulations?" Kyle held up the glass in salute.

"Maybe." Mace blew out a sigh. Hung his head and then looked back up, eyes glossy. "What the hell am I saying? Yeah, of course, it's mine. Got to be."

"Why would you think otherwise?"

"I guess it's the timing. She's about four months along. That means it happened right in the middle of everything exploding at home. We weren't exactly taking advantage of the marital bed. Hell, half the time I was sleeping on the couch. So how'd I get her pregnant?"

If this weren't Mace with his marriage on the line, Kyle would have come back with a sarcastic response. As much as he didn't want to talk feelings and marriage and crap, he couldn't abandon his friend in need.

"What does Amber say?" Kyle asked.

"Guess there was a night where alcohol was involved. A lot of alcohol."

Now he did laugh. "Sorry. That would make sense. You are kind of a lightweight, man. So she got you drunk, took advantage of you and now you're going to be a dad? Mazel tov! You've always wanted kids and you'll make a great dad."

Mace tossed his empty food basket on top of Kyle's and sat back. "You're forgetting one important factor. She left me. I'm here in Connecticut and she's at her parents—who hate me—in Wisconsin. I either leave the Navy or I get to be an absentee dad. You know sometimes I think Bryant is the smart one in this group."

Kyle choked on his water. "Did you hit your head on the plane ride home? Bryant smart? How do you figure?"

"He doesn't get involved. He's always got a lady, but they all know the score from the start, it's just for fun, don't expect any bended knee proposals, no rings or bells or promises of forever. Somehow, they're all okay with it too. You ever see that guy stressing over a woman?"

"I'm pretty sure the dude doesn't have a heart to give away."

"Still, I'm telling you. Take a page from his playbook. Whatever this thing is with Nic, stop it now before you lose your heart and end up hurt."

Yeah, Kyle thought, *it might be too late for that.*

* * *

Nic wiped down the elliptical and tossed the towel in her bag. She must have spent more time on the devil's torture device than she'd thought because half way up the stairs to the locker room she had to sit and catch her breath.

You're stalling, the little voice in her head said.

"Remember what the counselor advised," Nic said out loud.

With that she pulled up on the banister and sprinted the last few steps. Well, maybe sprinted wasn't the right word, but at least she didn't crawl on her hands and knees, which is what she had felt like doing. Before pushing open the locker room door she strolled over to the set of double doors that led to the long corridor that housed among other things, the entrance the men's locker room. A quick peek assured her no one else was around, at least that she could tell. She'd also been watching the stairs while working out. No one had gone up them to change in over an hour.

Still, when she entered the women's locker room she did a thorough inspection checking for any gaps, cracks or hiding places. Once she was convinced there was no way in this world a sequel could be made, she headed toward her locker. Lifting the edges of her T-shirt, she hesitated and looked around.

Was that the door creaking open?

Cripes. Here I go again. Deep breath out. *Just go look. You'll feel better.*

Nope, no one there. Back at the locker she lifted her shirt and tossed it on the bench next to her, then pulled her sports bra off and let it drop onto the pile. Black spots danced before her eyes. A click from the far side of the room had her spinning around. Falling back against the cold metal, she groped into her duffle until her hand landed on the soft cotton of her towel and she could wrap it around her.

There's no one here. It's just my mind playing tricks on me. Stop. Stop. Stop. Please, just stop.

Her breath came too fast, too shallow, and the room started to rotate. She had to get out of there. Air, she needed air. Using her hand to guide her, she stumbled around the line of lockers and yanked open the door. The force of the door flinging backward thrust her forward. Strong arms kept her from face planting. There was something oddly familiar about the striking hazel eyes staring down at her.

"I'm okay," Nic murmured from between her legs, the floor inches from her face. Warm hands ran circles over her back and a soothing voice kept telling her to breathe and she'd be okay.

"Slowly sit up. Take your time and if the room starts to spin or go dark, put your head back down."

Nic looked around and then at the two men standing beside her.

"You kind of passed out," the man with the hazel eyes said.

"I'm going to get someone up here to check her out, Jax." The other guy took a step and Nic's hand shot out and grabbed his leg.

"No." She waited a beat for her heart to settle and her voice not to squeak again. "Please don't. I'm okay."

The two men looked at each other and then back to her. The one called Jax took the lead. "Why don't you tell us what happened and then we'll determine if we need to call anyone else in."

Nic bent her head to wipe the sweat from her brow and that's when she realized she was sitting on the floor outside the locker room, on the edge of the indoor running track in yoga pants and a towel. Thank goodness it was summer time and the gym was mostly empty.

"Here, drink this." Jax handed over his water bottle. "We're not going anywhere until you explain what happened. It's our job."

"It's stupid. I had a panic attack. Thought someone was in there with me or filming."

"Ah." Jax's face lit up. "I didn't recognize you out of uniform."

Nic shrunk down into herself as she pulled the towel tighter. "Excuse me?"

"Chief Jackson Faraday, ma'am. We met on the *California* the day you pulled back into port. Miner checked the locker room and it's clear, ma'am. If you want we can get one of the female employees to escort you back in and stay with you while you get dressed."

"No." Shaking her head, she pushed up against the wall to stand. "Thank you both. I'll just grab my stuff and go."

"I can stand guard if you want, ma'am," Jackson offered.

Both men looked at her like she was a frail kitten to be handled with kid gloves. Given their size, she didn't know how well they'd do with the whole 'handle with care' thing, but she didn't doubt their ability to scare off the bogeyman. And she did appreciate the offer, but they'd already come to her rescue and delayed their own workouts on her behalf. She'd just go pull on her shirt, grab her stuff and go. Once she got back to her room she could take a shower in private.

"Actually, if you guys could keep this to yourselves, I'd really appreciate it."

Both men nodded and Nic thanked them again as she pushed open the door to the locker room and stepped inside. The *thunk* of the door as it shut behind her gave her a little start. This time she didn't look around; instead she stalked to her locker with the intent to grab her gear and bolt. But as she reached for her clothes her hand stayed.

If she kept running, she would never learn to stand her ground. Over and over she batted the counselor's advice around: don't push herself, take baby steps, trust her gut. She was tired of baby steps. She just wanted her life back. Wanted to use a public locker room, walk into the galley and not feel all eyes on her, not wonder what every person she met thought of her.

"Enough." She ripped the towel off and stepped out of her shoes and pants.

Five minutes later she was showered, dressed and heading out the door. She had done it.

Woot!

Granted it was the least relaxing shower of her life, and all the stress she'd had pre-workout was back. More of a baby step, but she'd taken it. She was clean, her hair was washed, and she didn't freak out. She might have showered and dressed at the speed of sound, but she didn't smell, so it still counted.

Maybe next time she could get in the shower without the freak out happening at all, then the time after that she could focus on taking a little more time.

Today, right then and there…she'd won the battle. Maybe not the war, but definitely the battle.

Stepping out of the room she felt light, almost giddy, a little like her old self and decided she deserved a reward. Maybe dinner out, followed by a trip to the mall for a new outfit or a mani/pedi. As she was making her plans, movement at the far end of the track caught her attention and she leaned against the wall, thankfully not for support this time.

The man slowed as he approached her.

"Chief Faraday, it's a gorgeous day out and yet you chose the indoor track. Kind of odd," she said.

"No odder than those down on the treadmills." He nodded to the people one level down. He didn't fool her for a minute. "You're looking better. Color's back."

"You didn't have to stand guard, but thank you."

"We're not all like him, ma'am. We're brothers and sisters in arms. We watch each others' sixes."

Chapter Thirteen

"I feel like your dirty secret." Kyle wedged himself between Nic's legs as he reached behind her into the open cupboard for something.

"What do you mean?" Nic lowered the cold beer bottle she'd been about to take a sip from and looked into his eyes.

Kyle dipped his head and scents of citrus, jasmine and something she couldn't name but that smelled wholly male filled the air around her. He flicked her ear with the tip of his tongue before biting down with just enough pressure to make her catch her breath. As quick as the foreplay had started, it had stopped and he turned back to the stove.

"I'm like your boy toy." The smile playing at his lips as he turned back to face her relaxed her nerves and sent them into a happy dance all at the same time.

Thank goodness he'd been joking. The last couple of weeks she'd had enough on her plate and the last thing she needed was to find out Kyle was in secret a high maintenance mistress. Or is that mastress? Paramour? She'd just stick to lover.

"Are you complaining?" She teased the front of his already hard male form with the tips of her toes and wondered if they'd make it through dinner before giving into the chemistry that sent most of their meals to the microwave.

"About the sex? Never."

"So what's the problem?" She dropped her foot and hopped down off the kitchen counter. She liked Kyle, a lot and didn't want to screw things up for them. They already had enough going against them.

"No problem." He pulled her into his arms and kissed the tip of her nose. "Occasionally, we Neanderthals actually like to take our women out.

You know, show them off to the other Neanderthals, prove our manhood, do something fun, even romantic once in a while."

She laughed. Something she did frequently in his company, among other things.

"I appreciate the fact that you've jeopardized your man card for me and as much as I'd love to let you take me out and parade me in front of the world, until this case closes I don't think it's a good idea. As it is, my mom called me today. She's had reporters hounding her for an interview, which she won't give, of course. I don't want to do anything that might bring more attention to me or cause my family any more embarrassment."

He gave her a quick hug and released her to dish up their dinner. With both plates full he led her to the couch where they tended to eat most of their meals. She curled up on one end, feet tucked under her and took the plate he offered while he sat at the opposite end. Princess had already claimed the middle cushion and neither had the heart—or was that courage—to disturb her.

"How is your family taking all of this?" he asked.

"About how you'd expect. Standing by me. My parents are quiet on the public front, refusing to answer any questions, as expected. With me they check in pretty much daily to see how I am. My brothers? They want to kick Stone's butt along with everyone else involved."

"Can't say I blame them. From what I hear it should be over soon. I've heard the investigators and attorneys have talked to everyone involved at this point. Now it's just a matter of getting on the calendar."

She pushed her food around on her plate, thinking about his words. One problem almost down and a new one to face. "How soon after the trial do you think the *California* will be scheduled for deployment?"

"Hard to say. Depends on the rotation of the other boats, who's already left, what's their mission. Stuff like that." He tucked a strand of hair behind her ear that had escaped from her braid and ran his fingers down her cheek, gently lifting her face so her eyes looked into his. "Hey, I know what you're thinking and we'll deal with that bridge when we get to it."

"I'm not sure what you think I was thinking, but I was wondering if I should start looking for an apartment or stay in the BOQ." Not for one minute would she admit it had struck her that she was going to miss him or how much or that seeing him with another woman when she pulled back into port would be like having a hot poker shoved through her heart.

"Oh, yeah. Stay in the BOQ. Less hassle, and then you can pack up and leave without having to worry about loose ends." He swapped the plate for the beer he'd sat on the coffee table. His throat undulated with every swallow and suddenly she didn't want to talk about family or leaving. She didn't want to talk at all.

Sadly, Kyle's earlier comments about feeling used came back to haunt her conscience. Instead of attacking him and ravishing his body like she wanted, she asked him about his week. Not nearly as fun, but she wanted him to know that she thought of him as more than sex on a stick.

"You know how it is. Same bullshit, different day."

Normally Kyle was an open book, but given the fact that Stone was one of his guys he could be getting some backlash over the ordeal. "Well I have some good news. Sort of."

She told him about the panic attack she'd had last week at the gym, complete with the Master-at-Arms Chief coming to her rescue and forcing herself to walk back in and face her fears. "Every day since then, I've been going to the gym and making myself use the shower there. I'd like to say that was the last panic attack, but two days ago I had a major setback."

She grabbed their empty plates and headed into the kitchen where she quickly washed them and grabbed a glass of water to steal a few minutes to pull it together. Just thinking about the attack on Wednesday closed the air off to her lungs and sent pretty little dark spots dancing before her eyes.

Scooping up Princess cat, Nic sat down next to Kyle where she felt safe.

"I was coming out of the shower as another woman was coming into the locker room, but I didn't know that at the time. I was still around the corner in front of the shower stalls with nothing but a towel wrapped around me when I heard Stone's voice through the open door. I thought he was in the room with me."

"Oh, baby." Kyle slipped his arm around her shoulders and pulled her in tight. A soft kiss on the top of her head made everything inside of her sigh. *Man, am I going to miss him,* she thought. *Oh, well, suck it up, buttercup. Such is the life you choose when you signed on the dotted line.*

"Yeah, but here's the best part. After I got done hyperventilating and peeled myself off the floor, I tore around the corner ready to flay him for crossing a line and entering a space he didn't belong. I wasn't afraid to confront him anymore. I may not be one hundred percent, but I'm getting my life back."

"I wish you would have called me Wednesday," he said quietly.

"There was nothing you could have done. It was over and done with in under thirty seconds, although at the time it seemed a lot longer. Besides, you can't always be at my side, Kyle. I have to face these fears and get over them on my own."

She kept her focus on the cat. Stroking her from her head to the tip of her tail, it was easier than seeing the disappointment in Kyle's eyes that she'd heard in his voice a minute ago. She understood where he was coming from and she really hoped he did too.

"I know. Tell me again, why aren't we out celebrating tonight? Steak. Lobster. Champagne. You deserve all three."

She laughed and snagged his beer. "I'll take this for now. We'll save the expensive night out for when I can walk into a public facility and not even think about the possibility of having my privacy invaded."

That day might never come and it wasn't just doubting herself either; the counselor had warned her there was no expiration date on trauma. Every person dealt with the damage caused in his or her own way. There was no quick fix. There was no one sure-fire resolution that worked for everyone.

No way would she say that out loud. Talk about jinxing yourself.

"Okay, I'll book a table overlooking the water at Latitude 41 for next week," Kyle said.

She turned her head to meet his mouth and kissed him. A quick, playful, loud kiss that made the tension in the air dissipate with their laughter. "Appreciate the vote of confidence. By the way, how are things with you and the mini-me going?"

He choked on his beer. "Mini-me?"

"You don't see it? He's like you without the mileage, and double the attitude. You're like Chris and Liam Hemsworth—not quite twins but damn close."

"You think I look like Thor?"

She rolled her eyes and took a deep breath. "Not even close. Answer my question."

He pulled her onto his lap and held her hands behind her back, forcing her forward until her mouth was mere centimeters from his. "He's warming up to me."

The door slammed, startling Nic so that she fell fully on top of Kyle, knocking their foreheads together. Keith took one look at the two of them, muttered, "Figures," and headed toward the hall leading to the bedrooms.

* * *

"Hey," Kyle said, "Where have you been all day?"

Keith turned and leaned his shoulder against the wall, his trusty backpack slung over the opposite shoulder. That thing was like his security blanket, or emergency go-bag, or maybe he had a million dollars stashed in it and was afraid if he sat it down Kyle would discover his dark secrets. Or maybe there were other things in the bag Keith didn't want Kyle to know about, like things that got Kenny thrown in the slammer. Keith looked at Nic and then to Kyle, boredom radiating off of him in waves.

"I'd think you'd have better things to do than worry about my whereabouts."

"Guess again, kid." Nic shifted, slid her leg off his and started to rise. Kyle laid his hand on her knee. He could use some backup, a united front, if you will. If he guessed right, his brothers were used to blowing their dad off. When you heard griping twenty-four-seven it all became white noise. Kyle knew firsthand how that went. "Mom called. Said you weren't answering her calls. She got worried."

"Didn't hear it ring. I'll go call her now."

"Right." He sat forward, arms resting on his knees. The kid was full of it. "I haven't seen you without your phone since you got here. Hell, you even take it into the head with you."

Kyle did a quick scan. Keith's pupils weren't dilated. His coloring was good. Arms weren't covered up. He didn't smell any funky smells. Well, except for grease like the kid had been around someone cooking, but otherwise he didn't look like he was baked or drunk.

But there were other things he could have been out doing that he shouldn't have.

"I know you think you're an adult and don't have to answer to me or anyone else, but you're wrong. This isn't Citrus Park where they'll turn a blind eye until you fuck up royally like Kenny. You so much as even look at a beer here and they'll haul your ass in. You get mixed up with the wrong people like Woody and there won't be anything I can do for you."

"Whatever. I was busy. Now I'm tired. Are you done with the interrogation?"

"Busy doing what, Keith?"

Nic nudged him with her knee. "I should go. It's getting late."

"No." He turned back to his brother. "Well, I'm waiting."

Kyle looked around the room quickly and upon only seeing the three of them, wondered how in all of Hades his dad's voice and words had come out of his mouth. Didn't you only turn into your parents when you had kids of your own? It was something he swore he'd never do... become like the old man, talking down to everyone around him, treating his family like slave labor and basically acting like a Class-A asshole. He didn't even talk to his junior sailors that way.

"I'm going to get something to drink," Nic picked up his hand and set it back on his leg and stood. "Keith, can I grab you a soda, bottle of water, anything?"

"I'm good, thanks." The kid's smirk spoke volumes.

He waited until Nic had disappeared around the corner and then walked over to his brother, putting them eye-to-eye. At the last second he sat on the end of the couch thinking standing in front of Keith might be too confrontational.

"Look, I'm sorry. Mom was freaking out. She's heard some talk around town about Woody and is convinced you and Kenny are in league with the devil. I guess being away, I forget how fast the tales back home can grow. But you got to cut me some slack, Keith. You've hardly said anything to me since you got here. You won't tell me anything and when I ask you a question, you give me attitude."

"Dude, you want me to spill my guts to you? I don't even know you."

"Give me a chance, Keith. I'm trying my best to be here for you."

Kyle clamped his hands together at the back of his skull. It was either that or punch a wall. No matter what he did or said, the kid shot him down. Every attempt he'd made to get to know his brother was met with a door slammed in his face—literally and figuratively.

"Can we do this brother bonding some other time? I'm tired and I have a double shift tomorrow." Keith picked up the backpack that had slid to the floor.

"Double shift? You found a job?" Kyle heard the shock in his voice and winced. *Way to go, Hutch. Show the kid how much faith you don't have in him.*

"I got *two* jobs." Kyle didn't miss the stress on those three letters or the exasperated tone and dead-eyed stare. "I'm lifeguarding over at the Y in the morning and then I've got the closing shift at Taco Bell, so don't freak when I'm not home by seven, *Dad*."

Nic's soft laughter floated across the room and both he and Keith glanced her way. "Impressive. Not even a month and already fully employed. Congrats, Keith. I see you share your brother's work ethic and sense of humor."

"That's not all we share." Without further explanation he disappeared into his room.

Shaking his head, Kyle held out his hand for her and nodded toward the sliding door to the small balcony. Outside where Keith couldn't hear, Kyle apologized for the second time. He shouldn't have put Nic in the middle of the two of them.

"That's the most he's said to me since he arrived," he said.

"Baby steps. So what was with his parting comment?" She dropped into one of the two green plastic chairs and propped her feet on the matching plastic table. The day had been hot and humid, a typical July in Connecticut. Now that the sun had set, the breeze off the Thames picked up and cooled her exposed skin from her shorts and T-shirt causing little goose bumps to break out.

"No freaking clue."

He leaned back, planting his butt on the railing, one foot propped on the table next to her pretty toes painted bright red with white spots. Her T-shirt matched her nail polish, which made him wonder if what was under the shirt and shorts matched as well. If baby bro had arrived a few minutes later Kyle would have found out. Maybe it wasn't too late. The tension from their exchange slipped away and Nic rubbed her foot up against him. A door somewhere inside slammed, followed a few minutes later by another door. Yeah, there was no way they were getting back to their earlier mood.

"I don't think he likes me much," Nic suggested on the third slam.

"I think he might like you too much."

"Kyle." She sat up suddenly as if a thought had hit her straight between the eyes. "Did you think to ask your mom before she shipped Keith off if he had a girlfriend or not? Maybe that's what wrong. Maybe my being here is a reminder of what he's missing."

Kyle looked over her head and through the glass door into the empty room. *Crap.* Why hadn't he thought of that? He'd make a point to ask Keith the next time he saw him. It could be that he was worried about their brother too; after all, the two hadn't spent any real time away from each other ever. Now, depending on the judge and evidence, Kenny could be in an eight-by-eight until he was middle-aged.

He'd call their mom in the morning, let her know Keith was doing great and had two jobs and see if he could get some more info out of her. Maybe then the kid would open up to him.

Nic nudged him with her foot. "A penny for your thoughts?"

He reached down to take her bare foot in his hands and began massaging it. "I think we should grab a blanket and head over to Dubois Beach. Everyone will have gone home by now and we'll have it completely to ourselves. It's a sure bet to cure a headache."

"Really?" Her eyes clouded with indecision. "Didn't you say I'd have to get naked?"

"Different cure. Fresh sea air, the sound of waves rolling to the shore, a cool breeze on your face—what every sailor needs." Slowly, he ran his hand up her bare calf, taking his sweet time before stopping at the hem of her shorts. "We'll save the Hutchinson Special for another time, when we won't be interrupted for hours."

"Sounds like a perfect plan, on both accounts."

Chapter Fourteen

Nic had never felt so…so unfeminine before in her life as she did facing the dozen drop-dead gorgeous young women standing before her on the pier, including Miss Connecticut complete with a shiny diamond crown. Even the male photographer looked more feminine than she did in his ripped jeans and plain white, V-neck T-shirt tucked only in the front.

Quickly she introduced herself and Petty Officer Wu, explaining that before they boarded the boat he needed to go over a few rules for their safety and security. She left Wu in charge and wondered over to the side where Kyle stood, arms crossed over his chest looking way too sexy in his khaki uniform. Really, that color shouldn't look good on anyone, yet he looked scrumptious. Maybe it was just left over pheromones from the weekend.

"Did you volunteer for this duty or draw the short straw?" she asked Kyle. She looked down at the gentle waves hitting the column beneath them, not wanting to think about how she compared in his eyes to the women standing before him, who were not only beautiful, but smart and talented.

"Are you kidding? Volunteered." He slid a little closer and let his hand drop down to fall in front of her and took her hand. "It was the perfect excuse to see you."

She couldn't help the small smile or ignore the race of her pulse at his words. Nor did she want to examine her reaction too closely. "Why are we giving them a tour of the boat?"

"Public Relations thought it would be a good chance to restore the image—shine the light on the positive—and the Group agreed."

"So I'm to be the poster girl for being all that you can be?"

"Think that's for that other branch."

She laughed. "So what you're saying is the admiral's daughter shouldn't promote the ground pounders? Someone's got to be the decoy while we sneak up on the enemy and do the job."

"Said like a true Submariner." He grinned at her and nodded toward the group. "I think Wu's in Heaven."

"Let's hope Mrs. Wu doesn't find out how much he enjoyed this assignment. With the exception of those sashes, they're at least dressed appropriately for climbing down ladders and going through tight spaces."

"Yeah. The brunette with the big...blue eyes," he pointed to one of the three women without a sash who was glued to Miss Connecticut's side. "We had to take a trip up to the NEX so she could buy a complete outfit. I can't believe their chaperone, the older woman who could pass as Helen Mirren's double, let her wear spiked heels and a skirt that barely covered her butt."

She'd have to keep her eye on that one.

"Looks like Wu is ready to head on board. You joining us for the fun and games?" She turned to look at him as she stepped forward, not wanting to let the group see the hope on her face.

"Wouldn't miss it."

Nic led the way, making her way swiftly down the ladder and into the control room where they'd start the tour. She moved to the far end of the room, near the hatch as the space swelled to capacity with the contestants, the chaperone, the photographer, and the two extra women whose role she had no clue of. Wu introduced Miss Connecticut, Gabrielle Davis, and then rest of the entourage to the skipper and stepped back to let him take the helm.

As the Captain had the audience's attention, Kyle slipped passed the women to stand next to Nic. The spicy scent of him hit her and every molecule of her being came alive. With every nerve, every fiber she craved his touch, his kiss. Giving into that craving would be bad considering where they stood. For now, she'd have to settle with the comfort... but no that wasn't right, because what she felt when he was near was anything but. No, he knocked her off kilter to where half the time she wasn't sure if she was coming or going and the other half had her head in the clouds or the gutter.

Depending on how one looked at it.

"How many other women besides Lieutenant Riley are stationed on board this submarine?" Miss Connecticut asked as she waited her turn to look through the periscope.

"At this time, she is the sole female member of our crew," the Captain replied. "However, female officers began serving on Ohio-class subs in 2011. Now we have enlisted as well, but Lieutenant Riley is a pioneer in the fast attack community and we hope now that she's breached the walls more will follow." Pride shone through the skipper's voice and Nic returned his smile; it was good to know the past few weeks hadn't spoiled his view.

"Can't the Navy just order the women to work on subs?" a petite blonde asked.

"It takes a special type of person to live on a sub, so service is voluntary," the Captain answered.

"Yeah. Crazy ones," one of the junior guys stage whispered.

There was no arguing with that statement. The group finished checking out the periscope and the skipper ran them through responsibilities of each person in the control room. Some looked a little lost, some interested, and a few, like the brunette with the big blue eyes, had their attention on the men, including Kyle.

"Okay, ladies and gentleman, next we're moving down a deck to show you where the crew eats and sleeps and the torpedo room. Before we go, any other questions for the skipper or the men in here?" Wu looked around the room and pointed to the brunette. "Yes, Kerry?"

She flashed him a sweet smile while she twirled a strand of hair around her finger. "How can you see where you're going when there are no windows? Aren't you afraid you'll hit something like a boat or a whale or something?"

Several of the men ducked their heads and Nic knew it was to hide the smirks they sported. Everyone who had been to Disney or saw *Twenty Thousand Leagues under the Sea* thought all subs had windows.

"That's a good question, Kerry," Wu replied. "We use multiple tools such as GPS, SONAR, maps, charts and an inertial guidance system, which tracks the boat's motion. So think of those crime shows where they look on a car's GPS to see where the car has been. It's kind of like that. We can see where we started and exactly what route we've taken and know where we're headed."

Nic heard her tell Miss Connecticut that she didn't believe them, that they had to have the windows covered so the group couldn't see the top secret stuff going on outside.

Umm, yep she was on to them.

Nic just rolled her eyes and nodded when Kyle offered to bring up the rear so they didn't lose anyone.

Wu looked back at Kerry but didn't say anything and Nic made a mental note to let his department head know how great he handled the tour.

"It's so big on the outside and so squishy inside," Miss New Haven said.

"Kind of like the reverse of a certain blue call box, except instead of one mad man we have many in our steel box," Nic said.

"Ohh, I like you. Quick, which are your favorites? Mine are Matt Smith and David Tennant."

"Christopher Eccleston, David Tennant, and Peter Capaldi."

"Impressive. Smart, beautiful, a Naval officer and great taste in TV and men. You should come hang out with us sometime."

Nic thanked Miss New Haven and stepped aside. Next stop was the gallery and mess deck where Chief Boone waited to show off his skills. On each table was an assortment of nibbles like crab puffs, bruschetta with thin slices of beef, miniature shrimp tacos and several other savory dishes, along with cookies, brownies, and the chief's signature Better-than-Sex Peanut Butter pie.

Chief Boone had pulled out all the stops. Too bad the desserts would be wasted.

Oh well, more for me, she thought eyeing the pie, which was probably the only reason her pants weren't falling off these days.

"Where do you store your food? There doesn't seem to be enough storage room to accommodate a crew of one hundred forty for four months." Miss Windham asked Chief Boone when he'd finished his spiel.

"We line the passage way and the crew walks on tops of the cans and boxes."

"No way. How do you stand up straight? I mean you're pretty tall and that hallway we came down didn't have a lot of headspace," Miss Windham said.

"I spend most of my time in the galley, but yeah. The first few weeks out can be a challenge."

"Excuse me, Chief, can Knut get a picture of you and me showcasing this wonderful spread?" Miss Connecticut, nodded toward the photographer.

Nic mouthed the name to Kyle and gave a slight shake of her head as his eyes lit up. Now she knew why Wu hadn't introduced everyone in the group to the skipper. Those guys in the Control room would have had a field day. For whatever reason, sailors tended to have the sense of humor of your average eight-year-old. Although, she'd admit it did help in surviving long deployments.

"Hi, I'm Kerry. Can I ask you a question? Is it hard to be the only woman on board? I mean it's got to be right? It'd be like being the only girl on an all-male campus."

"Not really. I have two older brothers who used to drag home every member of whatever sport team they were on at the time. Not much different. Lots of fart jokes, when conversations stop when you walk into a room, you know not to take it personal and do not ask what they were talking about, and be prepared to be the center of a practical joke or two."

"Sounds like the first grade class I student taught this past year."

"You're an elementary teacher?"

She smiled and bobbed her head up and down. "Starting this fall. Do you mind if I ask you a few more questions?"

Nic shook her head, hoping that the girl hadn't caught any of the news about her and that was were all this was headed.

"Is it dark under water?"

Lord, help the next generation, she taught.

"Very. Light doesn't penetrate very far."

"I bet buying headlights for a sub are expensive."

Those poor kids are doomed.

"Umm, kind of." Nic did her best to keep a straight face.

"Can you guys rollover like the fighter jets do?"

Kyle looked her way, a wry twist to his mouth, the coffee cup he was about to take a drink from suspended in space.

Glad he found the conversation amusing, but then again he didn't have to answer her without hurting her feelings and clearly telling her the truth wasn't something she would accept given her window comment.

"Uh-huh, we do barrel rolls all the time."

"Knew it. Tell me. Is that yummy Lieutenant Hutchinson single?"

"He's not married." Even though she wanted to tell Kerry no and steer her in another direction, Nic didn't dare take a chance that one of the crew would overhear. They'd been great through this whole mess, never showing anything except support and respect. Would they still do the same if they knew about her and Kyle? A part of her feared they'd look down on her, to question her morals if their relationship was exposed, especially if it came out how they met.

Kerry tucked the hem of her top in tighter emphasizing her big blue eyes and deep cleavage. "Thanks for the chat. Now I'm going to go see if I can change his Facebook status."

Nic grabbed a cup of coffee and a slice of the pie and leaned against the bulkhead to watch the show. If she could just press a button and fast forward a couple of months, then all of this would be behind. The boat could get back on schedule. People would forget and she and Kyle could enjoy a normal relationship. Or, as normal as you could get with two people on active duty.

Wu switched from answering questions to talking about some of the practical jokes the crew played on each other. Nic was as enraptured by his tale as the rest and didn't even notice Miss Connecticut approach.

"You know you don't have anything to worry about?"

"Excuse me?" Nic asked, baffled by the comment. She didn't have anything to do with the pranks Wu was talking about.

Miss Connecticut nodded in Kyle's direction, who not only had Kerry batting her lashes at him, but several other women.

"I don't think Kerry is his type and the others like to flirt with pretty much anyone in the male population." She nodded to the group as several had already turned their attention away.

"Are you enjoying the tour?" Nic really didn't want to talk about Kyle and what his type was or wasn't or watch women flirt with him.

"Yes, but I have a confession to make. When they told me about the boat switch, I was thrilled. I was hoping to meet you."

"Why?" It came out as a whisper.

Unfortunately, Nic had a good idea of the answer.

"I've been following the story of what happened to you."

Nic couldn't answer past the lump that had swelled in her throat. Would it never end? Would she ever reach the end of the tunnel and emerge into the light?

"Sorry. I shouldn't have said anything. It's the curse of being a psych major." She grimaced and looked down, her fingers playing with the edges of her sash as if it were choking her. "It's just that most people given the situation would have cut and run if they could, and I know you were offered a transfer. I've done some checking. But you didn't. You chose to stay and I admire your decision."

"Thanks."

"For what it's worth. I hope they hang him by his balls."

Miss Connecticut left her with that happy thought and returned to her group. They were headed to the torpedo room next and since that was Kyle's area of expertise he led the group. The women were more than happy to follow him. Wu hung back and waited for Nic.

"Eat one piece too many of Boone's pie? You're looking a little green, ma'am."

"Maybe a little too much sugar and caffeine on an empty stomach. You did a terrific job keeping them entertained and informed." Nic pressed against the wall to let a couple of crewmembers pass as they made their way from the mess deck.

"Thank you. Last year I had to do one of those career days at the elementary school. I just told the ladies what I told the kids."

"I bet the teachers loved you filling their students' heads with various pranks they could pull on each other."

"Yep. Not sure I'll be invited back. I better get up there with the Lieutenant. I may be overstepping boundaries here." At her questioning look, Wu looked toward Kyle and then back to her. "I don't think you have any worries in regards to the Lieutenant, ma'am. He's a standup guy and it would take more than a set of big…blue eyes to turn his head."

"Thanks. Go."

Of all the fuckity-fucking fuckups.

Had someone seen them on the beach this past weekend? Thankfully nothing happened worth videotaping.

They'd been so careful, she couldn't believe anyone saw them together. Nic hung back for a few minutes. As a kid her mom had taught all of the Riley kids about Karma and the law of three. It had scared Nic so bad she'd made sure to always be a good person.

Yeah, well clearly in a past life you were a bitch or a mass murderer or something and karma is collecting on your debt now.

She couldn't come up with any other explanation for the mess called her life.

"Why are there beds in here? I thought this was the torpedo room," one of the beauty queens asked.

"Space is limited so we have to use every inch we can," Kyle replied.

"Where do they keep their clothes and stuff?"

Time to dwell on that later, Nic pushed forward and stepped into the room in time to see Wu lift the rack.

"Right here," Wu said.

The group burst out in embarrassed laughter.

"Guess that answers my question." Knut draped his arm around his girlfriend. "What do they do to fill their free time?"

Swallowing a groan Nic hung her head and swore in her head. The rack was filled with adult mags and toys. There went their restored image.

"And that's a wrap." She lifted her head to meet Kyle's laughing eyes. "We hope you enjoyed the tour.

Chapter Fifteen

Nic chewed on the edge of her thumbnail as she made her way up to Sub Support, wondering what her entire family was doing here. She should be overjoyed. It'd been ages since she'd seen her brothers, since all three of them were home at the same time together, but a niggling in her gut told her this wasn't just a "Hey, we were in the area and decided to drop by" visit.

Rounding the building she spotted Kyle's Charger and remembered they'd had plans for the night. She had no idea what because Loverboy refused to tell her, only that it was a surprise. She pulled out her phone and hit the message app.

Need to cancel tonight. Fam showed up unannounced.

Come over after. I'll be up.

Will you now?

Always for you. ;-)

Smirking, she pulled the heavy door open and hustled up the stairs to the command conference room. Her mom sat at the end of the long table, surrounded by men, all of whom looked ready to do her bidding like that of a queen at court. She stood and all the men followed.

You'd think her mom outranked them all.

The commanding officer and his next in command excused themselves, offering up the use of the room for however long the family needed it. As soon as they had the room to themselves, Nic relaxed and hugged her mom first. Despite the smile that greeted her she didn't missed the pinched look of maternal concern. The one that said you're not eating enough, sleeping enough, and you're making me worry too much. It was a look Nic was used to seeing.

Still wondering about the sudden visit, Nic took a closer look but her mom gave no clues. She looked the same as always: chin-length black hair, not a gray hair in sight, smooth skin with just a touch of eyeliner and lipstick, and impeccably dressed in black capris with a sleeveless top. Everything an admiral's wife should be: classy.

Liam and Reece were both dressed in civvies and pretty casual at that, with jeans and T-shirts, which ruled out some kind of military function for them. They gave her quick hugs before stepping back to let their dad take center stage.

Nic didn't wait for her dad's hug or greeting. Her nerves were fraying by the second.

"Pops, what are you all doing here?" Unlike the other two, he was in uniform. "Did you have another ceremony to attend? Why didn't you tell me you were coming? I would have arranged for time off." She rambled not wanting to discuss what really brought them to see her.

He wrapped her in his bear arms and hugged her. "Breathe, Lily-Pad."

"I am." She pushed free. "You guys are kind of freaking me out. We don't just show up unannounced, en masse without a reason. That's not our family. Do you all know something I don't? Oh my God! Did someone die?" Tears sprung to her eyes.

Her whole body shook as she fought to control her emotions. Legs like water, she groped behind her for a chair, almost falling when she missed. Liam slipped an arm around her waist and guided her to safety.

"Chill, little drama mama. No one's dying," Liam said.

Oh, she was going to smack the smirk right off his face. At her steely-eyed stare of death, he laughed and stepped back a step missing a punch in the arm by an inch.

"Stop." Her mother's voice brooked no argument. She might be little, but the lady was mighty. "You two." She wagged a finger at them both. "Why can't you behave for once? Act like the adults I raised. Lily, your brothers are home on leave. Since you missed your father's birthday, I decided we'd all celebrate now, together. I didn't think how this might seem. We should have called. But now we're here and we're going to enjoy our family time."

The last of her comments was directed at Liam, who shrugged like he had no clue what she meant.

Reece pulled up the chair next to her and dropped into it. "What's the deal with you and this guy, Hutchinson?"

"Have they set the trial date yet?" her dad asked.

"Yeah, what is up with you and Hutchinson?" Liam pulled up another chair and took up the space on the other side of her.

They all asked their questions at the same time, sending Nic's head reeling. Finally she held up her hand. "None of your business, no, and none of your business."

"When do we get to meet him?" Reece asked.

"Isn't this the command he's attached to?" Liam's eyes gleamed with mischief.

"Mom, make them behave." Flashbacks to her teen years sent her heart pounding.

For some reason her parents just grinned and did that parent look where they could read each other's minds. Maybe they were having flashbacks too, the happy kind from when all three of them were little and the worst thing to happen was a toy got broken or the three of them fought over the TV. Easily fixed problems that didn't rip at a parent's heart as she imagined this mess of hers did to them every day.

"You two will leave Kyle alone. The fact that I like him is exactly why you are not going to meet him. How long are you here for?" Nic asked the group in general.

"Sunday night. Reece needs to get back to Kings Bay and Liam is headed to DC with us for a few days."

She turned to her annoying oldest sibling, giving him her most innocent look. "Sucking up again? You know you were already taken out of the will; it won't do you any good. Or is it you Trident boys have it so easy they don't need their XO on board these days? Oh wait. I forgot you're on shore duty and living the good life these days."

"Green isn't a good color on you *Lily-Pad*," Liam reached out and poked her in the ribs, knowing it was her ticklish spot.

"I don't know how either of you survived to adulthood without Mom or Dad killing you off." Reece shook his head and looked at his watch. "Fifty-four hours to go, until I either lose my sanity or we see if they finally crack and kill you two."

"Well you two have had Mom time and I haven't. So I'm stealing her away and we're going shopping while you all go do manly stuff elsewhere. Then we can meet for dinner." She smiled sweetly at her brothers, knowing the men in her family hated shopping while their mom adored the pastime.

Leeann Riley picked up her purse, kissed her husband and sons goodbye and looped her arm through her daughter's. Just as they reached the door her dad's booming voice stopped her in her tracks.

"Lily-Pad, while you're out give Hutchinson a call and invite him to dinner tonight. Your mom and brothers would like to meet him."

Her brothers smirked, thinking they'd got one up on her. So of course Nic did what any sister would do in her situation: she stuck her tongue out at them while trying to think of a great reason why Kyle wouldn't be available for the entire weekend. The flu? A family emergency? A free trip to anywhere away from her brothers?

* * *

Kyle closed the message from Nic and looked down at the contents of his grocery cart. He'd planned on surprising her with spicy shrimp tacos for dinner, followed by chocolate molten cake that would lead to a round of wild monkey sex to take her mind off the stress of waiting for the trail to be set. He could work with the change of plans. Skip the tacos. Go straight to dessert and then a round of sex.

Much better plan.

He switched out the ingredients in his cart, paid for everything and headed next door to the Navy Exchange. It wouldn't hurt to pick up a few items to set the mood like scented candles and flowers. Chicks loved that stuff. While he was thinking of it, he should hit the Package Store and find a good wine to go with the dessert.

Rumors were circulating that Stone expected a slap on the wrist instead of jail time. No telling what her mood would be like if she'd heard the news, plus time with her family.

His would be shit if the situation were reversed. Then again from everything Nic had told him the Rileys sounded like a nice, normal family who actually liked one another. Unlike his family, where the only bond was shared DNA. He did appear to be making some kind of progress with Keith. They had moved past the terse, forced conversations to something bordering between apprehensive neighbors and irritating siblings. They'd even managed to eat in the same room together last week—a first. Their debate over sports teams resembled a Boston fan and Bronx fan trying to convince the other their team was the best, but it was a start and he'd take it.

Taking the stairs two at a time—not for health reasons, but because the escalator was broken as always—he headed for the home goods section of the store only to come up short at the sight of a smile that sent his heart racing.

Detouring to ladies' clothing, he peered over Nic's shoulder at the dress she held up. "Not that one. It covers up too much of the good stuff," he said.

Nic spun around with her hand on her chest. "Jeez, Kyle. Give me a heart attack. And I really don't think my family wants to see the 'good stuff' during dinner."

"In that case, that one's fine, but go with the red. Black is boring."

She put the dress back and pulled out the color he suggested. "Shouldn't you be at work? It's the middle of the day."

"Command picnic today. I bailed, given my mood."

Dark clouds passed over her eyes. She reached out and cupped the side of his face. "Work or home?"

He kissed the palm of her hand. Either she hadn't heard or just didn't connect the dots. In case it was the first, he didn't want to be the one to ruin her weekend. "Things at home are actually better. Everything okay with your family?"

"Supposed belated birthday celebration for my dad." She waved it off like it was nonsense. "So why the anti-social mood?"

"My girl ruined my surprise for tonight and now it's just me and Princess PITA. Not the same thing."

Her eyes lit up. "Think of them as delayed, not ruined."

She put the boring dress back and pulled out the one that was cut low and probably could pass as a long shirt even on her. He smiled and nodded. She looked it up and down, shook her head and put it back on the rack. "Maybe when all of this is over. It can be my celebration outfit."

"You could get it now and do a trial run when you come over to my place tonight."

"What did you have planned for tonight?"

"Nope, not telling. It's a surprise and that dress is perfect. That dress screams sex." He kissed the tips of her fingers, sucking one into his mouth before gently biting down on it.

Nic's eyes widened and her face went beet red.

"What dress?" A smaller, older version of Nic elbowed her way in between them. The woman inspected Kyle, her lips compressed in a tight line as she took in everything about him. For several moments she quietly stared into his eyes. Not sure what he saw, but the sudden smile let him breathe again. "So you are Kyle Hutchinson."

"Mom, meet Kyle. Kyle, meet my mom, Leeann Riley."

Mrs. Riley didn't give him a chance to say anything before she turned and plucked the dress off the rack. "Buy it in red," she said to Nic. "Your young man has good taste, but don't wear that tonight. Your father will keel over in his pot roast. You will be joining us, won't you, Kyle?" She'd turned those sparkling almond eyes on him and he felt himself melt.

He didn't know what he was saying yes to, but he knew he couldn't say no.

Which is how he found himself walking across the parking lot of the Daniel Packer Inn later that evening dressed in pants and a button-down shirt when the temperature still read 101 degrees on the dash of his Charger. Sweat dribbled down his spine and dampened his undershirt.

Great. Way to impress the lady's family, Hutch. Smell like a locker room.

Nic turned to wait for him as he stopped to tug his shirt away from his sticky body and then tuck it back in. Women had it easy. Throw on dress and they were done. Did she even have anything on underneath? The dress she'd chosen was one of those thin strapped ones that didn't allow for a bra so he knew at least half of her was only one layer away. The loose skirt left him guessing on the lower half. And it was red. She looked like a siren and he could feel her pull. He'd gladly risk his life for a taste of her.

"You didn't have to dress up. It's just family."

"Your dad found me alone in your room. Your mom's first impression was of me talking about sex. I'm not blowing it with your brothers too." He pulled her into his arms.

"She also said you had great taste." Nic wove her hands behind his neck and kissed him quick. "Relax. Liam and Reece will like you and even if they didn't, they don't get a say in who I date."

Right. She might say that now, but when push came to shove he'd bet a month's pay she'd cave to her family's wishes. There was no way she could live without their approval. He saw it in her eyes when her dad showed up on the boat and earlier when he'd met her mom, not to mention when she talked about them.

The thought of losing her struck him hard and fast. They'd weathered the past couple of weeks, but a person could only take so many blows before they caved. How many more before she called mercy? What would it take for her to give in and take her dad up on one of his many friends' job offers? He'd taken the job in Groton because of her. Stupid since they weren't even dating at the time and now, he didn't know what he'd classify his feelings as. He just knew he wasn't ready for it to be over.

"What's wrong? You look like you've seen a ghost." She glanced up at the former inn, now a successful restaurant. "They say it's haunted."

He kissed her. Not some quick, barely there kiss. A kiss that seared his brain faster than the scorching August temperature. One hand slid up her back to cradle her head while he slipped the other around her waist and pulled her in tight up against him. He wanted to feel every inch of her. Hell, he wanted to pick her up and haul her back to his place, strip the sexy, little red number off her and kiss every inch of her. For now, he'd settle for her soft lips under his, her sweet taste that called to him like honey to a bee.

When he released her she staggered back a little, eyes glazed. She lifted her fingers to her mouth and ran her tongue over her bottom lip.

Maybe he could talk her into skipping dinner?

A piercing whistle cut through the night causing Nic to sigh and roll her eyes. She grabbed his hand and started walking.

"That would be Liam telling us he's hungry and to hurry up."

They greeted her oldest brother at the door and followed him to the table. Walking behind Liam, Kyle couldn't help notice the guy's impressive size. The dude was huge, with shoulders meant to take down opposing forces and forearms that could crush a guy's head like a walnut.

Reaching the table, where the Vice Admiral and Mrs. Riley sat, along with Nic's other brother, Kyle made a mental note not to piss off either one. Apparently the Riley men were all from the same mold. The only difference being neither of the brothers sported their mother's dark hair nor their dad's red. Kyle wasn't sure of the proper term, chestnut maybe, brown with red and where Liam had the same eyes as Nic, Reece had ice blue ones like his dad.

While Nic introduced him to Reece and he said hello to her father, Kyle watched Liam take his seat at the table. Kyle could either sit in between the brothers or one of them and their dad. Very strategic.

Nic tapped Liam on the shoulder. "Will you please move over a seat?"

"Have Reece move. I like the view from here."

"Liam, she asked you first. Plus, I need to talk to Mom about some stuff," Reece said.

They were good—surround the enemy and separate him from his only ally. He imagined if he'd had a younger sister he'd do the same. Kyle pulled out the chair in the middle of the two brothers and smiled. "It's fine. I'll sit here. This will give you a chance, babe, to catch up with your dad."

The table went deathly silent for a split second. Normally not something one would notice, but this was the summit meeting and every move, ever word was a calculated choice. He got that.

The waitress appeared as soon as they were all seated and took their drink orders, rattled off the daily specials and answered Nic's questions about the haunted history of the inn. They exchanged the normal pleasantries while everyone perused the menu and then made their choices when the waitress popped back over. He wasn't sure which tactic they'd take, but he was ready.

"Kyle, where are you originally from?" Mrs. Riley asked.

"A small town in Northern California, ma'am. Citrus Park is mostly farmland and not a place you'd find on the state's attraction list."

"My family were farmers back in Korea before they came here. Tell us about your family," Mrs. Riley said.

He gave them the basics, skipped over the part about his brother being in jail, and even to him his family sounded normal, almost boring. Just like they should be.

The rest of the family let their mom run the conversation, but he noted all eyes were on him. Nic worried her bottom lip, chewing it until he was sure it would start to bleed. The vice admiral seemed interested yet preoccupied, while the brothers studied his every move, probably looking for a sign of weakness.

"Mom, Pops, did you two finally decide on where you were going to go on your vacation?" Nic absently buttered one of the rolls, purposely passing the basket to her dad instead of Liam who had reached for it.

Apparently irritating sibling syndrome took place in every family, not just the dysfunctional ones like his.

Her dad snorted and ripped his roll apart to lather it with a couple of tablespoons of butter.

Her mom clapped her hands in glee. "We did. We're going to take a cruise down the Rhine River next spring. I'm so excited. I've always wanted to go on a cruise, but your father always balked and said he went on cruises all the time. That it was no vacation."

"Well, it's not," the vice admiral responded.

"It's not the same, Pat and you know it." She swatted his hand before he could take a bite out of the roll and snitched it out of his hand. Calmly she scraped off all but a smear of the butter and handed it back to him, an 'I-dare-you-to-complain' gleam in her eye. "For one thing, this boat doesn't go underwater."

"At least you hope it doesn't, Mom." Liam winked at her and took the breadbasket that had finally made its way to him and set it far out of Nic's reach.

"I'm with Pops, why would he go on a cruise? They don't submerge, no angles and dangles, and no shooting your enemies. There's also rumor you get liberty every day or two and see daylight out your window," Reece said.

"I raised a bunch of smart asses." Patrick looked at him. "Do you talk to your father this way?"

"Only if I want to get smacked upside the head, sir." He said it jokingly, keeping to himself that he'd suffered his fair share and then some of head smacking as well as getting his butt beat a time or two. If there was anything the old man didn't tolerate, it was lip of any kind.

"See, now here's a man who knows how to show proper respect. Unlike you, boyo." Patrick jabbed a finger in his youngest son's direction.

"Boyo? Watch out world, Patrick Michael Sean *O'Riley*'s letting loose his Irish, even though he's never lived on the Emerald Isle a day in his life," Liam's attempt at an Irish accent had the whole table busting up as it sounded more like a cross between a drunken leprechaun and every American on St. Paddy's day.

Nic started laughing. "Next he's going to break out into song with 'Danny Boy' or what's that lullaby he used to sing to us, 'Too-Roo-Loo-a-Doo.'"

"'Too-Ra-Loo-Ra-Loo-Ral,' and I'll have you know, you slept like an angel when I crooned to you at night." Patrick shoved another chunk of roll in his mouth, glaring at his offspring.

"Aw, Pops, if we didn't give you a hard time you wouldn't know we were yours. You'd be accusing Ma of making hay with the milkman when you were away." Reece's accent was a little more dead-on, but brought on more fits of laughter especially from his siblings.

"It's called nature vs. nurture, brother dear and I'm still not sure you are blood related. Unlike me—who's clearly Mom's—I'm not convinced they didn't rescue the two of you from a band of baboons."

The three of them went back and forth, slinging good-natured insults at each other while their parents sat back and watched with amused looks on their faces and sparkling eyes. Kyle had to wonder if he had stayed put, instead of escaping the minute he graduated, if he and twins would be as close. Not once during their little tirade had he felt any heat behind the words, no intent to hurt the other, just simple teasing.

Maybe he and his brothers would have reached this point. Hopefully he and Keith would get there sooner rather than later.

The waitress arrived with their food and the group settled down while she got everyone situated, but he could see Nic and Liam giving each other looks. On the ride over, she had given Kyle the run-down on her family. Liam, in her eyes, was a perpetual teen, always looking for the fun in life and avoiding anything too serious. He might be that way with his family and even in his personal life, but no one with that attitude made it as far and as fast as he did.

Reece was the forgotten middle child. Quiet, observant, serious enough for them all and then some. Yet, Kyle had seen more such as his sense of humor and a protective streak, especially when it came to his baby sister. Every look he gave Kyle said "Dude, you aren't good enough for her."

Maybe so, but she had picked Kyle and he wasn't arguing with her.

The waitress left and Liam stole a fry from Nic's plate. She promptly stole one of his in retaliation.

"Children," Leeann Riley's sharp tone brought them both to a stop. "Behave. And to think they've eaten at the White House before. Thank goodness they didn't act like this then."

Kyle glanced at Nic, his brow arched in question. She'd eaten with the President of the United States? Nic shrugged and dug into her dinner. Hell, his family didn't dine with the president of the Elks Club.

"Pops, I need your advice," said Liam. "I've got a young sailor. Twenty-one. At work, he's the poster child for the Navy. Does his job—4.0 across the board on his last eval—shows promise as a leader, nice kid. The kind you'd want to clone because they make your life easier."

"Like a mini-you, except for the nice part and wanting to clone you," Nic responded.

Instead of giving her shit, Liam nodded. "Pretty much. The problem is when he clocks out for the day. He goes from exemplary sailor to frat boy. So far he hasn't broken any laws, just skirted the edges and I think it's only a matter of time."

"What's his LPO say?" Patrick's forkful of pot roast sat suspended in air as he waited.

"Petty Officer Maynard doesn't seem to know or won't say. The chief's talked to him, the COB's talked to him, I have. None of us can get anything out of him except he's letting some steam off but knows what he's doing. The thing is, I can see it in his eyes, the pain. Something's off."

"Does he have a wife, fiancée, or girl back home?" Reece asked between bites. "Maybe there's a family member who's sick and he doesn't want to face it or is feeling helpless being so far away. He wouldn't be the first to drink his troubles away."

Liam turned to him. "Kyle, your thoughts?"

"It could be any of those. Or he might be experiencing his first taste of freedom away from a controlling family. He's on task at work, because if he screws up there, it's back to the control freak parents. But once quitting hour hits, he lets his freak flag fly and is having fun, but not enough to land him in trouble."

He'd known a few kids like that in college. The kind of who never stepped out of line at home while growing up, never gave their parents an ounce of trouble, joined the clubs, played sports, volunteered for everything and then they were set free. Suddenly they had all these options before them and no mommy or daddy telling them what to do or which option to pick or that they couldn't stay out until five in the morning, so they did it all. Most dropped out by the end of their freshmen year. A few mellowed and some didn't make it to see another day.

"Talk to his friends," Kyle and Nic said at the same time.

Their eyes met and locked and he didn't need to look around the table to know everyone else watched the two of them. The weight of their judgment, the questions flashing through their minds could be felt throughout his entire body. The silence hung heavy until Nic's mom laughed.

"Well, there you go. You have your answer." She pushed her empty plate away. "I don't know about any of you, but I'm ordering the flourless chocolate torte for dessert."

Looking at the plate that once held a good-sized serving of pasta, he now knew where Nic got her healthy appetite from, which was fine with him. He loved to cook and he loved women that loved to eat.

All three kids and Patrick Riley laughed and groaned.

"Mom, I don't know how, but you can still out-eat me and Liam. I'll stick with coffee," Reece said.

"Me too. Some of us have fitness standards to meet," Liam pushed back and turned to Nic. "Suppose you're going to make the rest of us look like wimps too?"

"You bet. But I'm getting the chocolate fudge brownie sundae." She gave her brother an evil grin.

"That's low, sis." Liam turned to Kyle. "I love ice cream and can't eat it. She never passes on a chance to torture me."

"Kyle, you up for dessert or—"

His phone cut her off. Keith. He excused himself and answered thinking his brother needed a ride home early from work.

"You what?" Kyle's blood boiled as he listened to Keith on the other end. He tried to walk away, but his feet were glued to the floor. His head spun. "Yeah, I'll be there as soon as I can. Just keep your mouth shut and your hands to yourself."

He hung up the phone and met five pairs of questioning eyes.

Crap.

Of all the lamebrain stunts and piss poor timing.

"I'm sorry, I'll have to pass on dessert." He shoved his phone into his pocket, dreading what was next. "My kid brother needs me to pick him up. Thank you for dinner. Nic, can you get a ride home with your family?"

"I'll come with you."

"No, stay and enjoy your sundae. There's no reason for you to cut your time short because of my family."

"It's okay. I'm getting a little tired anyway," she persisted.

Great. What was he going to do? Wait and tell her in the parking lot if she came with him it might be while before they got home? Better to come clean now and take it like a man. She'd tell her family eventually.

"Then you really should catch a ride with them. It's going to be a while before I can get you home."

Walking up to her, he dropped his voice and leaned into her to explain the situation convinced once she knew the truth she'd let him slip out and make his apologies to her family. Nope, he should have known better. The argument went on for several minutes, the whole time he was fully aware of the awkward conversation at the table.

"Kyle, is your brother stranded at work?" Leeann asked.

Nic raised her brow and gave him a look he wasn't sure how to interpret. Tell her the truth or lie? Not a fan of the second option, he went with his gut.

"No. He's at the police station."

Everyone stilled. Neither brother looked up. Her parents looked at each other. It was exactly what he expected and feared deep down. He didn't belong with a woman like Nic Riley. She was a league above him and even if they did have a good thing going, her family would never accept him. Who wanted their daughter to get mingled up with a family of jailbirds? Because that's what his family was, and even if he had escaped, their taint was all over him, constantly pulling him back into the mix. Hell, her dad probably had some up and coming young politician already picked out for Nic.

After a moment, she made her way around the table to kiss her mom, give Reece a shoulder squeeze, and ruffle Liam's hair, before stopping back in front of Kyle. "I'm coming with you. I don't know why he's there. I don't care, but I'm standing by your side."

An hour after leaving the restaurant, Kyle, Nic and Keith were all back at his apartment. Keith hadn't muttered more than thanks since they'd walked out of the Groton Police Department. Nic had refused to go back to the barracks. The whole way home her hand had rested on his leg. She hadn't attempted to make small talk, rather she'd left the brothers alone with their thoughts and he appreciated her silent strength next to him more than he cared to admit.

Keith made a beeline to his room.

"Stop," Kyle ordered.

He turned around with a sneer on his face. "What? I said thanks for picking me up."

"Yeah, but you didn't explain why you were there." Kyle crossed his arms in front of him, his legs spread shoulder width apart.

"It's no big deal. I got off early and stopped a couple of buildings over to talk to this girl I'd seen around. They were having a party. Guess someone called the cops. One minute I'm standing there talking, the next she hands me her drink and says she has to use the bathroom. Then some jerk grabs me by the shoulder and whips me around. The elbow jab to his face was an automatic reflex."

"You were drinking and assaulted an officer?" He should never have let his mom talk him into this deal. Keith was as much trouble as his twin.

"Do you ever listen?" Keith jabbed his hands into his hair and spun around. The kid paced down the hall, drew his fist back and stopped it within an inch of hitting the wall. He walked back to the living room and looked at Kyle and Nic. "I wasn't drinking. Yeah, I hit the cop but I didn't know he was a cop until after the fact."

"I warned you—"

"Look, I did what you said. I did what Mom said. I've been clean since I got here. I've done nothing but go to work and come back to this boring ass apartment."

"Keith—"

"I'm not Kenny. We may look alike, but we don't share a brain. Got it?" Before Kyle could respond his brother disappeared into his room and slammed the door shut.

"Guess he's not ready to hear the part where I say I'm sorry?" Kyle dropped on the couch and looked at Nic, who had curled up in the chair with Princess PITA in her lap.

"I might wait until morning. Give him a chance to cool off and for the embarrassment to fade."

She sat the cat on the chair as she got up and came around to the back of the sofa. She put her hands on his shoulders.

"Planning to strangle me and put me out of my misery?" He dropped his head back until it rested between her pert breasts.

She bent forward until they were a few inches apart and stared eye-to-eye. Her hands caressed the sides of his face. "No, just a suggestion. Try to have a little faith in your brother. He's not a bad guy and he's a hard worker."

She dropped a kiss on his mouth and slipped her hands back to his shoulders, gently kneading the muscles, working the knots that had formed during dinner.

"How do you know?"

"I might have made a run for the border and spotted him working one night. We had a chat during his break. He's really proud of you and what you've become, Kyle. He might not say it or show it, but he respects you and looks up to you as to what he can do if he puts his mind to it. He simply needs some time and guidance to figure out what that *it* is."

The muscles started to relax under her skillful hands and the headache that had been building on the way home faded.

"You amaze me."

"Why thank you, but in what way?" Her laugher chased the last of his tension away.

"My family doesn't exactly have a sterling reputation. I mean, there's zero chance they're going to be invited to the White House to dine, yet it doesn't seem to bother you."

"Wait—no more dinners with POTUS? I'm out of here."

She wrapped her hands around his throat and shook him until he cried mercy.

"For the record, I ate there once and I wasn't the one invited, it was my parents, and it was kind of boring. Sure the food was delicious and it was kind of cool being in the White House, but the conversation was superficial. Beside, everyone's family has some kind of secret. Even us."

He craned his neck around to look at her. "Yeah, what skeletons are the mighty Rileys hiding?"

She came around, curled up on his lap and wrapped her arm around his shoulders. Leaning into him, she kissed him and whispered, "I'll tell but remember this is top secret." Another kiss, this time on the cheek. "The official story says that Granddad Riley left Ireland chasing a skirt… not

Gail Chianese

my dearly departed Grandmother's either. However, there's a rumor that the real reason he left his beloved homeland was to escape the British Army and a cell for involvement with shall we say… a certain group that believed in a united Ireland and might have gone about it the wrong way."

"You're saying your dad's father was a criminal?" His voice rose in shock.

She laid her finger across his lips. "Shh, 'tis a secret I'm telling. And don't be letting Liam and Reece fool you none. They might be all proper now, but as lads they… well, let's say they took an awful lot after their granddad and were always up to no good."

He laughed at her faux Irish accent and slipped his hands behind her head to bring her in close. Somehow this woman got him. Knew what he needed, when he needed it and without him knowing it had worked her way under his skin. Suddenly he understood his friend Mace a little better and sympathized a heck of a lot deeper with the man. How did he make it through the days with his wife so far away? How was he going to deal with Nic being deployed and him being left behind?

His chest ached at the thought and he held on tighter.

"Hey, is everything okay?" she whispered.

The emotion was too new, too raw, and it closed his throat off, leaving the words stuck. He silently nodded and slid an arm under her legs and lifted her. Without a word he carried her into his room, and laid her on his bed thankful he'd taken the time to clean up the place earlier. Not that she hadn't seen his room in all states before, but tonight was different. He lit the candles he'd bought that afternoon and toed his shoes off into the closet.

"Ooh, flowers. Are these for me?"

He turned to find her leaning over the vase he'd forgotten about on his nightstand sniffing the bouquet. The candles cast the room in a soft glow transforming it from a basic room to something romantic. But it was the smile on her face that sent his heart skipping a couple of beats. He'd seen some magnificent sunsets before, but none were as breathtaking as Nic Riley when she smiled.

Not knowing what to say that didn't fall smack in the middle of a cliché or sound so stupid she'd break out laughing he simply nodded.

"Come here." She crooked her finger at him. One moment he was across the room and then the next he stood before her at the edge of the bed.

He didn't know how to describe everything going on inside his head—his body, yeah sure that was pure chemistry—but his brain was another thing. It was like Nic had cast a spell and when she looked at him he couldn't refuse her anything, his mission was to see to her every want and need, to protect and to love.

Did that make him whipped?

If so, he didn't care.

"Let me love you, Nic."

Her eyes grew big, turning from a warm honey brown to dark chocolate. She reached up to undo his shirt buttons as he slid the zipper down on her dress. He slipped the barely there strap off her shoulder, following its path with kisses before turning his attention to the other side. She had the sweetest, smoothest skin he'd ever felt.

The dress fell to the bed and he sucked in his breath at the sight of the matching red silk panties. They took their time undressing each other, exploring, as if this were their first time or last time and they were committing every curve, every dip, every texture to memory. They exchanged sweet, lingering kisses and deep passionate kisses until both were panting for air.

Dipping his finger deep inside her, he found her more than ready for him, but held off taking her until he brought her to orgasm.

"Kyle, inside me. I want to feel you fill me up."

Only then did he slip inside, and it was she who filled him. With each stroke he came closer to home. Nic wrapped her strong legs around him and dug her fingertips into his shoulders. His muscles strained as he held back his release, alternating between shallow and slow deep thrusts. Nic threw her head back, her eyes half-mast, and arched into him as she whispered his name. The contractions wrapped around him and moments later he plunged into the abyss.

While his physical energy had been spent his mind whirled as he lay with Nic curled up against him. Everything about tonight had been different. Not better. Not worse. Just different. Maybe it was the knowledge that with the trial coming up, she'd be deploying shortly after. The thought turned everything inside him into knots and he pulled her in tighter, the emotions forcing those words to the surface.

"Nic, I—"

The Imperial March sounded from other room and Nic slipped from his bed.

She grabbed his shirt and pulled it on. "I'll be right back. That's my dad and if he's calling this late, it's got to be important."

Chapter Sixteen

Nic walked back in the bedroom with the phone to her ear, listening to the bombshell her dad had dropped. Her gaze shifted to Kyle lounging in bed. The sheet had fallen when she got up, leaving him more than half exposed to her viewing pleasure. As her dad's words hit her, she turned her back on Kyle and hung up.

He had to be wrong.

This couldn't be happening.

It had to be a lie. A sick, twisted lie.

The candles flickered, shadowed flames licked across the walls threatening to burn the place down. The room grew hazy and air refused to enter her lungs. Her dinner pushed its way up, catching in her throat, unable to make it past the lump lodged in the way.

"Nic, what's wrong?" Kyle's soft, warm voice grazed across her body, leaving her raw and exposed.

It took several moments for her to register he was crouched in front of her and she was sitting on the floor with the phone clutched to her breasts.

It had to be a lie.

The slate gray eyes studying her that had not long ago been filled with passion were now filled with concern. This man before her couldn't betray her in such a way.

Could he?

"Nic, honey? Is someone hurt? Sick? Let me get dress and I'll take you wherever you need to go." He looked around, probably for clothes and she reached out for him.

"Everyone's okay. That was my dad. He got a call giving him a heads up on the case. Stone has named a new accessory. Actually he's named an officer, saying he was following orders to videotape me and disperse the tape. That this officer didn't want me or any woman onboard submarines and thought this was a good way to show the problems it would cause."

As she spoke, she leaned forward and snagged her dress off the floor and pulled it on. She stood up and searched the room for her underwear.

"That's bullshit. Every officer on the boat supports the rights of women to be on submarines." He stood and pulled on a pair of jeans from his closet, not bothering to button them or put on his boxer-briefs.

Any other time and she'd be turned on.

Frustrated, she flipped on the light and started flinging the sheets around to find the rest of her clothes. Spotting a flash of red as the sheet settled, she reached under and snagged her panties.

"Before all this happened, I would have said the same of the entire crew," she said. "Stone proved that notion false."

Now dressed, she looked around for her shoes and purse.

"Did he say who the officer was behind this scheme?" Kyle asked.

She froze, her gaze glued to the flowers on the nightstand as she answered. "You."

A string of profanity so impressive it would have caused the saltiest of sailors to blush burst from Kyle. Nic didn't interrupt. She took one last look and walked into the living room, where she slipped on her heels and grabbed her purse. Kyle met her at the door.

"You believe him?" His voice was filled with pain and shock.

Nic blinked twice and it hit how her reaction and actions must have appeared to him. Yes, initially doubt ran through her mind, but when she looked into Kyle's eyes she knew it for what it was... a lie.

"No, of course not. It's just my family. Well, my parents are understandably upset. I need to talk to them."

"Do you want me to go with you?"

He kept his hands to himself and she missed his touch.

She ran her hand through her hair and laughed. "Umm, not a good idea. Not yet anyway. Liam sounded a bit upset and Reece was far too quiet. You might want to steer clear of them until they leave town. I hear Block Island's a lot of fun. You should check it out tomorrow."

"So guilty until proven innocent?" He crossed those arms over his chest when what she really wanted was them wrapped around her.

"No, it's not that at all. They're overprotective. Big brother syndrome. You get that, right?"

"Yeah, sure."

But his body language said the opposite. Anger, hurt, and disappointment all radiated off of Kyle in tsunami-size waves. If it hadn't been for pure willpower she would have instinctively stepped back. Instead she reached out and cupped the side of his face.

"I'll call you tomorrow after they leave." With a quick kiss she was out the door.

* * *

The way she'd left things with Kyle last night didn't settle well with Nic. All through breakfast her stomach turned and twisted whenever she thought of the look in his eyes as she stood at the door to leave. Damn Stone for putting doubts in her mind and shame on her for letting him.

If she showed up on Kyle's door and he closed it in her face, she wouldn't blame him one bit. After all, what had he done to deserve her lack of faith in him? Bust the guy selling the video. Stand by her side through it all. Give her a shoulder to cry on? Yep, those were all perfect reasons for her to cast aside the past few weeks and paint a big black V for villain on his chest.

She was pretty sure the amoebas on the fleas on a hyena's butt could look down on her, and she'd have no right to complain.

"Lily Nicole, are you in there?"

"Oh, what?" She pulled herself out of her self-recrimination and met her mom's worried look. "Sorry, was thinking about work."

"I asked if you've spoken to Kyle since your father called you last night."

Well, yeah because I was in his bed...nekkid at the time.

"Uh, yes. We did talk. I mean I told him about the accusation and assured him that no one in my family believed such nonsense about him." She shot Liam a steely-eyed dare.

"Why are you looking at me?" Liam held up his hands in surrender. "Why does she always think the worst about me? What about Reece?"

"Well, you did chase off most her of her dates in high school when you came home to visit," her mom supplied.

"Where is Reece anyway?" Nic looked around for her other brother, who hadn't met them at the restaurant.

"He'll be here soon." Her dad said setting down the menu. "He had an errand to run."

"Trust me, big brother, I told Kyle to steer clear of both of you," Nic said. "Neither of you are very good at keeping your noses out of my business or listening to me for that matter." She turned to her dad, before Liam could respond. "Pops, you don't believe Stone, do you?"

It doesn't matter what they think. I'll stand by Kyle, just like he did with me, she thought but deep in her gut her family's opinion and support did count. Sure she rebelled growing up, did her own thing like any other teen and when it came time to decide on life after high school she went Navy against all their wishes. The choice hadn't stemmed out of disrespect for their feelings, but out of pride in what they'd done, the sacrifices they made on a daily basis for their family and country.

She wanted to follow in their footsteps, stand by their sides, and know she contributed to this great country. And she didn't want to do it tucked safely behind a desk far from the action either.

Her father took so long to answer that she started to worry. A rebel she may be, but her dad had never let her down in his judgment of others.

"Based on what I've heard about Lieutenant Hutchinson, our conversations and more importantly from the way I've seen him look at you, no. There are some things you can fake and others that you can't."

"What do you mean?" She asked slowly. How did Kyle look at her? Other than with lust in his eyes and oh man, she really hoped that's not what her dad meant.

Liam chuckled and her mom blushed.

"Lily-Pad, if you don't know the answer by now either you're not ready to know the answer or not paying attention." Her dad's eyes sparked as he took his wife's hand and kissed it.

They ordered their food when the waitress arrived, not waiting for Reece. He knew the rule: you snooze, you lose. While they ate the conversation bounced all over the place from her dad's birthday party that she'd missed, to current affairs, to Liam's new duty assignment, his lack of a girlfriend and the grief it brought her mom because it meant no grandchildren in the foreseeable future, to her mom's pet projects.

Breakfast wrapped up and the golden child still hadn't made an appearance.

"Is Reece avoiding me?" Nic looked at both of her parents and then turned to Liam.

"He said he had something personal to handle this morning. I think he and his girlfriend are fighting and he stayed in to call her." Her mom waved it off with a sigh. "He'll join us later. Oh, look at the time. Your father and I have to go. We've been invited to coffee with friends. Give Liam a ride back or why don't you two go find something fun to do. Today's too nice to be locked up inside."

With quick kisses her mom headed toward the door, leaving her dad to pay for breakfast. Nic and Liam followed outside and waved the parentals off.

Nic turned to him, shaking her head. "I almost expected for her to remind us to be home in time for dinner."

"It did sound like a slip back in time. I don't think she always sees us as grown-ups." He slung her arm over her shoulders. "Sis, let's walk. It's been a while since I've been up this way and I've always loved the old buildings here."

The playful tone she associated with Liam was gone and in its place was that of a man with a lot on his mind. Hopefully not all because of her.

"Is everything alright with you? Work going okay? I mean you rocked your XO tour on the boat, or at least that's what Mom said," Nic said. They strolled through the crowds at Mystic Seaport, stopping to stare at a couple of passing kayaks on the river.

"Four point zero across the board on the eval, so yeah. It's all good and I've punched all the right tickets to make Commander." He popped a couple of coins in a penny press machine and started to crank the wheel, causing it to stretch the penny out. "I'm worried about you. Mom said you've been having panic attacks."

Nic blew a puff of air out, sending her stray hairs fluttering. "One of these days that woman will learn to keep a secret." Nic accepted the souvenir coin from her brother and tucked it into her pants pocket. "They're getting better. Not as frequent, not as severe. I still feel uncomfortable using public facilities, especially on the boat or the gym, but it is getting better."

"The media is going to have a field day when they get ahold of this new development. And you can bet Stone will make sure they have it. Are you ready for all that?"

"I'll just ignore them like last time. They'll go away as soon as something else more sensational happens, which will be about fifteen minutes later."

"Nic, sweetie." Liam stopped her and pulled her out of the flow of traffic. "This is going to be different. This time you're dating the man accused of being behind the whole ordeal. How's that going to look?"

"Exactly what it is. A lie." Even as the words left her mouth she knew it wasn't true. The old "innocent until proven guilty" went out the window a long time ago and Kyle would be tried and convicted through the lens of a media camera.

"You know better."

"All the more reason why I need to stand by his side, to show the world I believe in him and they should too." She poked him in the shoulder to drive her point home.

He stepped back further away from the other tourists into the shadows of the trees and out of her reach. *Chicken.*

"Let me ask you something and don't get mad. Could he have used you to get close to Pops? Set this whole thing up, come to your rescue, be the big hero in the hopes that our father will be so thankful he'll give Hutchinson a career boost?"

"Wha…" she sputtered, not even able to get the word out. Talk about your ludicrous ideas. Finally, after all these years she had proof her oldest brother had been dropped on his head and had serious brain damage.

So then why can't you just say no?

Because all three siblings had earned the T-shirt, "Been there, experienced that, people suck." Yet something inside her told her Kyle wasn't that person. Maybe it was because she'd seen something in the way he looked at her, something he couldn't fake like her dad said. Or maybe it was wishful thinking.

Or maybe not.

She really wished Lindsey or Cherise were available to talk to right about then, because her brother had her head spinning.

"But wait, Liam, there's a flaw in your grand scheme. Pops did offer Kyle a billet in D.C. and Kyle turned him down. So if this were some elaborate ruse to fast track him to whatever, why would he do that? Being on Pop's staff, hand-picked no less, that's like finding the golden ticket."

Breakfast wasn't settling in her stomach and the discussion had given her a killer headache.

"I don't know. Maybe he's playing hard to get," Liam replied.

"Seriously?" She shook her head and started to walk away. "You weren't just dropped on your head as a baby. Mom played basketball with your head."

* * *

Kyle dropped onto his couch with a bowl of Captain Crunch, propped his feet on the coffee table and stared out the window as he ate. Princess PITA hopped up onto the back of the couch. She purred into his ear while her tail flipped back and forth smacking him in the face. He'd slid open the glass door to let the morning breeze in, grateful to turn off the AC for a while. Outside laughter from the complex playground filled the air.

Had he ever been that carefree?

He couldn't recall a time when there hadn't been something or another—bills, his old man's attitude, chores—to worry about and that was before the twins arrived.

At least back then if you screwed up or even if you were an innocent caught in the crosshairs the punishment lasted only as long as it took for some other matter to detract his parents' attention. Now everything he'd worked for since that fateful day at Tomlinson's store could be ripped away from him and there wasn't a whole hell of a lot he could do. It would be Stone's word against his.

Keith stumbled through the room and into the kitchen. Kyle didn't attempt a conversation. He'd discovered right away that baby brother needed caffeine and time before his brain allowed coherent speech upon waking. The sounds of the fridge opening and closing, cereal pouring into a bowl told Kyle everything he needed to know for now. The kid had an appetite; he was fine.

How was he going to explain this mess to his family? After all, they sent Keith here to keep him out of trouble and for Kyle to be a good example. So much for that stellar plan.

"Hey." Keith dropped into the chair and propped his feet up next to Kyle's. Princess immediately abandoned him for her new BFF. Traitorous cat. He'd probably been sneaking her cans of tuna. "Where's Nic?"

"Gone." His voice was gruff, his answer short, just like his mood.

Keith's brows arched. "Gone, gone or just gone for the moment gone?"

Million-dollar question. Sure she said she'd call, that she didn't believe the accusation, but she also wasted no time getting the heck away from him after her dad's call.

"Dunno." He didn't want to talk about it either, so he kept eating his Crunch Berries.

"What did you do, buy the wrong flowers or pick the wrong candles?" Keith ran his hand from the cat's head down her back sending her purr motor into overdrive. "You know if you don't treat your girl right, she'll find someone who will."

Kyle eyed the cat, then his brother and shoved his empty bowl onto the table. He let out a deep sigh and closed his eyes. The walls were closing in. Maybe he'd grab a bag and head out to Block Island for the day, or hop a train and lose himself in Manhattan, or go rent a boat and sail for the day. No way could he sit around here waiting.

"Dude," Keith's shocked voice trailed off. "Look, I was only joking. If you two fought, I'm sure she'll be over it soon and you guys will make up. Just hang a sock or something on the door so I don't walk in on it."

"Ha. You're a real comedian, kid." Kyle peeled one eye open. "You working today?"

Keith nodded. "I've got a full shift at the Bell. If you need, I can make myself scarce after work."

"No, don't worry about it. Think I'm going to get out and enjoy summer. Was thinking you'd come along, but work comes first."

"About last night." Keith waited to continue until Kyle sat up and looked at him. "Sorry I was a jerk and thanks for coming down to get me."

"No worries. I'd say being a jerk is a family trait because I was one too. Call it even, and forget about it?" He stuck his hand out for a truce, relieved when his brother took it and grinned.

"Guess we get that from Dad." He sat back, quiet for a couple of moments before speaking again. "I talked to Mom yesterday. Kenny struck a bargain with the DA. He's giving them evidence on Woody's operation and in return they're giving him a clean slate. Whatever he knows is good enough that they're putting him in witness protection. He wanted Mom and Dad to go with him, but you know those two. Citrus Park is home and no one is chasing them off."

"If they're putting him in WITSEC there must be a credible threat."

Kyle sat staring at his brother, trying to comprehend this new twist in his life. One brother was here so he could keep him safe, the other hidden by the authorities and his parents were sitting ducks. And there wasn't a fucking thing he could do because with Stone's lie he wouldn't be allowed to take leave.

Could his life possibly get any more screwed up?

"I'll call Mom later and see if I can talk some sense into her," Kyle said. "Maybe she can convince the old man to go on vacation, take a cross-country road trip out here or somewhere far away." The veins at his temples pounded.

"Thanks. I've been ordered to stay away, which is fine. I don't ever want to go back. That place is like a living graveyard. People don't even know they're dead until they cross the town line."

"Yeah, tell me about it. Have you thought about checking out the community college I told you about? "

"I looked it up online. Out-of-state tuition is crazy expensive and more than I'd make in a month. I might enroll in some online classes at one of the CC's from California though. Get my grades up, apply for a scholarship when the time comes."

Kyle grabbed his bowl, grabbed Keith's as well, and then headed into the kitchen. He contemplated coffee or water, choosing the later before heading back to the living room. "Do you have an idea what your major would be?"

"Not yet. Thought I'd take a few of those test that help you figure out where your strengths lie, other than wrapping a mean burrito."

"Not saying you have to join the military if you take it, but the ASVAB is a good one for guidance. Helped me choose my path in college. The Navy just kept me the hell away from Citrus Park."

A knock on the door had both turning their heads. Keith grinned and set the cat down. "I'll check it out. In the meantime, I'll get out of your hair while you two make up."

But when Kyle opened the door, it was Reece who greeted him.

"Morning." Kyle held his hand out, only to be ignored. "I thought you were having breakfast with your sister."

His guest stood scowling for several seconds without uttering a word. Probably learned that trick from his father and Kyle was sure many junior sailors had caved under the look. He'd make a great commanding officer someday. Too bad Kyle's old man had scowling down to an art form and his grandfather could have stared a priest into confessing, even if he didn't do anything wrong.

Kyle held his ground.

Keith joined him at the door. "Oh hey, you must be Nic's bro." He held out a hand. "I'm Keith, and considering he's keeping you standing on the door, I probably shouldn't admit it, but I'm Kyle's brother."

Reece grasped his hand in a quick shake and Keith stepped back. "You should come in before the cat escapes. Can I get you something to drink?" His brother called over his shoulder, not even looking to see if Kyle stepped aside or if Reece followed.

Kyle stepped back and allowed Reece to enter and close the door.

"Thanks for the offer, but I'm good," Reece replied.

"Suit yourself." Keith dropped back into the chair and looked up. "Must have been one heck of an argument if Nic sent her big brother over. You here to pound Kyle into the floor? Cause if you are, I'm obligated to take his side. Unless, he hurt Nic, then I'm going to get in line behind you and help you kick his butt."

"Don't you have to get ready for your shift or shower or bribe the Princess?" Kyle hooked his thumbs in his front pockets and leaned back against the edge of the couch. He wasn't afraid of Reece, although he was fairly sure the guy was up for some punching bag practice using his face as the target.

"Nah, I got plenty of time." Keith settled in, determined to find out what was going on and there wasn't a lot Kyle could do short of telling him to get lost.

"Does she know you're here?" Kyle asked.

"She might by now. Are you going to deny the charges against you?" Reece stepped into Kyle's zone. Knuckles popped, voice even, the guy was pissed but holding his anger in check.

"Would it make you feel better to hear me say it?" Kyle gave a slight shake of his head catching his brother's confused look. "Fine. It's a trumped-up charge and Nic knows it. What else can I do to ease your mind? Swear on a stack of bibles? Pinky swear? Cross my heart and hope to die?"

"Stay away from my sister."

Kyle's head jerked back, as if Reece had physically punched him. Was he joking? The whole situation felt juvenile and if it weren't so serious, he would have laughed. But one look at the hard line that was Reece's mouth, the pulsing of his jaw as he clamped down and released as well as the fact the his body look like he was strung tighter than a guitar string had Kyle thinking twice.

"Don't you think Nic should have some say in this?" he asked.

Reece dragged his hands through his hair and spun around. He walked over to the small dining table and hung his head. "Hey Keith, if that offer for coffee is still good, I could use a cup. Black, please."

"Look, I get it. You and your family think I'm some kind of low life who used and betrayed your sister—"

Reece held both hands up stopping Kyle. "That's not true. Not entirely. Liam is still on the fence about you. The rest of us like you, which is why this is hard, plus Nic's crazy about you. But if you care about her, you'll stay away from her until this is all over."

Keith came out with the coffee and Kyle gestured to the chair while he took up his normal spot on the couch, fully aware of his brother at his back.

"I don't see what point my staying away serves, other than to make me look guilty."

"Guess you haven't watched the morning news, have you?" He sat on the edge of his seat, holding the cup like a lifeline. "You made the lead story. It's only a matter of time before they leak the next part and that's how you're dating the alleged victim. By the time the trial starts in a week,

Nic will have gone from a target to co-conspirator or even the mastermind behind a foiled sex tape plan. Her reputation and career will be ruined."

Kyle let the words sink in, swirl around and filter through his brain. Such BS. All of it. Nic had nothing to do with Stone's plan. He had nothing to do with it, but would the viewing public believe them? They had no proof, just their word against Stone's. The Navy itself wouldn't do anything against Nic, they had no grounds for a case, but he got what Reece was saying.

Perception.

People loved a good scandal. They loved to see others fall from grace. *We may not go to public hangings or beheading and cheer on the hangman/axman anymore, but we still loved a public execution.*

"It's a little late to hide our relationship. The damage has been done—"

"Not really. From what she's said to our mom, you've kept things pretty much under wraps and only a select few really know the truth. Trusted friends, a few co-workers. You both could spin it as you were friends, as her sponsor on the boat you were helping her navigate the area, giving her tips on where to look for housing, where to stay away from. That kind of thing. Purely platonic."

"Who's selling Nic on this plan?"

"Liam."

He chuckled. The two of them butted heads non-stop last night at dinner. Something told him both were going to end up with a killer headache after this discussion and he had a feeling he knew which one was going to win the skirmish. While neither he nor Nic might like it, they had their own battle they were about to enter and if they were smart they'd listen to her brothers.

Several minutes passed in silence as all parties let the conversation settle over them. It wasn't Kyle's career or life he worried about, although he should.

A smart man would walk, would think about all the hard work he'd poured into the past sixteen years of his life, would think about his own family and the issues going on with them. Those alone made his head spin. Then again when didn't his family drive him to the edge with a firm hand at his back and only his will kept him from falling into the black, bottomless pit of nothing.

He'd spent years working his butt off so he wouldn't land back in the middle of drama central called home. Yet that's where he'd landed. Apparently if you would not go to the drama, it would come to you and wrap its greedy claws into your body and attempt to suck your life away.

Talk about melodramatic, Hutch. It's a friggin' week, not a life sentence.
He looked up into Reece's expectant eyes. "I'll do what I can to keep
the limelight away from her."

Keith had kept quiet during the conversation, which had surprised him,
given his earlier offer to jump straight to Nic's defense against him.

"I've got get ready for work." He headed out of the room, mumbling
what sounded like dumbass to Kyle.

He'd have to ask later if he meant for agreeing to stay away or what.

Reece and Kyle spent a few minutes discussing Stone's game plan and
Kyle's response to the accusation. Should he keep quiet, make a statement
to the media, find a witness to clear his name, or get a lawyer and take a
chance they'd do their job.

Nothing like playing Russian roulette with his freedom and future.

He saw Reece to the door and returned to his spot on the couch, no
longer interested in getting out for the day. If convicted, the judge could
toss him in jail for up to twenty-eight years, bust him to the lowest rank,
take all his pay, and then give him a dishonorable discharge.

He needed to find someone to clear his name ASAP.

Grabbing his cell, he shot off a text to both Mace and Bryant and told
them he needed their help. Since they were still on the boat, they might
have heard talk that could help or question the crew for him. The Group
would do their own investigation, but he couldn't sit on his haunches and
do nothing with everything in the balance.

Keith came out of the bedroom, his trusty backpack swung over his
shoulder, the cat in his arms. "How much trouble are you in?"

"I don't know yet. How much of that did you hear?"

"All of it."

"And?"

Keith sat the cat down, hitched his pack higher on his shoulder, hanging
on with one hand. "And nothing. You'd never betray Nic like that. I know
it. She knows it. I'm in your corner, bro. Whatever you need."

Kyle stood. He clamped a hand on Keith's shoulder, his throat tight
with emotion at his brother's words. "Thanks. I won't make the same
mistake as last night again. The same goes for you—whatever you need,
I'm here for you."

"Great, cause I could use a ride to work."

Kyle laughed at his brother's smirk. Should have seen that coming.

"Yeah, give me a minute." The phone rang and Kyle grabbed it.

"Lieutenant Hutchinson? This is Commander Williamson. I need you to meet me at my office in the Group 2 building as soon as possible. If you need a ride, I can send an escort."

"Not necessary, sir. I'll be there in twenty minutes."

He hung up and looked at Keith. "Let the games begin."

Chapter Seventeen

Tired and cranky didn't even begin to cover Kyle's mood. He could take on a grizzly and win. Throw in hunger, as he hadn't eaten anything except a bowl of cereal six hours ago, and the fact that his freaking car AC decided it wanted to blow out lukewarm air on the hottest day of the year. So, yeah, call him Kyle the Grouch.

He slammed the car door shut and headed across the hot pavement of his apartment complex, wanting nothing more than a cold beer, a cold slice of pizza, and fifteen minutes under the spray of a cold shower. Maybe then he'd be fit for humankind.

Thank goodness Keith was at work. The mood he was in, he'd probably bite the kid's head off for breathing. A couple of hours of peace was exactly what he needed to get his head clear and his mood out of the black.

"Excuse me?" A pretty blonde with a microphone and a guy toting a camera approached. Kyle held up his hand and kept walking. "Kyle Hutchinson? Lieutenant Kyle Hutchinson? Amanda Clarkson with Channel Four News. We'd like to talk to you about the case against Petty Officer Stone videotaping Lieutenant Lily Riley aboard the *USS California* and your role in the incident."

He counted to ten and forced his hands to relax.

"You'll need to talk the base public affairs office. I have no comment."

He kept walking. His CO and the investigator were crystal clear; he was not to talk with anyone about the investigation, especially the press. He'd actually snorted with laughter at their instructions. Like he'd talk to the media. He didn't even do PR work under the best of circumstances. Some people wanted to be in the spotlight, be the poster children of the Navy. Not him; he simply wanted to do his job and do it well, advance as far as he could, as fast as he could so that when he hit twenty he could retire and start a second career doing whatever he wanted.

Right about then running a bar on some unnamed beach in the tropics sounded like heaven to him.

"Lieutenant Hutchinson, did you instruct Petty Officer Stone to make that tape?" the reporter persisted.

"No … comment." It killed not to answer. Would Nic understand when she saw the news clip? Would she care or believe him even if he had answered? Speaking of people seeing the news, he'd better call home before the bullshit made its way to his mom. That's the last thing she needed with everything going on with Kenny and her heart.

"Lieutenant, how many other women have you and Stone made videotapes of?" The woman stuck the microphone in his face, while the cameraman blocked his path.

Holy cripes. If he followed protocol he'd sound as guilty as hell to the world. Say none and it made it sound like he was defending Stone. The CO was going to have his nuts on a chopping block for disobeying his orders come Monday morning. Kyle stopped and looked the reporter in the eye.

"I can't speak for Petty Officer Stone. As for myself, the answer is none. If you have any other questions, you'll need to direct them to the PAO. If you'll excuse me." He stepped around the camera and kept walking.

She caught up. "Why is Stone saying he was following your orders?"

Vindictive jerk. "No comment."

He didn't know how they found out where he lived, but in case they hadn't actually gotten his apartment number he didn't want to lead them to his front door. He stopped abruptly and the camera guy ran into him, mumbled sorry and backed up a few steps.

"I'm hot, tired, and we're done," Kyle said.

"Is it true that Stone worked for you?" the reporter asked.

"No comment."

"How did you learn about the video if you didn't have anything to do with the creation of it?"

"No comment."

A couple that lived across the hall from him scooted around the three of them, ducking their heads so the camera wouldn't catch their faces on film, but not before he caught their confused and horrified looks.

"Is it true that you're dating the victim, Lieutenant Riley?"

It took the effort of a saint—something he'd never been accused of—not to tell the reporter where she could stuff her microphone at the mention of Nic's name and their relationship. He didn't know who her source was, but they'd better remain anonymous or he'd be tempted to toss them into the middle of the Thames River with an anchor strapped to their ankle. As he'd used up his share of restraint and then some, temptation was a sure bet as the winner.

"No comment," he gritted through clamped teeth.

"Lieutenant Hutchinson, don't you think people deserve to know the full truth? Don't you want them to know your side?"

She had no idea.

"What I'd like is for you to respect my privacy and rights and the Navy's request that you contact the Public Affairs Office for comment. I know you have a job to do, but I have orders to follow."

Without another word, he turned and walked off. Not to his apartment, as he was sure the little hungry shark would just follow him and shout more questions through the closed door and drive him and his neighbors crazy. Following the path that led from his building around the complex to the main building, past the pool, tennis courts, dog park and through the playground he took his time. It had to be around a hundred and ten, or more with a humidity factor pushing the heat to a thousand and twenty or more.

If Lady Luck could cut him a break, the duo would give up and he could go enjoy that beer, pizza and shower. Rounding the corner he said a silent thank you when their van was gone and he bounded up the stairs to his apartment.

The door opened before he could slide the key in.

"I thought those two would never leave." Bryant left the door open and dropped into the chair and picked up a beer.

Mace came out of the kitchen with a bowl of chocolate gelato and took up residence on the couch.

"Make yourself at home." Kyle tossed his keys on the table and headed to his room, where he stripped and walked into the shower. Ten minutes later he was dressed and had a beer in his hand.

"When did you two get here?" Kyle asked.

"About ten. Your fan club pulled up right behind us. How did it go with the interview?" Mace stretched, pushing Kyle further down the couch and clasped his hands behind his head.

"Like you'd expect. Bare room with me cuffed to a chair and a single bare bulb swinging overhead. Bad cop, stale coffee, lots of answering the same questions over and over topped off with a little waterboarding for fun. Then cut me loose with orders not to talk to anyone."

"Man, you have all the fun, Hutch." Bryant flashed him a playful grin trying to lighten the mood.

"Hey, if you want I can tell them you were the mastermind. I'm not greedy. I'll share in the fun and be sure to tell them the only way to get you to talk is with electrotherapy."

"Nah, I'm good man."

They hashed out theories on why Stone had named him and what the game plan would be going forward.

"I'll do what I can, maybe enlist the COB or Boone to listen for chatter among the crew." Mace paused for a moment. "If Stone shared his plan, and I'm betting he couldn't keep it to himself, someone will talk. Since I did the initial investigation I've already gotten a message to report in first thing Monday to talk to Williamson—"

"Me too. Got it right after the reporter showed up." Bryant reached down and picked up the cat to settle her in his lap. Spoiled thing. His roommate wouldn't know what to do when he returned from patrol and found out the Princess had actually turned social. "Do you think he suspects that because we were roommates that all three of us were in on the deal?"

Both guys snorted in response.

"What has Nic said about all of this?" Mace asked, ignoring Bryant's question.

"Not a lot. She doesn't believe it. Her brothers have warned me off of her, at least until the dust has settled down and the trial is over." The pizza he'd been craving turned to cardboard in his mouth and he tossed the paper plate onto the table.

"Did she agree to that plan? Because from what Cherise told me, Nic has a habit of ignoring her family's wishes and usually does the opposite." Bryant's strokes had Princess PITA purring like a racecar and Kyle made a mental note to keep an eye on her when he left. She might be ready to defect.

"I haven't talked to her since the suggestion was delivered. Doesn't matter if she likes it or not, until my name is cleared and the media hounds find someone else to sniff around, her invitation to Casa Hutchinson is rescinded."

She'd see his reason and agree and it couldn't be any worse than being locked in a tin pig for weeks, being within reach and not being able to touch her. At least this go around was only seven meager days and they wouldn't be bumping into each other left and right and front and back, for that matter. A week was a picnic.

* * *

By lunchtime on Monday exhaustion threaten to knock Nic on her butt. She'd been on the run since arriving at oh-six-hundred. There was no reason for her to get up with the sun or report in almost two hours early, except she'd gotten tired of counting sheep. Meditating hadn't done a darn thing except prove her mind didn't know how to relax and the chamomile tea she'd drank at bedtime had multiplied in volume and caused her to get up and pee seven times throughout the night.

Everything she'd need to do for the next three days was done and the XO had told her to get lost as his inbox was overflowing and he didn't need any more work to sign off on. Instead of leaving and going back to her room to nap, or just curling up in her bunk on the boat, she went in search of Mace and Bryant.

Both were in their stateroom/office poring over reports.

"Hey guys, how's it going?" She leaned into the doorway, effectively blocking them both in, which was a good thing because they both looked like startled deer ready to bolt at the sound of her voice.

"Good, just getting ready for work-ups. You ready to go back out?" Mace had swiveled around to study her. Not in a sexual, perverted, I've-seen-you-naked kind of way, more like he was looking for signs of stress. Couldn't say she blamed him. She didn't really want to be trapped underwater with someone having a nervous breakdown either.

She gave his question serious thought before answering. Both had a right to know if she wasn't up to par. Not only her safety depended on her being honest, but so did that of the crew. The panic attacks were fewer and farther between when she used the base gym. Most days she held her head high as she walked through the Exchange shopping or the Commissary getting groceries. Only every now and then did she question a look or feel the tightness in her chest. Although she hadn't managed to hang out in the public areas of the barracks when others were around, nor could she stop herself from sprinting down up the stairs when she heard voices or encountered others.

So stupid.

But it was getting better. She was getting better and she'd win this battle yet, it just might take a little longer than she'd originally anticipated.

Both men sat, waiting for her answer.

"Honestly, I think I am ready for patrol. I can't let what Stone did jade me or worse, stand as my baseline for how I judge others." Saying it was one thing, putting it into action was whole other challenge.

"Let us know what we can do to help," Bryant offered.

"Thanks. By the way, did either of you talk to Kyle this weekend?"

She cringed inside. Why couldn't she have just kept the conversation work related? Now she sounded like an insecure girlfriend checking up on her guy.

"Uh, no not me. You, Mace?"

Boy, Bryant was a lousy liar.

"I think he said something about heading out of town. Maybe checking out Block Island or the beaches down on Long Island." Mace picked up the report he'd been working on and glanced down at the paper.

"Guess that means you didn't hear about the latest development and Stone's accusation then?" Her gaze bounced back and forth watching the two of them sweat as they racked their brains, probably trying to remember what they were supposed to say to her.

"Yeah." Mace recovered first. "We got called in for questioning this morning. Look, Nic, I know you're worried about him, but he's not in the brig or anything. His command probably has him lying low until this is cleared up. Give him a few days and I'm sure he'll call."

Just as she suspected. Her brothers got to Kyle.

Dirty-rotten, overprotective, pains in her rear.

Well, if they thought they could pull her strings and treat her like a puppet, they'd better think again.

"No, I'm not worried. Not about the accusation." She picked at the doorframe, not meeting their eyes least they see that she was lying. "He and Keith... well, it doesn't matter now." She left them with their reports, grabbed her bag and checked out for the day, courtesy of the XO. The sun shone overhead, a cool breeze was blowing and she was in the mood for a little Mexican and then maybe some beach time.

An hour later she sat in what was becoming her regular corner table while waiting for Keith to finish up his shift. She'd popped in one night on her way home from shopping, not knowing Keith was working, and he'd asked her to wait around until he got off. Turned out, the kid was lonely and concerned about his brother back home, his mom, and didn't have a clue how to talk to Kyle.

Knowing what it was like to be the new kid in town, she'd given him her phone number and told if he needed to talk to call. He'd texted her his schedule and she'd came by a couple of times at the end of his shift or for a couple of minutes during his break. They'd generally sit in this same booth or outside and talk about nothing in particular or life in the Navy, and once in a while his family.

Last time he'd brought up his twin, he'd been worried about the case against him and that he might never see Kenny again. Apparently the guy he'd gotten mixed up with was seriously bad news.

"Where have you been all weekend?" Keith slid into the chair across from her and set his lunch on the table. "You hungry? I'll split this with you or order up your favorite for you."

Just what her hips didn't need...more fast food.

"I'm good. My family was in town. What's going on with you? You look happier than when I saw you last."

Which would be when he and Kyle were shouting at each other last Friday night.

Keith brought her up to speed about the turn of events with Kenny and his and Kyle's discussion Saturday morning. When he hesitated in his story, she gave him a little nudge.

"Were you there when my brother showed up? Want to swap?"

He laughed and shook his head. "Nah. Reece is a little too intense for me."

"Don't let him fool you. He's really a big pussycat...with claws and fangs and sometimes smelly breath and feet."

She had him laughing, which had been her goal. "I'm glad you and your brother made up. That's what I really came by to find out. Things between Kyle and I might get a little weird. This video case—"

"He told me about the accusation," he interrupted.

"Yeah, there's that, but I don't know. Call it women's intuition. I think we're about to sail through some choppy seas and it may take us a while to reach calm waters again. Whatever happens between your brother and me, it doesn't change the fact that I'm your friend and if you need me, call me."

He shoved his food away. "He's a dumbass—"

"Keith."

"Sorry, but he is. I told him too. Even so, don't give up on him yet. He's crazy about you."

"I haven't given up on him or us. Trust me, I don't fold that easily." She nodded toward his food. "Now eat your lunch and tell me what you've decided to do when summer ends."

At the end of his break, Nic gave Keith a quick hug and assured him Kyle wouldn't flip at his decision. Even if he did, it was Keith's life and like it or not, he was an adult and could make his own choices. Now, if she could just convince her family of the same in regards to her.

She pulled up and parked in the visitor parking after a quick search confirmed Kyle's car was in his assigned spot. Big Brother One and Two may have kept the two of them apart over the weekend, but enough was enough. She wouldn't let them or Stone dictate her life any more.

Nic knocked on the door and waited. After several minutes, she knocked again. Inside she could hear Princess meowing like she was talking to someone when she was hungry, which was most of the time, and Nic would swear she'd heard someone bump into a chair. Since Keith was at work and Kyle's roommate was still out to see that left one person.

Uh-huh. Or did it?

Maybe Kyle wasn't home alone.

She knocked again. They did say three times is the charm.

The lady across the hall opened her door and smiled at Nic. "I don't think anyone's home. I haven't seen Kyle since early this morning when he went running."

"His car is parked in the lot and I know his brother doesn't have it today. He should be here."

"It's been pretty quiet today, unlike this weekend when those reporters kept showing up. Maybe he got a ride with a friend?"

Nic shrugged and headed for the stairs, stopping at the sound of a cough behind Kyle's door. "Yeah, maybe."

Or maybe he was avoiding her. Funny, he hadn't struck her as the type of guy who scared easily. So was it something else keeping him away, something like a guilty conscience?

What was she thinking? This was Kyle, not one of her exes who was more concerned with his top score in whatever video game he was playing than her. She'd seen how torn up he'd been after he'd discovered the video. From what she'd heard, Mace and Bryant had to pull him off of Stone.

He'd never betray her.

Chapter Eighteen

Kyle's phone went sailing through the air and landed with a thump on his chest Wednesday night.

"Yo, dawg your phone is ringing." Keith stood over him, glaring. "You can't ignore her forever."

"I know. I'm not." He sat up and swung his legs off the couch and stared at the missed call message.

After Monday's unanswered visit she'd hadn't called until today. It had taken everything in him not to open the door and pull her into his arms, but he couldn't risk even more crap raining down on him. When he'd reported in Monday, the CO had called him into his office and in no unmistakable terms told him to go home, keep a low profile, keep his mouth shut, and he meant it this time and above all else, stay away from Lieutenant Nic Riley.

If Kyle couldn't follow those orders he'd find himself restricted to a barracks room with a guard outside his door.

"Hey, since all you're doing is sitting around moping, can I use your car to go to work tonight?" Keith asked.

"I'm not moping and the answer's no, but I'll drive you."

"Whatever. I've got to be there in ten. So maybe you could put some clothes on and brush your hair and your teeth, cause dude you're breath reeks."

Brothers. Who needed them? Definitely not him, but he got up and did as Keith suggested. Not because he agreed with his brother, but he had plans to meet up with Mace and Bryant for dinner and see if they learned anything new. If they didn't find someone soon to punch holes in Stone's story he didn't have a clue what he'd do.

He walked into the living room while Keith shoved his phone into his backpack. It pinged a couple of seconds later and when Kyle mentioned it, Keith shrugged it off. Normally he grabbed his phone like a lifeline when it rang or a notification sounded.

"Let me drive," Keith said and held out his hand.

Kyle clutched the keys all the way to the car as his brother needled him about driving, only relinquishing them after the kid promised he wouldn't say a word during the five-minute drive. Something was up. Keith wouldn't look him in the eye and then there was that strange business with his phone.

Had he heard more from home that he didn't want to share? Probably found out Kenny's WITSEC story was pure BS and was too embarrassed to tell him. Kyle still needed to call home, except what was he supposed to say— "Hey Mom, guess what? Not such a good role model after all." Yeah, the old man would eat that news up.

Lost in thought, Kyle hadn't paid attention and realized they'd arrived at Keith's job until his brother turned off the ignition as he got out.

"Why in the hell did you turn off—" Kyle asked as he slid out of the passenger seat and came to a stop.

Nic.

His heart ached at the sight of her.

She smiled and turned away.

"You better get inside before you're late and we'll discuss this later, Shyster," Kyle said.

His brother loped off across the parking lot, leaving the two of them standing alone with dead air filling the space between as Kyle came to rest next to the driver's door. He reached out for Nic, but the message was loud and clear as she stepped back out of his reach.

For once in his life he didn't know what to say. Everything that came to mind sounded like a cliché or a knockoff from some campy movie where he'd apologize and she'd forgive him and they could carry on like he hadn't been an idiot for the past couple of days. His intentions might be good, but his execution sucked and he knew it.

"Come here often?" He waggled his eyebrows, trying to make it into a joke to cut through the chill.

"Had an uncontrollable taco craving."

"Not craving anything else are you? Like pickles and ice cream?" He gave her one of his best grins. "Or me?"

"No." She looked down at her watch. "Haven't had much of an appetite for anything lately. Definitely nothing sour. Probably wouldn't have given in to the taco urge if your brother hadn't sent me a text saying he desperately needed to talk. Figured it had to do with Kenny or your mom, until you got out of the car."

He stepped into her space and with each step she took back, he took one forward until she was pressed up against the passenger door of her car.

"I didn't put him up to the ruse."

"Didn't actually think you had." The ice in the air had reached her eyes and her voice cut deep as she hit her mark.

"Let's go get a real meal and talk. Somewhere nice."

She glanced down at his T-shirt and shorts and rolled her eyes at him. "Is it just everyone else you listen to?" she asked.

"What's that supposed to mean?"

What the hell had he done now? His mind raced, trying to connect asking her to dinner and how that played into listening and what had he missed. Nic placed her palms against his chest and shoved him away.

"Never mind, Einstein."

"Nic, please. I've missed you."

He had, too. The past five days may as well have been a full-on deployment for him. Being stuck in the apartment was nothing compared to the restriction from Nic. He hadn't taken her calls knowing he'd cave and break orders. He missed her smile, the scent of her hair, the feel of her skin, the sound of her laughter.

He missed cooking for her and the look on her face when she tasted something new and liked it even though she'd been convinced she'd hate it. Then there was the way she'd purr when he'd rub her back and wiggle her toes to keep from laughing as he skimmed his fingertips over her ticklish spots. Most of all he missed the way he felt inside when she was next to him like all was right in the world, and he could handle anything life threw his way.

A horn honked and Kyle looked up to see Petty Officer Wu wave to them from the adjacent parking lot. A good reminder this wasn't the place for them to have this conversation, as anyone could drive by and see them.

"If you don't want to go out, we could go back to my place and I'll whip up shrimp tacos," he said.

She shook her head and took a step away, then stopped and turned back to him. The resigned look of disappointment killed him.

"I'll pass. Your silence the last couple of days has pretty much told me everything I need to know. It's over. It was fun and now it's time to move on. I'll talk to Keith and tell him not to play matchmaker again."

"It's not over, Nic." He took her hand and held on like a lifeline. "Did you talk to Reece, by chance, before he left?"

"About?" Her eyes narrowed to thin slits.

"His visit to see me."

"His what?" She exhaled a deep breath. "Start talking and don't stop until you've told me every. Last. Detail." Arms crossed, she leaned back against her car, one brow cocked, lips purse and steam coming out of her ears.

He told her everything: Reece's concern, his proposed solution, the reporters showing up, right down to the CO's orders to stay away. During his confession she never said a word.

She'd gone unnaturally calm, like the air right before a hurricane leveled everything in its path.

* * *

Of all the egotistically, alpha male, control-freak, stupid, cockamamie ideas her brothers had ever come up with, and there'd been some doozies before, this one took the cake. And to top it off, Kyle had agreed with them.

What had she ever seen in him?

He was just like them.

Oh dear, God! She'd been dating a clone of her brothers.

Well, that was going to stop right here and now.

She was tired, beyond tired of the men in her life deciding what she should do and how she should live. They meant well, she wouldn't argue that they didn't have the best intentions, but sooner or later and it better be sooner, they had to realize she could make her own choices.

"Why didn't you tell me all of this Saturday or Monday? You were home Monday when I stopped by, weren't you?" she demanded.

He flinched. It was there and gone in a heartbeat, but she saw it and his admission hurt more than she expected. Oh, yeah, she knew he'd been home. Call it women's intuition. Having him admit it was like pouring salt in the cut and rubbing it in.

"We didn't think you'd agree with our plan."

"You figured I'd get hysterical and unreasonable and I don't know, throw myself at your feet and beg you not to leave me alone for a week?" She couldn't help the laughter. The thought was ridiculous. Even her thirteen-year-old self would have scoffed at the idea of throwing a fit over some *boy* ignoring her.

"I had thought you might miss me."

She paced between the cars. It was either that or throttle him in front of every passing car on Route 12.

"Do I look like a china doll? Someone who needs to be handled with care? Who will break if life gets a little rough?"

Before he could respond she shot him a warning look and made another rotation.

"I warned you about my brothers. Told you they were overprotective, but did you listen to me? No. You meet them once and you're what? best buds now? Are you linked up on social media? Exchanged phone numbers?"

"It's not like that, Nic." His denial just pushed her irritate button harder.

"Oh sure it is. Reece came to you with some scheme to keep me *safe* from getting hurt and you fell in line with their plans. You and he decided I didn't need a say in my life. That I wasn't capable of handling the stress or I was too delicate given what happened before."

He opened his mouth to respond and she held up one finger, silencing him. He laced his hands at the back of his neck and looked skyward. She was probably trying his patience. Well good, because he'd tried hers and if he didn't like the outcome, he should have thought of that when he threw in with her brothers.

"I can accept Liam and Reece treating me like a kid. To them, I'll always be their baby sister whom they have to protect. It's their job and that was drilled into them from the time I was born by our parents, but you. I think the worst part is you treated me like a mindless puppet, instead of your equal."

Tears sprang to the corners of her eyes and she fought to keep them from flowing. Embarrassed, she turned away, hating that her emotions got the better of her, proving him right in that she couldn't handle the pressure.

"Nic, I'm sorry." His soft voice caressed the side of her neck.

"I thought you were different, that you didn't look at me and see a victim. Guess I was wrong."

His warm hands squeezed her shoulders, but she refused to turn around and face him.

"You're one of the strongest people I know."

Her head whipped up and she glanced at him from the corner of her eye. "Then why? Why cut me out?"

He slid his arms around her middle and pulled her back against his hard chest.

"I don't know how this is going to turn out. It's my word against Stone's, unless I can find someone to prove he's lying. The judge can decide to set an example and throw the book at us. I could end up in the brig for a long time. Not to mention that reporter who showed up knew about you and me. I don't want your name dragged through the mud again. What if they find out about my brother? How's that going to look?"

"It doesn't matter. I believe in you and I'm not ashamed to be seen at your side."

"Do you really want to be on the ten o'clock news with the man accused of videotaping you in the shower? A man from a family of criminals? How will that look for your father? For Liam or Reece? Do you think the reporters will leave your mom alone then?"

Damn him for knowing her weakness and playing it against her.

"So tell them your side," she pleaded as she turned to face him, searching his eyes for a sign of hope, but what she saw instead caused her to step back.

Cold determination and distance stared back at her.

"No." He let go and shoved his hands in his back pockets.

Emotions and thoughts she didn't want to face or deal with slammed through her body, swirling around her until she thought she'd explode. Fears and doubts shoved their way out of the box she'd locked them away in to the forefront of her mind and demanded to be seen, heard, and addressed.

"And what if I said that you were right, that I wasn't strong enough to deal with this week and the trial on my own? Would you still stand there and say no?"

"You and I both know you'll be fine."

"All that talk about standing by me. What was that, just lines to get me into your bed?" She hated herself for asking, if only she could ignore the doubts, if only they'd let her.

His jaw clenched and he looked away without responding. His entire body looked like a coil ready to spring.

While her heart felt like it did indeed belong to a china doll and was one blow away from shattering into a gazillion pieces.

"Answer one last question for me, Kyle. Did you have anything to do with the video?"

She held her breath, and prayed to every known deity she'd ever heard of, made promises and bargains, and cursed herself for asking. A day ago the question wouldn't have crossed her mind, much less her lips. Heck, an hour ago it wouldn't have been voiced.

Chills ran over and through her, even though the temperature hovered around ninety-five. Her stomach rolled and the longer he took to answer the sicker she felt.

"If you have to ask, then you're right. It was fun and now it's time to move on." He sauntered to the driver's door of the Charger and didn't even bother to look back at her. "See you around, babe."

The car door slammed, delivering the final blow shattering her heart. The taillights of the Dodge disappeared down the road, as Nic stood alone in the parking lot. She had no idea how long she stayed there staring into the night before she got into her car and drove dry-eyed to the base, handed the gate guard her ID and then parked in the barracks lot. One minute she had been watching his car leave and the next she found herself alone in her room, her plain, beige-walled room that she hadn't bothered personalizing.

What would have been the point?

As soon as the trial was over the boat would be back on schedule and out to sea, until then she had been spending every free minute at Kyle's place. Talking, cooking—well, he cooked, she ate—watching movies, normal stuff people do, but it had felt extraordinary with him. Special. Fun.

She'd missed him the last couple of days and not just his cooking—even though he had skills gifted by the gods—or his backrubs. It was more like the way he laughed at her silly stories of her and her brothers' antics growing up, the way he made her feel like she was the only person on the planet and he wouldn't want to be with anyone else. She'd missed playing with his silky hair and how he'd snuggle into her and the smile that would grace his face, his tough guy attitude with Princess and yet how he never missed a chance to scratch behind her ears or slip her a treat.

It was over.

Was any of it even real for him?

Or was Liam right and it had all been a well-planned scheme to advance his career and bank account? She didn't want to believe it, but he hadn't denied it even when she'd asked him flat out.

Everything inside of her broke at once. The tears rushed down her cheeks, great sobs of sorrow escaped as she slid into her bed.

She'd been such a fool.

It couldn't be true.

She argued back and forth with herself in her head as tears soaked her pillow until there was nothing left inside of her. Her head pounded, but it took energy to get up and get the aspirin from the bathroom, energy she didn't have.

Her phone buzzed and she pulled it out of her back pocket. It was Keith asking if she was okay. No, she wasn't. She was a long cry from okay, but give her a couple of days or weeks, maybe months and she'd pull through this too, for what didn't kill you made you strong. She wasn't dead, and at the rate she was going, she could take on Hercules and kick his butt.

Chapter Nineteen

The following Monday morning Nic took care getting dressed. She wore her uniform like a shield created in a special lab or sent down from Valhalla. Perfect creases, ribbons over her left breast, hair pulled back into a tight bun so no strands could escape, she was the Naval officer poster child. Ignoring the well-meant advice from some to choose pants and downplay that she was different from any other officer on the boat, Nic had opted for her uniform skirt.

She had no intention of letting the judge, trial counselor, or the defense forget for one moment this wasn't about an act against an officer; it was a personal attack by a sexual predator.

If Stone and Tarasov walked with no more than a slap on the wrist, what would happen next? Who would be their next target? A minor? Groups of women? And would they stop at voyeurism or escalate?

The prosecutor had warned her that she'd be called to testify, to tell her story. It wouldn't be easy. She'd have to expose herself in front of so many people. Yet if it meant the two of them could never do this to another, then that knowledge would be her strength as she took the stand.

Pain lanced through her heart at the realization that Kyle wouldn't be there and she'd truly be on her own today. Shoving it away, she opened her room door.

"Surprise!" Lindsey's high bubbly voice shocked Nic, making her take a step back as the petite blonde threw her arms around her.

Nic laughed and returned the hug before releasing her and turning to her companion, Cherise, who enveloped Nic into a mama bear embrace.

"Hey, Sugar. Didn't think we'd let you face today without us, did you?"

Man, have I missed these two.

Nic stepped back in the room and wrapped both friends in another hug and cried happy tears and then cursed, as she'd have to fix her eye make-up again.

"You have no idea how happy I am to see you both, but I didn't expect this. Not that I'm complaining." Nic dropped down on her bed, relief coursing through her.

"We wanted to get here early yesterday, but the first flight we could get on had us landing at eleven last night. However, we come bearing gifts." Cherise held up a familiar bakery bag and the smell of chocolate hit Nic's senses.

"Oh that's right." Lindsey bolted out of the room and came back in with a carrier and handed her steaming cup of chai tea. "And this morning, Miss Prim and Proper wouldn't let us arrive without breakfast in hand."

"I still can't believe you're here."

"Are you kidding? When we went to ask for leave to come up it was denied. Seems special liberty had already been arranged and approved and we're both here representing our boats' support of you." Lindsey dropped into the spot next to her and laid her head on Nic's shoulder. "You are so not alone, my friend."

Cherise pulled up the single chair in the room and sat. "Your brother set it up with our commands. Not that my XO admitted that nugget of info, but I saw your brother down at the boat the other day. Girl, tell me he's single, because those shoulders of his...mmm."

"Eww. That's my brother you're talking about and trust me, you don't want to date the overbearing idiot." Nic sighed and laughed. "Although on second thought. He needs a strong woman he can't bully around to straighten him out. I'll text you his number and where he hangs out, along with all his weaknesses."

"Now that we've got Cherise's love life planned, you need to bring us up-to-speed on what's been going on with you. Then we can talk about hooking me up with your other brother, 'kay?"

Between all three of their schedules they hadn't been able to connect since Nic had pulled back into port. She started at the beginning and filled them in on everything that had happened since reporting onboard the *California*. The shock of seeing Kyle, which earned Cherise a glare from both her and Lindsey.

"Hey, y'all told me not to tell you what I knew."

"I know. My bad."

She told them about the challenge of fitting in, which had them both nodding in agreement and even more when she told them about the moment after the security drill where she'd finally felt like a part of the crew. Then watched the horror on their faces as she described the details of the how everything fell apart from there.

"I can't believe you've had to deal with this on your own, sweetie." Lindsey gave her a squeeze and handed her a chocolate donut with chocolate frosting. Exactly what she needed.

"I haven't been totally alone."

She filled them in on Kyle: the good, the bad, and the ugly.

"I'm sorry Mr. Hot-One-Night-Stand turned out to be Lieutenant Douche," Lindsey said.

"Lindsey," both Nic and Cherise admonished.

"Fine, Lieutenant Dirtbag." Lindsey pulled out another donut and bit into it.

Nic and Cherise made eye contact and laughed. The way Lindsey had ploughed through the Boston crèmes you'd think it had been her heart shattered in the parking lot. For all her talk, Linds had the softest heart of them all and was the biggest romantic she'd ever met.

"That's my sea story." She stood and brushed the crumbs off her hands. "Not quite how I pictured making Naval history and I hate that this will be forever tied to not just me, but to my dad and brother's historical notes too."

Cherise dropped her empty cup into the trash and stood too, smoothing out her skirt. "I doubt that any of them have even given it a thought and I don't envy those working with them today. I'm sure they're fit to be tied at having to stay away instead of being here to comfort you."

"Dad and Mom have already called…twice. We better get moving or I'll be late."

"Let me wash the chocolate off my hands first," Lindsey said and then disappeared into the minuscule bathroom.

Cherise turned to Nic and said, "Can I stick my nose where it doesn't belong?"

"Um, sure."

"Bryant called me last week, so I knew what was going on, especially the part about Kyle. Nic, I don't believe he had anything to do with the video."

Maybe not and she said as much to her friend, but he had his chance to respond. Plus, there were other factors to take in. She may not have liked the way thing went down between them, but with all the free time she'd had lately and distance giving her hormones a rest, now she saw it was for the best.

It's what she kept telling herself on the short drive from the barracks over to the Trial Service Office. When they arrived, she turned off the ignition and sat, unable to move. Heart beating like the wings of a hummingbird, she looked to her friends.

"I don't know if I can do this, if I can face Stone or listen to his lies and see the pity in the judge and everyone's eyes." Tears burned at the backs of her eyes. Damn it. She was so sick and tired of crying. It seemed like it was all she did anymore. Fanning her face, she looked skyward. "I want my life back."

"Sugar, I can march in there and tell the prosecutor that you can't testify if you want." Cherise took hold of her hand and Linds scooted forward to place her hand on Nic's shoulder for support.

"Sweetie, with or without you, they're going to pay for what they did." Lindsey had practically climbed up on the console between the seats to get Nic's full attention. "But with your testimony they'll get a harsher punishment. We'll be there for you the whole time. You're not alone and you can do this."

That's what Kyle said and where was he now that she needed his strength? Nowhere in sight.

Neither friend pressured her any further. They laid out her options and left it for her to decide. They trusted her to do the right thing. To choose wisely.

Unlike the men in her life…and then it hit her. Sitting there, thinking about not testifying, thinking she couldn't do it, that she wasn't strong enough was exactly what she'd accused them of thinking about her. She was living up to their expectation of her failing.

Well, screw that and the idea of taking the coward's way out.

Her mom didn't raise a quitter. It took a woman of strength and determination to stand up to the likes of her dad, and she'd been known to do so on multiple occasions. She pulled a tissue out from the pack she kept in her glove box and wiped her eyes, then rubbed her cheeks to bring the color back to her face and reached for the door handle.

"Let's go show these boys what real women are made of."

Nic and her bodyguards, at least that's how she thought of them as Cherise and Lindsey flanked her on each side, followed the Legalman through the office to the conference room used for hearings. As she rounded a corner her eyes locked with Kyle's. For a moment time stood still, everyone around them disappeared, sound ceased, it was just him and her. They could have been anywhere and for that briefest of moments they were back in the bar in Boston noticing each other for the first time.

Nervous, happy butterflies danced in her belly, heat stole over her and the memory of his soft lips trailing kisses down her neck while his hands did amazing and erotic things to her body.

Then the blue of his eyes darkened to stormy clouds, the corners of his mouth turned down and he looked away. Soft voices rushed at her ears. The click-clacking of heels on tile and the distant ring of a phone jolted her back to the present.

They passed the door Kyle had disappeared into and rounded another corner and went up the stairs. The place was like a maze. The last thing she expected to see as they reached the top was the crowd of people outside the conference room. Not just any crowd, but members of her crew: officers, chiefs, and enlisted.

Had the counselors planned to call everyone in as witnesses?

They'd be in court until winter.

Master Chief Ronquillo stepped up to her first. "Ma'am, Commander Holloway and Lieutenant Commander Ward are already in the room. Until I've testified, prosecution has asked that I wait downstairs."

"Of course, Master Chief."

He shot a look over his shoulder. "If they could, the entire Goat Locker would be here to lend you support." Another look at someone in the crowd and a shake of his head and he was off down the stairs.

Odd, but then most people were in one way or another. Bryant worked his way out of the crowd of men with a smile on his face at the sight of Cherise before disappearing as he turned to Nic.

"No one wanted to wait at the boat, but the skipper won't let everyone in for the hearing. As it is the prosecution is making Mace, Kyle, and me wait in separate rooms downstairs until he calls us to testify. Remember no matter what is said in there today, you're one of us. You've earned the right to serve and none of us would have it any other way. We are family. Got it?"

"Got it." She nodded and he held out his hand and did some kind of complicated handshake, or at least tried to, until they both laughed and he promised to teach it to her on their next deployment.

Excusing himself, he pulled Cherise to the side and Nic looked around for Lindsey who had disappeared a moment ago. Nic didn't know if she was supposed to go into the conference room, a.k.a. courtroom or wait out here. The trial counselor had gone over every step with her, but that was days ago and a fuzzy memory at this point.

The crew talked quietly giving her space, a few flashed smiles and asked how she was holding up, but most sensed that what she really needed this morning was their presence and not the chatter. With the exception of Stone and his buddies, the rest of the guys were great. Sure there were a few who if she'd met at a party or in some other social environment she'd steer clear of, a couple of others she didn't know too well as they were the quiet ones, and of course the braggarts. No family was perfect.

But they were hers.

And she was theirs.

Over the past few weeks, especially when the panic attacks hit she had thought of quitting. Calling in on one of her dad's favors.

Not letting down her crew is what kept her coming back each day.

She almost let them down that morning. Thinking about what was to come she wandered over to a corner to read or rather stare at a plaque on the wall. As much as she appreciated everyone's support, the walls were inching in and air was getting a little scarcer.

Closing her eyes, she counted backwards from twenty while picturing herself standing in the middle of an empty meadow. With each count she focused on slowing her breathing down, on thinking happy thoughts and when it didn't fully work the first time she started over at twenty and repeated the process.

The squeak of a door brought the conversation to a stop. Nic closed her eyes, said a prayer and turned around to see the trial counselor. He made eye contact and then turned back to the room at large.

"I'm sure that I speak for Lieutenant Riley when I say thank you all for coming today. Your show of support is what makes us a superior fighting force. However, I'm sorry to say we cannot accommodate everyone in the courtroom for the trial. There is a large conference room down the hall that has been set up for your use, complete with coffee."

As each officer made their way past her they gave her a high five, fist bump or a love tap on the shoulder.

"Ma'am." Petty Officers Wu and Brooks stopped in front of her and she smiled. "We want you to know that we, the enlisted crewmembers, have your six, ma'am. What Stone, Tarasov and even Smitty did was wrong. We'd stay and wait in the conference room with the others, but we have to get back to the boat—"

"Someone's got to work," Brooks cut in.

"I appreciate you both coming down today. Thank you," Nic said.

"Master Chief Ronquillo has promised to keep the crew updated throughout the day or there would have been a mutiny." Wu chuckled. "We think you're a great officer and leader and we're proud to serve with you, ma'am."

Both snapped to attention.

Nic returned the salute and released both men, touched by their words and actions. She knew she had to face Stone today and the guys had made it easier for her. The verdict was still out on whether she could handle an underway or if the panic attacks would sideline her. If they did, at least she wouldn't have let them down on this day.

"Lieutenant, I brought you a little something to help you through the day." Chief Boone handed her a brown paper bag. "Figured you wouldn't eat much before this started and I know you've got a soft spot for my blueberry muffins."

At his words she peeked in the bag and then held it up to her nose and inhaled deeply. Cinnamon, sugar, and sweet Maine blueberries. She didn't know why some lady hadn't swooped him up yet because he had skills in the kitchen. Normally she'd be diving in, but this morning her stomach threatened to rebel if she so much as took another look. She rolled the bag shut and tucked it into her purse for later.

"Thank you. I'll just save this for after I get on the stand."

"You'll do fine." He fidgeted for a moment, shifting from foot to foot either not sure what to say or do. "I'll go in now and if you start to get nervous, look at me. I know this is hard…had a sister who was mugged once. Facing her attacker in court, it was rough, but she did it and you're a lot like her. Tougher on the inside than you look."

"I thought the master chief ordered you all to stay at the boat today."

"He did and he can write me up if he likes." A spark lit up his eyes as he glanced at the courtroom. "Then again, I might forget how he likes his favorite meal too."

"Consider it an order from me to stay, Chief," Nic said.

As the man slipped through the conference room doors Nic found herself chuckling quietly. Shocked at her ability to find her sense of humor at such a time she looked around to find the waiting area cleared out. Faint voices from down the hall from where her crew had adjourned to kept her from feeling completely alone. Not a peep came from the courtroom and after a few minutes Nic started pacing. How long did it take to read the charges against Stone? She'd never sat in on a court martial before so the exact proceeding details were unknown to her.

Probably a lot like regular court and both counselors had to talk first.

For a second, she thought about putting her ear up to the door to see if she could hear what was going on, then changed her mind and resumed her lap around the room. About half around, she jumped when her phone buzzed in her purse. Her brothers. She considered ignoring both of their messages since neither had enough guts to actually call her after their stunt with Kyle. It would serve the two busybodies right to sweat it out.

Groaning, she clicked on the icon and read first Liam's note and then Reece's and smiled. They may be interfering idiots, but they were hers and she loved them. Both wanted to be there today for her, and would have if it hadn't been for the direct order received from their father to stay away. Both made sure to tell her that was the only reason they weren't standing by her side. She understood.

Not the first sacrifice they'd made as a military family, most likely not the last.

If he could, if it wouldn't jeopardize the outcome of the trial, Pops would be here for her. But not everyone would see him a Patrick Riley, father. The defense could claim he used his position as SUBLANT to sway the panel or judge. No way were they giving Stone anything he could use in an appeal.

Like it or not, he was going down today.

She sent a quick response to her brothers and turned off the phone before shoving it back in her purse. The last thing she needed was the constant buzzing as they sent follow up texts asking for updates while sitting on the stand.

"Lieutenant Riley?" She spun around to face the young Legalman who had brought her upstairs. "They're ready for you."

Nic took a steadying breath, pressed her hand against her rebelling stomach and nodded. With her head held high she walked in and followed the trial counselor's instructions to take the stand.

She refused to make eye contact with Stone.

Damn the rule that prohibited women from wearing their hair down. If she didn't have to pull it back she could have used it as a curtain and completely blocked him from her vision.

Instead she focused on the others in the room, including Commander Holloway—this couldn't be easy on him or Lieutenant Commander Ward. It happened on their watch and ultimately everything that went on under their command was their responsibility. She hadn't even thought to ask if they'd received any backlash.

Chief Boone sat with Cherise and Lindsey, all three giving her supportive nods or thumbs up. A pair of striking hazel eyes met her surprised glance. Chief Faraday, the MA who had come to her aide at the gym and who had escorted the prisoners off the boat, gave her a small smile.

To her right sat the military panel or jury, two female officers, two male officers and one male master chief.

Then there was the judge and of course, the opposing counsel.
The people who would determine a man's fate.

People who would pry into her life.

They had prepped her for this, told her what to expect, what they'd ask, but it hadn't equipped her for coming face to face with the man who had come damn near close to destroying her career and disrupted her life and so many others.

Out of the corner of her eye she could see Stone's smirk as she answered the prosecutor's questions.

Cold rage burned inside her. If she could reach across the room and rip his eyes out...she would. Never before had she been filled with such anger and hatred.

The prosecutor, Lieutenant Commander Marsh, led the conversation to how her life had changed since the discovery of the video and asked her to describe those changes to the court. Words stuck in her throat

The moment had come, the one she'd been dreading all week where she'd have to confess to these brave men and women what a coward she'd become. Would the skipper have her declared unfit for duty when he found out? Words clogged up in her throat at the thought of bringing more shame on her family or letting down her crew. She looked up, met Chief Boone's solemn gaze and told her tale.

When she was done describing the anxiety attacks, the counseling, the sidelong glances and everything else she'd endured she glanced around the room and for the first time looked Stone in the eye. The smirk had disappeared. His shoulders slumped forward. The tips of his ears could outshine a certain reindeer.

Maybe he was starting to get that this hadn't been a game or some harmless prank or whatever had gone on inside his head. Maybe there was hope he wouldn't repeat his mistake. Not that she didn't still want him to pay for what he did, but the fury inside of her dissipated a little, sort of like going from a category five hurricane to a three. She wasn't ready to settle down to tropical storm level just yet.

"Lieutenant Riley, one last question. Given what you've been through and the difficulty you have with public facilities, do you feel you can continue to perform your duties as a submarine officer?"

The million-dollar question.

Could she go back to sea on a sub or any ship for that matter? Did she even want to? What was left here for here? A ruined reputation. Sure her co-workers had her back, but that didn't mean the respect extended to their significant others or to the people in the community. She'd seen some of the online comments, and not everyone faulted Stone for his actions.

Some believed it was to be expected—men and women couldn't control their natural urges when in close confines. Other said she probably asked for it by dressing in too-tight uniforms or flirting with him.

Hard to believe that even now, in the advanced age of technology, enlightenment, and equality many people still blamed the woman.

She didn't really have friends here, other than Kyle and his brother, and now she didn't have them either. This one incident had overtaken her life, cast a shadow over every aspect, leaving very little time, energy, or confidence to seek out new friendships.

If not for Kyle, she would have been a recluse for the past eight weeks.

Maybe it was time to throw in the towel and take her father up on one of his offers? But that was a decision for another day, for now she'd go with the truth.

"Can I fulfill my duties?" She let her gaze land on every face in the panel and the audience before answering. "At this time, I do not know."

Lindsey gasped, Cherise sat rapidly blinking and Chief Boone got up and left the room, but not before Nic saw him wipe the corner of his eye.

The prosecutor sat and turned to the defense attorney, who stated no questions. Nic was excused and they called in Kyle before she'd even taken her seat in between her friends. Lindsey held onto her hand and both said something soothing, but Nic's brain focused solely on Kyle as he took the stand.

He took her breath away in his summer whites.

They ran him through all the expected questions and through it all he kept his calm.

Professional. Precise. Detached.

She could have been anyone to him as his gaze skimmed over her, landing anywhere but on her. Tired of hearing the same questions, Nic focused on Kyle, specifically his body language looking for a sign, any sign that she or the trial affected him. He sat up straight, eyes on whomever was asking him the question, then meeting those of the panel members before turning back to the original person. His responses were concise and clear. No emotion, no stuttering, no stopping to think.

His hands didn't clench in rage like hers had.

No clamped jaw, flattened or curled lip, high color in his cheeks or raised voice to show he was angry.

Wasn't he?

Didn't he hate Stone just a little for what he did? Or had Liam nailed it on the head when he suggested Kyle really was behind it all? Even with Kyle's non-answer, she still had trouble swallowing that story whole.

Not that it matter now.

"Lieutenant Hutchinson," the defense said and paused. "What is your relationship with Lieutenant Riley?"

Kyle's eyes met hers, locked on and for a brief flash she saw what might have been pain or regret. He turned to the lawyer. "Nothing more than a former crewmember."

Pain seared through her heart at his words and denial of what they'd shared. Not that he'd ever said those three magical words, but she had thought they might be on their way to exchanging them.

Nothing more, the words ricocheted around her brain.

Lindsey leaned into her. "Nic, are you okay?" she whispered.

Nic nodded, but didn't look up.

"Sugar, we don't have to sit in here and listen to this crap." Cherise nudged her to move.

Nic squeezed both their hands. "I have to stay. I have to see this finished."

It was only then that she looked up at the squeak of the door and realized Kyle had left as they brought in Petty Officer Tarasov.

Nic sat up straight as they swore in the witness and stared the man down, daring him to look away.

The trial counsel had at him first.

"Petty Officer Tarasov, did you help the defendant, Petty Officer Stone in the creation and distribution of the video involving Lieutenant Riley?"

"Yes, sir. I was his lookout and would warn him whenever anyone headed his way while he was filming her in the shower."

"When did Petty Officer Stone approach you to help him?"

"Initially we talked about it a couple of weeks before we deployed. Just one of those strange conversations while knocking back a few brews at Sally's. I mentioned that money was tight and he said his girlfriend drained his bank account and he needed a way to supplement his income." He turned to the judge before continuing. "We batted some ideas around— all totally legit—and then this guy sitting a few seats away started talking about black market videos and all the money in it." The prosecutor tapped his notepad with what sounded like a pen and looked up at the witness. "How did that lead to the idea of taping Lieutenant Riley when she wasn't assigned to the boat then?"

"It didn't at the time. Stone laughed and said maybe he could get his girlfriend to star in some homemade flicks and that was the end of the conversation." Bright red patches formed on Tarasov's cheeks. "Then the day after we got underway he brought it up again, only this time he'd tape the Lieutenant using the crawl space next to the officer's showers, but he needed me to act as lookout. If I helped him, he'd split the money 60/40 with me."

Tears streamed down Tarasov's face.

"Petty Officer Tarasov, did you and Petty Officer act alone in this endeavor of yours?"

"Yes. I know he's accused Lieutenant Hutchinson of ordering him to make the film, but that's a lie. He wanted me to back him up. I have to live with the mistake I've already made and there's nothing I can do or say to make up for it. I can apologize, not that I expect you to accept it, but I don't have to compound the wrong I've already done with another one."

Stone and his attorney bent their heads together, whispering frantically between each other.

"Lieutenant Cruz, would you like to cross examine the witness," the judge asked.

Stone's attorney stood up. "No, sir. My client would like to change his plea to guilty."

Chapter Twenty

Kyle's tossed his phone onto a chair as he entered his apartment. He'd made one freaking stop on the way home from the Trial Service Office and the phone had been buzzing since he'd walked into the minimart. All he wanted was a beer or six, and the peace of his living room.

"Dude." Keith popped his head out of the bathroom before coming out with a towel wrapped around his bony hips. "You're back early. What happened? Did they nail his nuts to an anchor and drop him in the sound?"

"So much for my peace and quiet." Kyle ignored his brother and unloaded the two six-packs into the fridge, grabbing one before heading into his room to change.

His personal puppy followed.

"So, what's the verdict?"

Kyle stripped off his uniform. Keith leaned against the doorjamb.

"Bro, I've got to be at work soon. You're killing me." He looked away and then glared at Kyle. "I'd text Nic and ask, but yanno... You threatened to kill me and then kick my ass back to California if I made contact with her. Not that that made any sense."

"I don't know. I left." He took a long pull on his beer and relaxed as the cool liquid hit his parched throat.

"Okay." Keith stepped back and disappeared into the bathroom only to pop his head out a second later. "You do know your phone is blowing up, right? Who's texting you?"

"Don't know." Kyle dropped onto the couch and took another drink. "Don't care either. I was ordered to testify and then go home and stay here until I heard otherwise from my command. No one said I had to stay sober."

"What if that's your boss?" Keith looked nervously to the phone.

"If you're so worried about it, check and while you're at it, grab me another." Kyle downed what was left in the bottle.

Keith picked up the phone on his way to the kitchen. He came back, handed him the bottle and tossed the phone into his lap. "You might want to read those messages from Mace. If I didn't have to work, I'd celebrate with you."

Hitting the message icon, Kyle read through the messages including the one from his CO telling him to be back to work in the morning.

Relief should be coursing through him.

He lifted his bottle in salute to karma and laughed. He and his friends had searched all week for someone to clear his name with no luck and yet the person they failed to see was right under their noses and in the end he came through on his own.

There had been no need to cut Nic out of his life to protect her. All he'd done was ruin a good thing. And then he remembered their conversation in the parking lot and her question.

Did you have anything to do with the video?

If she had to ask then ending the relationship was the best thing to do. Without trust they wouldn't make it a year, much less fifty. Just look at Mace and his wife. All their problems boiled down to Amber not having faith in her husband.

Kyle didn't need that kind of bull in his life. He had all the drama he needed and more from his biological family, which reminded him he needed to try to call his mom again and find out what was going on with Kenny.

He took another slug of the beer. Yep, time to put his focus back on his career and family. Having Keith around had been a wakeup call. He might hate the drama and his father drove him up a wall, down the other side and clear across the field, but he missed them.

Keith and Kenny needed him. His mom needed him. Nic didn't.

"Crap."

Kyle turned his head toward the hall waiting with bated breath to find out what the new crisis was all about. He didn't have to wait long before Keith rushed out of his room, his trusty backpack flung over his shoulder. Kyle didn't bother asking, he'd hear anyway.

"I'm running late. Can you give me a ri—" He cut himself off and headed toward the door. "Never mind."

"Here." Kyle dug into his pocket and tossed him the keys to the Charger. "I'm not going anywhere. Just don't scratch it."

His brother thanked him and slammed out the door. Finally the peace and quiet he'd craved all morning. He could get blissfully hammered and not have anyone yammering in his face, asking him questions, or lambasting him for making—what they considered—stupid mistakes.

He finished off the second bottle and had settled on the couch, remote in hand when Princess PITA jumped into his lap. "Ah, now you want my attention and love, now that the other one has gone." He stroked his hand down her back and closed his eyes, lost in the sensation and trying not to compare her fur with Nic's silky hair. "I don't know why we put up with you traitorous females."

Flipping through channels, his third beer sat—untouched—on the table in front of him. Where getting drunk had sounded like a great idea earlier now he didn't care, just like he didn't care what he watched, which was why he'd stopped on... What? The Weather Channel. Great, he'd turned into that guy. Next he'd find golf exciting to watch and have half-dozen cats of his own.

He'd be the crazy cat guy and all the kids in the neighborhood would make jokes about him, egg his house at night and dare each other to ring the bell and run.

Princess purred under his stilled hand bringing his attention back to his surroundings. "Yes, I know. It's all about you."

The phone buzzed and he read the text from his brother:

Call Nic and apologize.

"What the hell do I have to apologize for? I'm not the one who lacked faith in her." He looked down at the cat who meowed in return.

"Flipping A, now I'm asking a four-legged furball for advice." He shook his head and wrapped his hand about the ball of fluff as he leaned forward to grab his beer when the doorbell rang.

"So much for getting peacefully drunk in the sanctity of my home." Holding on to the cat, he headed for the door thinking it was the guys since he hadn't responded to their text messages yet.

All the air in his lungs rushed out as he stared at the last person he'd expected to see. She'd been crying, not hard enough to leave her pretty almond shaped eyes bloodshot, just enough to gloss them over and turn the tip of her nose pink.

"You left before the trial ended." Her soft voice held a touch of sadness and uncertainty.

"Didn't see a need after I testified." He stepped back to let her enter.

"You missed all the fun with Tarasov's testimony. Stone pled guilty. I'm not sure if five years in prison, with a reduction to an E1, all loss of his pay and a dishonorable discharge is justice or not." She scratched the cat's ears and wandered in to the room.

"You think he should have got a longer sentence?"

Considering the man was charged with four felonies, Kyle thought they should have given him the max. Even then, twenty-eight years didn't seem long enough.

"A year for each offence plus one wouldn't have been enough this morning before I took the stand, but now... Does it matter? It's over. You've been cleared of any wrongdoing. A week from now everyone will be back to their normally scheduled lives, but will the sentence reverse the damage he caused?"

"No." Kyle gestured to the chair as he and Princess resumed their spot on the couch. It was the only way he could guarantee he'd keep his hands off of Nic, because even though his fingers itched to pull out the pins holding her hair in place and then feel their silky strands, he wasn't ready to forgive and forget.

"There's a reason for that old saying, the pen is mightier than the sword." Nic glanced at his beer and scrunched up her nose. "It's barely noon and you're drinking?"

"It's happy hour somewhere." He lifted the bottle he had no interest in and saluted her before taking a drink. "Why are you here? The guys already told me the outcome, so if that was your intention, thanks but I'd rather celebrate on my own."

She scowled again at his bottle. "I'm sorry."

That stopped the next drink. "For?"

"So many things." She laughed, but the sound was somewhere between desperation and frustration. "For you getting dragged into this mess, listening to my brother, but mostly for even thinking for a moment that you could have—"

"Leave."

The shock on her face should have had him apologizing; instead it fed the fire stoking his anger and disappointment.

"Excuse me?" She sat there, stunned.

"Look, apology accepted. Now, can you please leave?" He sat the cat aside and stood, prepared to walk her to the door.

She stood and didn't walk to the door, but walked right up to him until they were within an inch of each other. Until he could smell the vanilla and warm sugar that was distinctly Nic without taking a deep breath.

He could see the strain lines around her mouth and the faint smudges beneath her eyes.

"I think that's the first time you've lied to me, Kyle Hutchinson, because your tone says you clearly don't accept my apology. Your choice, but I'm saying it again. I'm sorry. I was wrong. I was mad and scared and I missed you, so I let my fears and insecurity rule my mouth instead of my head and my heart."

He grabbed her arm when she stepped away. "Is that why you practically ran from my bed when your dad called to tell you about the allegation? Because you can't say you missed me then or that I had done anything to warrant your doubts. If Mace and Bryant hadn't showed up when they did, I would have been the one on trial for assault and wouldn't have cared, because he violated you. You *were worth* throwing my career away for."

Tears shimmered in her eyes and he released her.

She came to apologize, all he had to do was say okay and they could go back to where they'd been before, but he didn't want a relationship based on great sex and casual friendship. He wanted a woman who loved him enough to throw it all away for him, the way he *had* felt for Nic.

Had.

Were worth.

Past tense because no matter what he had felt for her or what he might still feel, he'd accept nothing less than a full partner who was willing to invest, sacrifice, and believe just as much as he was in them.

And the painful truth was Nic was that person.

She backed away, tears slipping down her face.

"You have every reason and right to hate me. I don't blame you either because I did act like an idiot." She made it to the door and stood with her arm outstretched, hand on the doorknob. "I made a mistake, a huge one, and now I have to pay. Unlike, Stone's punishment, mine will be a lifelong sentence."

By the time his brain registered the words, Nic was out the door and gone before he could ask what she meant.

* * *

Standing in the conference room, with a cup of coffee in his hand, Kyle observed the beehive of activity on the pier outside. A twinge of envy twisted inside him. Shore duty was great. What wasn't to love: regular office hours, going home to sleep in a king-sized bed, picking your own meals, and fresh air and sunshine every day. Ask any submariner, as much as they longed for shore duty, every time a boat pulled out, it took a piece of their heart with it.

"You're missing it already." Mace joined him at the window. "It's only for a couple of weeks. Ask nicely and maybe your CO will let you join us."

"Yeah, doubt that." Kyle took in his friend's profile and relaxed stance. "You'll miss it soon enough. Put your resignation in yet?"

"Nope and not going to either."

Kyle turned away from the window to focus on the man next to him, but not before he caught sight of a slight build in a baggy overalls. She'd lost more weight. He'd have to make a quick call down to Chief Boone. Maybe he could double up on Nic's cookie supply.

Mace nodded toward the boat. "Have you talked to her since last Monday?"

"No, but that's not important. Why aren't you dropping your papers? What about your reconciliation with Amber? The baby?" He gestured to the empty seats around the conference table but Mace declined.

"Turns out I'm not going to be a father."

Kyle reached out in support and Mace shook his head.

"Oh, she's going to be a mom. I'm just not the father of *her* child." His voice wasn't filled with any of the emotions Kyle expected to hear—anger, jealousy, pain. How could Mace be so zen when his life was falling apart? He started to ask, but Mace looked out the window and down at his watch.

"Look, I made a mistake and didn't fight for my wife or marriage. That's on me. Learn from Uncle Mace. You love the woman. Go after her. Beg her to forgive you, whether you made the initial mistake or not. Forgive her and move on with your lives…together. Or be a bonehead and be miserable for the rest of your life." He clapped Kyle on the shoulder. "See you in a couple of weeks. I expect chocolate and flowers waiting for me on the pier, unless you smarten up and decide to give them to someone else."

Kyle turned back to the window, his gaze instantly seeking out Nic's form as she gave orders before heading for the boat. She turned once, looked in his general direction—not that she could see him—and gave a little salute.

He stayed in place until the boat disappeared down the Thames River.

For the rest of the day he was useless, Mace's word replaying over and over in his head. Was he making a mistake letting her go? The question plagued him all the way home. Opening the door the smell of pizza greeted him first, then a loud meow from Princess PITA, which must have alerted Keith to his arrival.

"Good, you're home. I'm starving." His brother handed him a bottle of water and a plate. "Long day?"

"Aren't they all these days?" He loaded up his plate and sat at the table they never used sensing something was coming.

"Mom called. They arrested Woody and his men in an early morning sweep. Kenny will stay in the safe house until he's testified, but the DA is going to do everything he can to keep them all in lock up until then and push the court date up. She and Dad send their love."

Right, more like Mom sent hers. Then another thought hit Kyle square in the chest and he pushed the pizza away.

"Does this mean you're moving back home?"

Could Nic have been any more right when she'd predicted that within a week of the trial everyone would be back to their regularly scheduled lives? With Keith out from under his feet, Kyle could get back to his: focused on his career, no cares, and no responsibility outside the job.

"Aww, you sound like you'd actually miss me, big bro." Keith smirked and then turned sober on him. "I'm touched, but no. There's no future for me in Citrus Park. The farms are drying up, there's no industry, no jobs. I've been talking to Nic about what comes next for me. She's been a big help."

"Did you decide to enroll at the community college for fall?"

"No, I enlisted in the Navy."

Kyle chocked on his water. "Excuse me?"

The smirk returned to his brother's face. "Yep, signed on the dotted line this morning. You're looking at a future Damage Controlman."

"Subs or surface?"

"Subs, if they'll have me."

Pride filled Kyle's chest at his brother's choice. He'd miss the kid though. Taking a bite out of his pizza, Kyle couldn't stop smiling at Keith's news. After the way everything else had been going lately, he was sure his brother would have headed back to dead-end Citrus Park and gotten mixed up with all the wrong people like Kenny. He'd hoped for Keith to enroll in college, but understood it wasn't the right path for everyone.

"So, now that we got me settled, what about you?"

"What about me," Kyle asked around a mouthful of cheese.

"Are you going to fix things with Nic when she gets back?"

"Here I was thinking how much I'd miss you. When do you leave?"

"In a month. Plenty of time to make sure the two of you don't screw things up again."

Kyle left his brother to the rest of the pizza to change clothes, but what he'd really changed was his attitude. Family wasn't so bad, sure they could complicate your life and bring about headaches and stress, but they also made you smile and had your back when you needed it. Sort of like a submarine crew.

Yeah, he'd miss his brother when he left for boot camp, but if Kyle played his cards right, he'd have a new roommate to keep him on his toes by then. First, he needed to correct a few mistakes of his own.

Chapter Twenty-One

The underway went smooth as silk…with a few almonds thrown in to keep Nic on her toes. Her first time using the officers' shower, she might have broken a speed record after she inspected every crack and crevice. Silly, but necessary to keep the anxiety at bay. And bless the crew, they had treated her no different than they had before her world had imploded on the last trip.

Of course the soft serve ice cream machine had to break, which meant she caught flak from the whole crew and especially the skipper.

They teased, pushed buttons and played practical jokes on each other. Exactly what she'd expect. The skipper had declared on the 1MC that morning he was proud of the crew and the training patrol had been a success.

So why then was she sitting cross-legged on her rack dreading the return home?

Life was back to normal.

The rest of the crew buzzed around the boat, happy chatter keeping them going as they slipped through the water home. Chief Boone had kicked his cooks out of the galley for a bit and made cookies for the whole crew. Hers, of course, had been twice the size and loaded with chocolate chips and nuts. Every time she saw him, he handed her some kind of fattening treat and her uniform showed the proof.

A knock on her open door brought her head up and a smile on her face. "Doc Corbett, come on in."

He pulled out the lone chair and sat with his elbows resting on his knees. "Feels good to be going home, doesn't it?"

Not really, but she'd keep that to herself.

"Is your family meeting you on the pier?" She smiled. "Homecomings, especially seeing the excitement on the kids' faces always get me. You'd think after all these years I'd be immune."

"I hope that never happens, after all, they're the reason we do this. The sacrifice we make, it's all about keeping our country and our loved ones safe." He rubbed his jaw, which was probably sensitive as most of the crew didn't shave while underway until the day they pulled into port. "I think the wife and kids will be there. What about you? Who's meeting you on the pier?"

No one and she had no one to blame but herself.

Mace and Bryant both tried to talk to her about Kyle, but what they failed to realize was that she had tried to mend the rift between them. Neither accepted her response and called both her and Kyle all sorts of foolish.

"Not this time. I expect my parents might come up when we return from our next full deployment, but not for training ops."

His face scrunched up in confusion for a minute. Maybe he forgot she was single and what it was like for those who didn't have families nearby.

"Huh. Well it's a gorgeous day out and you'll enjoy the sun as we pull into port. The Captain wants you topside when we do. I pulled the first kiss ticket."

He excused himself and left Nic smiling. Lucky guy.

Maybe someday she'd have some to enter her name in the raffle.

Twenty minutes later she was topside and watching the pier with all the families come into sight. The skipper had told her she was to disembark after the first kiss and first hug winners. Normally all the pomp and ceremony was saved for deployments, not training patrols, but given how their last time out, she could understand the change in routine. Boost the crew's morale.

The tug pushed the boat at a snail's pace toward their slip. Music blared from speakers set up under a tent and friends and families cheered. There were welcome home banners and bouquets of flowers and balloons. Kids jumped up and down and pointed, waving to their dads. The crew held rank. The closer they got the bigger the smiles on the boat grew.

She would have rather waited in her stateroom for the rest of the crew to take liberty. Not because she disliked homecomings. She hadn't lied to Doc about how they got to her. She still cried happy tears when the kids rushed into their dads' waiting arms, when sailors laid eyes on their babies for the first time or the sweet look of joy that overcame couples when they were once again in each other's arms.

Since she'd be one of the first ones off, she'd offer to take pictures for people as long as they didn't mind a few blurry photos. Then she'd head back to her room and do... what? Get a good night's rest and start living the rest of her life, that's what. Somewhere around the halfway point of the patrol she'd decided she could handle the close confines and was able to put the last couple of months behind her, so now it was time to start living. Find an apartment. Make friends. Get involved in the community.

All the things she'd done prior to BS (before Stone).

She didn't need Kyle to fill her time or make her happy.

At the thought of him her gaze darted to the building he worked in. Was he up there watching them pull in? Did he miss her half as much as she missed him?

She'd call Keith too. Not to check on his brother, but to check on him and see if he followed through with his plans to enlist. It was also time to call her brothers and put them out of their misery, or maybe that was add to it. After all, it was a sister's job to harass her siblings. She had left without clearing the air between them and it hadn't set well during her time away. Pains that they were, she loved them and could only make them pay for so long.

Not that she expected either to learn a darn thing from the silent treatment.

Maybe she'd talk her mom into flying up after she found her own place and the two of them could go shopping for furniture and supplies.

Lost in her own head, making plans, Nic hadn't noticed they'd docked until the XO nudged her. She went through the motions of asking permission to leave, saluted the two officers and made her way down the gangplank. She smiled at Doc surrounded by his wife and two teenagers, scooted around Petty Officer Wu and his wife, who had won the first hug, and looked around.

A giant bouquet of flowers came down in front of her. She spun around to tell the giver they had the wrong person only to come face-to-face with Kyle.

"Welcome home, Lieutenant Riley." His warm, husky voice made her smile.

"Are the flowers from my mom or Keith?" *Please say neither*, she silently begged.

Seeing him, all she wanted to do was wrap her arms around his neck and beg him to forgive her.

He looked confused. "Did you want them to be from my brother?"

She shook her head, not trusting her voice at the moment.

"A few of months ago I thought I had everything I wanted or needed in my life, and then this amazing woman I met in a bar showed me I was wrong."

"Kyle—"

"Shhh." He put one finger on her lips. "Give me a minute and then you can tell me to get lost. Okay?"

She nodded.

"I've made mistakes in my life, Nic. A lot of them. The first was running from home and not looking back or thinking of how it would impact my family. I thought leaving would be the best for everyone, but it wasn't, especially my brothers. Thankfully, my mom forced Keith on me and I was given a second chance to be a big brother."

"He's a great kid who looks up to you."

"And you. He told me how you've helped him deal with Kenny, the separation from home, opening up to me and his future. Thank you. There have been other mistakes, mostly small, inconsequential ones that have been forgotten over time. But the only other one that really matters is the mistake I made with you."

"I think we both made mistakes." Her voice dropped low. She was afraid that the next words out of his mouth would be that he was leaving.

"We did and we've paid our penance. We were under a lot of stress, and I don't know about you, but I was scared out of my wits. My career was on the line, I didn't know how to fix the problem and the woman I loved doubted my moral compass. Not that—"

"Wait." She held her hand up. "You loved me?"

"I did, I do… I love you, Lily Nicole Riley and if you'll forgive me I'll spend the rest of our lives showing you exactly how much."

She couldn't breathe. There were too many people around, with too much noise and her pulse pounding in her ears. She had to be imagining words that hadn't been said.

"What are you saying, Kyle?"

"Marry me, Nic?" His eyes sparked with desire and love as he lifted a small gray box up to her. "Open it. Say you forgive me, that you love me. Say yes."

Nic bit down on her lip and chewed. Her gaze was glued on the box. Could it really be that easy, forgive, forget and say yes? With trembling hands she took the box and opened it. Inside was a beautiful white diamond set in the middle of a love knot made out of rose gold.

"Make me a promise and I'll do the same." She'd learned a lot over the past few months. Most importantly that life was better with the person you loved at your side, but it took work. "Next time life gets stressful, and we both know it will with our lifestyles, we'll talk. No shutting each other out. No making decisions without consulting the other. No listening to my brothers. We each have faith in the other and in ourselves."

Kyle looked over her shoulder and grinned ear-to-ear. Mace and Bryant were probably recording this whole thing for him. Whatever, she didn't care; because right now what mattered the most was the man in front of her and his answer.

"I promise." Kyle kissed her on each cheek, then her forehead and finally on the tip of her nose. "Is that a yes?"

"Yes, it's a yes." She laughed and threw her arms around him. Looking him in the eyes she whispered for his ears only, "I love you."

They sealed the deal with a kiss that left Nic breathing hard and wishing they were back at his apartment.

"I think maybe I should put the ring on before you change your mind or I before I lose it out here. Then there are some people who want to say something to you."

She held up her hand and Kyle slipped on the ring. It was a perfect fit. He kissed her again, framing her face in his hands.

"I love you, Nic. Now, tomorrow, and forever."

Clapping and cheers broke out nearby and he turned her around to find not just Mace, Bryant and Keith, but her whole family.

Tears of happiness sprung to her eyes and she laid her head on Kyle's chest.

"Seems you were either pretty confident in my answer or darn right ballsy, Lieutenant Hutchinson."

"No risk, no reward and hearing you say yes was worth putting it all on the line. And if you didn't say yes, I had a plan B."

She looked into his steel-gray eyes and grinned. "Do I want to know?"

"It involved getting naked."

The smoldering look in his eyes caused her heart to stumble and trip over itself just like the night they met. Once again she had a desire to grab his hand and make a mad dash to be alone, but where she had once only saw a quick interlude, now she saw a lifetime of love and happiness.

If you enjoyed *Love Runs Deep* be sure not to miss Gail Chianese's

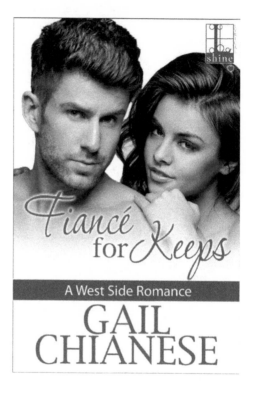

*With one cancelled wedding, one weekend fling,
and a lot of history behind them, can a
career-minded former couple finally get on the
fast-track to true love—with each other?...*

Tired of working long hours with no one to come home to, ER doctor Denise Saunders accepts a chance to compete on a reality dating show. But there's only one person she trusts to review the contract—attorney Brody Nichols, the man she left at the altar five years ago. Needless to say, Brody is floored. Unable to convince her to opt out, and unwilling to stand by while she risks getting burned by the spotlight, he can only think of one way to protect the woman he's never stopped loving...

Denise expected some surprises on *Finding Mr. Right,* but she's beyond shocked to meet the last contestant: *Brody.* She doesn't know whether to feel punk'd, pissed, or relieved. Yet as a series of hot hijinks and dueling bachelors ensues, Denise can't deny he's The One—and always has been. She knows she'll have to come clean about their past to the show's other contestants—and to Brody. But once she tells him the real reason she played the runaway bride, Brody may be the one to walk. Is honesty a risk she's brave enough to take?...

Read on for a special excerpt!

A Lyrical Shine e-book on sale now.

Chapter 1

"I've got good news and bad news for you, kid." Dr. Denise Saunders looked down into the hopeful eyes of her twelve-year-old patient, Johnny. "The good—you're going to live. The bad—you may die yet. Give your mom another scare like today and she just might kill you herself. Justifiably so."

"I almost had it," his small voice murmured as Johnny looked up through ridiculously long lashes at her and his mom.

"Almost had it?" his mom squeaked. "You're lucky you didn't break your neck. I still don't understand what in the world you were thinking."

Denise slid the X-ray into place and turned on the light to show her patient and his mom. "See this dark line here, running across the white? That shows you have a simple fracture of the radius—a broken arm. That's good, because we don't have to operate, but you will have to wear a cast for about six weeks while it heals." She turned to Johnny's mom, a woman about her own height of five-six, with darker brown hair and eyes that seemed well beyond her years. "Thankfully, kids heal pretty fast. He shouldn't have any long-term effects."

The thanks Mrs. Ford extended didn't reach her eyes. "So listen up, Blaze," she teased, using the last name of the superhero the boy had tried to emulate. "If you promise me you won't try any more super stunts, especially without supervision and protection, I won't dress your cast in Hello Kitty wrap. Deal?"

"They make it look so easy," Johnny grumbled, slinking down in the sterile bed.

Denise reached out and ruffled his hair. "Of course they do, silly. Johnny Blaze signed a pact with the devil and the Human Torch was mutated. Plus, they have the magic of Hollywood behind them."

"Johnny, honey, what are you talking about?" his mom asked.
"*Ghost Rider* and *Fantastic Four,*" Denise and Johnny
answered together.
"Are you kidding me? You could have been killed. You're never
watching those movies again," his mom choked out.
Denise gave Johnny a sympathetic smile before turning to his mom.
"Mrs. Ford, this is going to take a couple of minutes and we need to wait
for my nurse, Jenna, to gather up the supplies. Would you like a cup of
coffee or tea? We have a break station just outside the room."
Normally, Denise would have passed this task—wrapping Johnny's
arm—off to an intern with her nurse's assistance, but things were quiet in
the ER, as they had been for the past couple of weeks, so she could afford
to take the luxury of talking to her patient's mom and seeing this through
to the end. It was kind of a nice change of pace. Mrs. Ford cast a long,
frustrated look at her son and stood up. "I'd love some, thanks."
Denise led her outside the room and to the little causeway next to
it that allowed staff to zip from one side of the ER to the other, to get
patients ice, water, Jell-O, and the occasional snack to hold them over
on long shifts.
"Do you have kids, Dr. Saunders?"
Denise shook her head and ignored the tick-tock of her internal clock,
reminding her that birthday number thirty-three would soon be here.
"It's a challenge, especially with only one parent. Still, I wouldn't
trade one moment of motherhood. Well, maybe I'd skip a few, like when
he gets these wild ideas that he can be a superhero."
Denise pointed to the coffee and tea carafes and told Mrs. Ford to help
herself, and pulled a bottle of water out from the minifridge for herself.
"Do you mind my asking, what does his dad do for a living?"
"John Sr. was in the Navy. They said he was a hero when he gave
his life to save what appeared to be an innocent family. The woman and
children were decoys and John shouldn't have been in the sandbox to
begin with. He joined the Navy, not the Army or the Marines. He belonged
on a submarine. Safe. Away from land mines and suicide bombers." Mrs.
Ford looked to Johnny's room before exhaling a deep sigh and turning
back to Denise. "That was two years ago."
"Ah, I see." And she did, because this had been Johnny's third time in
the ER in the past two years after pulling a dangerous stunt. It all made
sense now, and her heart broke, knowing what this child had lost and all
he'd continue to miss out on in the coming years. "You're doing a great
job with your son."

"But if I don't do something soon, he might try something even crazier."

"I'm not a psychologist, Mrs. Ford, so take this with a grain of salt." Denise took a sip of her water. "Kids tend to deal with loss differently than adults do; they lose themselves in books and movies. They block events out and sometimes they try to prove nothing bad can ever happen to them."

"What do I do?" Mrs. Ford whispered, tears shimmering at the corners of her eyes. "I've tried talking to him. He tunes me out."

"There's a group of psychologists here in Providence who specialize in children. They practice behavior therapy, so they could help Johnny funnel his pain, confusion, and anger into acceptable— and safe—activities. I'll get you their card before you leave."

"Thanks." The mom stepped toward the room and stopped. "Would you really wrap his cast in Hello Kitty?"

"In a heartbeat."

Thankfully, she didn't have to resort to drastic measures as Johnny apologized to his mom as soon as they walked into his room and promised both women he wouldn't try any more stunts on his own. In short order, they got his arm wrapped in the cast and sent the boy and his mom on their way, with the psychologists' card tucked safely in Mrs. Ford's purse.

"I think you have another admirer," Jenna Beck, nurse and confidante extraordinaire, informed her as she cleaned up the mess in the exam room.

"Now, if only I could find a guy over four feet tall and of legal age who's as easily impressed."

"It might help if you didn't look like you were still waiting to graduate high school. Do you still get carded?"

"All the time."

"So not fair." They walked out of the room and headed to the nurses' station. "I'd like to find a guy who doesn't want to play doctor when he finds out I'm a nurse." Jenna pulled a syringe out of her pocket, hit the end, and turned it into a pen. "Of course when I whip one of these puppies out, they tend to change their tune rather quickly."

"Sheer genius." They joined two of the other nurses, Valerie and Kris, along with her fellow resident on duty, Dr. Shad Davis, at the desk. "Anything new come in?" Denise handed over the hospital copies of Johnny's discharge paperwork to Valerie.

"Nope. Time to enjoy the calm before the weekend storm, where we'll all put in overtime. Thankfully, Valentine's isn't as bad as New Year's or the Fourth of July," Kris said.

"It's not like I have a social life anyway. May as well work." Denise could remember a time when she'd had that someone special in her life to share the day's stories with, to go out to dinner or a show with, but she'd given it all up for the dark side. Only there weren't any cookies, just long hours, cold nights, and her own internal clock ticktocking away, reminding her life was slipping by.

"Tell me about it," Shad chimed in. "I figured because I never have time to hang with friends outside of here, I'd join the social media bandwagon and sign up on Facebook. At least then, in between patients and while studying for my fellowship, I could catch up with family. Big mistake."

"What did you do, get addicted to one of those games?" Jenna asked as she dropped into the free chair.

"I never made it that far. I picked a night after a particularly long and emotionally draining day. Got as far as filling in my profile and uploading my picture before I fell asleep at my desk. The next morning I woke up to over a hundred e-mails in my in-box with some interesting and creative suggestions. They even uploaded pictures. I think I saw more naked bodies in one day than I have in my entire medical career."

Jenna shot her a raised eyebrow and started laughing. Valerie and Kris, who were older and a bit on the conservative side, exchanged quiet smiles.

"Doesn't sound like Facebook to me. Not that I'm on there." Denise pulled her water bottle out of her pocket and took a long drink.

"Well, the site started with an *F* and had the word *book* in it." Shad turned about ten shades of crimson.

"You didn't?" All four women asked before breaking out in laughter.

"My next-door neighbor even responded. With a picture. Au naturel. He's eighty!"

Denise choked on her water. Tears streamed down Jenna's face, while Valerie covered her mouth with her hand.

"Do you know how awkward it was running into him at the mailbox? I mean, what do you say when you've seen your eighty-year-old neighbor naked, with an offer to do bad things to you?"

"How's it hanging? Oh, never mind. I already know," Kris suggested innocently.

Denise lost it then. The laughter stole her breath away, and the quieter she tried to be the harder it was to breathe. "Clearly you need to disappear, Shad. Change your phone number, delete your e-mail, maybe even move to Nome, Alaska. If anyone asks if you're Dr. Shad Davis from Providence, deny, deny, deny. I could hook you up with a good plastic surgeon. A little nip on the nose and chin, a little tuck around the eyes, and you might be able to return in about ten years or so."

"I've learned my lesson. The Internet is evil. I'm never going on social media again. My friends and family can reach me the old-fashioned way, via phone or in person." His phone pinged in his pocket and when he pulled it out and looked at the screen, Shad hung his head. "I'm going to go delete my e-mail account."

"Poor guy." Denise wiped the tears away and took in a few deep breaths. "But strangely, I feel better about my life all of a sudden. I'll be in the breakroom if anyone needs me."

As Denise walked away from the desk, where the three nurses were still chuckling, she made a mental note: do not attempt social media. Which really wasn't much of an issue for her anyway, except for Pinterest. She loved skimming the recipes. Not that she had the time, energy, or desire to cook real meals. Maybe if she had someone to share the food with, she'd be inspired to try some. As it was, cooking for one didn't require a lot of thought.

Pop a DiGiorno in the oven and twenty minutes later—better than delivery.

The breakroom was empty and Denise grabbed a packet of PopTarts—unfrosted of course—and dropped onto the sagging couch. She never noticed the beeps and hisses of the machines while on the floor. After all these years, it was white noise. But the minute she walked into the deserted lounge the quiet enveloped her, at times almost suffocatingly so and at others calming her nerves, allowing her to center her mind and energy. A must to survive the busy shifts in the emergency department.

Today it brought peace. They told you not to get emotionally attached to patients, yet it was hard, especially with the kids. And Johnny. . . well, he'd stolen her heart the first time he'd been brought in. He'd fallen off a ladder while trying to take Christmas lights off the front of his house. His mom had been at work and he'd wanted to surprise her. He'd looked up at Denise from beneath those ridiculously long dark lashes and said he was trying to help, so his mom could relax when she came home. How could her heart not go out to him?

The story of his dad had done more than touch Denise's heart; it had ripped it to shreds and reminded her of how lucky she was to have all her family. It left an overwhelming need to hear her mom's voice, see her sisters, and feel her dad's strong arms around her. She made a quick call to her mom, left a message when voice mail came on. Next she shot off a couple of texts to the not-so-forgotten middle child, Elysia, and the baby, Rhachel, asking when they were free for a girls' night out. Both lived within ten minutes of her, but their schedules kept them miles apart. Because she knew her dad, who worked as an airport ramp agent, wouldn't be able to take her call, she made a note to pick up flowers and stop by to see her parents over the weekend.

Nibbling on the pastry, she pulled up her e-mail and worked her way through sales notices, sexual stimulant ads, and invitations to engage in illicit affairs. The last e-mail in her box had one of those oddly familiar names she couldn't place right away. For several minutes she racked her brain trying to put a face with the name or at least place how she knew them. Her finger hovered over the Delete button as she debated whether to Open or Discard.

"What the heck," she said to no one in particular and held her breath as she clicked open the message. Her eyes locked on the first line.

Dear Denise, Congratulations! You've been selected to be the next Ms. Right on Finding Mr. Right.

Wow! Really?

She had put the show out of her mind. Who wouldn't have, after six months of not hearing anything? And, well, a few months ago she'd thought her days of being single had ended. As evidenced by the no social life and volunteering to work on Valentine's Day, things hadn't worked out as she'd hoped. A quick scan of the contents had her heart pounding, her palms sweating, and her stomach jumping up and down. Basically, it was like her first day as an intern— scared spitless and as excited as a kid on her first trip to Disneyland.

A second read-through and she noted the schedule. Filming began in three weeks. A crew would arrive in two weeks to film her intro, as they wanted to capture the "real" her, both at home and work. She would need to read the attached contract. Sign it. Complete the nondisclosure, eligibility, and release forms. Sign them. Complete the medical history form—easy-peasy. Sign it—okay, she got it, sign her life away. She couldn't pull up all the documents on her antique phone, but she got the feeling her head would spin when she did. Three weeks didn't leave a lot of time to put your life on hold. Good thing she didn't really have a life and had a lot of vacation days saved up. Not to mention she needed to shop for a new wardrobe and lose those ten stubborn pounds.

"Hey, whatcha doing?" Jenna poked her head into the breakroom.

Denise waved her in and put her finger to her lips. "You're never going to believe this." She filled her friend in on the e-mail contents while keeping an eye on the door to make sure no one else popped in. "So, what do you think? Should I go?"

Over the summer it had seemed like a great idea. Take a little break from the monotony of work. Hang out by the pool. Go on surreal dates with gorgeous men who were hot for her. Travel to exotic locations. Find someone to share her life with without all the fuss and muss of blind dates or hanging out in bars. Now? She was torn. Not that anything had really changed. One incredible weekend didn't change the past or—clearly—her future.

"Yes! Are you crazy? First, you get to escape the cold because that stupid groundhog saw his shadow. We should feed him to the wolves. Second, you'd get to live in that amazing mansion with that beautiful pool. Not to mention you'll go on cool, fun dates and visit new places. Why would you say no?"

"I don't know about that. According to the e-mail, they're moving to a mansion in the San Francisco area for a change of pace and scenery. It can still be pretty cold there in March." The second question was the issue, and while it was easy, it wasn't simple. Mainly, her job. She'd worked long and hard to finish her internship and residency at the hospital. "What if they won't give me a leave of absence? Then I'm out of a job and there's no guarantee he'll be the guy of my dreams."

"You won't know unless you go. Unless you're still hung up on Brody."

"What?" Her head reared back and she looked at her friend like she'd lost her mind. "Why would you think that?"

"Oh, come on, Denise. I know he was the guy from the wedding who you spent the weekend with in October." Jenna popped the last piece of Denise's Pop-Tart in her mouth and gave her a look, daring her to deny it.

"I never said it was Brody."

"You never said it wasn't."

"Okay, so what? I spent a wonderful, romantic weekend with my ex-fiancé. And maybe I thought—hoped—it would be the start of us rebuilding our relationship. Obviously, by his silence, that isn't what Brody was looking for."

Jenna crossed the room and pulled a bottle of water out of the fridge, tossed Denise a fresh one, and grabbed one for herself. She took a couple of sips with a questioning look on her face. The woman was worse than an amateur sleuth in a cozy mystery when she didn't know an answer.

"So he didn't call you after the fact?"

"Nope." Denise slunk down farther into the couch, knowing what was coming next.

"Did you call him?" her friend asked point-blank.

"It's complicated." Denise pulled the elastic out of her hair, ran her hands over her head, and rebound her ponytail, pulling it good and tight. "No, it's not. Hon, you walked out on him the first time. Doesn't it make sense that he might have been waiting for you to call? For you to show that this was more than a weekend fling?"

Denise hung her head between her pulled-up knees and groaned. She'd been wondering about this very thing for months. Hearing her friend say the obvious out loud made her feel like a scared idiot.

"If you're going to go on the show, you need to make sure your heart is available, my friend."

"What are you suggesting, o wise one?" She pretty much knew, but it was always good to get a second opinion.

"You know you need to see Brody, because I think he's the one. Either complete the circle and move on, allowing yourself an honest chance with Mr. Right, or try to work things out with your ex. I vote for option two."

Jenna made it all sound so simple. Nothing with Brody had ever been simple and Denise didn't believe in soul mates. Yes, the man drove her nuts—in all the right and the wrong ways. Passionate, honest, fun, loyal to a fault. Yet stubborn as a mule and when mad, a jackhammer couldn't get through the walls he threw up. None of that meant he was the only guy for her. Denise dropped her head back against the couch as she thought about all that had gone on in the past few months and years—they had a complicated history—and made her decision. Before she could change her mind, she grabbed her phone, typed a response, and hit Send.

"What did you just do?" Jenna asked.

"I told them I couldn't be more thrilled to participate." She shrugged her shoulders as she stood up. "Maybe I'll find my dream guy, maybe not. I don't believe Brody and I are meant to be together. We had our chances. If I'm wrong, maybe this will get him up off his duff and come after me for once."

"And work?"

"I'm on my way to Simon's office now. Wish me luck."

She practically bounced down the hall to her supervisor's office. Denise gave him the rundown of the offer, reminded him of her accrued leave and, a few minutes later, had his reassurance that it shouldn't be a problem.

***

Brody smiled as he listened to his mom rant about his lifestyle. It was an old argument, one he heard at least once a week and one he knew was delivered out of love and not disappointment.

"Mom, I'm fine—"

"Brody Andrew Nichols, wipe that smile off your face and stop mollifying me. You need a life. Working sixty-plus hours a week, an occasional barbeque with the boys, or a quick game of lacrosse before you return to your office isn't living."

"How do you know I'm smiling?"

"I'm your mom. I know all."

"Really? What're the winning Lotto numbers?"

"Don't sass me, young man."

"Mom, you do know I'm thirty-two, right?" By the silence on the other end, he knew he had pushed her buttons. "Okay, then I'll ask you an easy one. What's the secret to a good life?"

"Unconditional love. Which, at the rate you're going, you'll never know."

His smile deepened. She'd hit part one on the head but was so wrong on the second half. "Then I have a great life, because I have you and you've loved me unconditionally even when others didn't."

"That's not enough. Someday I won't be around and then who will you have? Jason and Dave will always be there for you, but they're starting families of their own. Being alone is a lonely, sad way to live. It's not really living, it's existing, and don't tell me you date because you don't. Not really. You may go out once in a while, but when was the last time you went on a second date or a third? You need to get over Denise, honey. I know she was the love of your life, but that was five years ago. Or forget what happened and ask her for another chance."

He didn't want to talk about his ex-fiancée. Not now, not ever. And especially not with his mom or even his buds. "Who?" Hoping she'd get the hint. "I'm fine, Mom. When the time is right, I'll find someone. You don't have to worry about me."

"Yes, I do. It's in my job description. It doesn't matter how tall you are, how old you are; you'll always be my baby and I love you." He heard the love and concern in her voice and hated that he'd put the latter there.

"I know. How about I take my favorite girl to dinner on Sunday? Let me show you my appreciation and that I don't work too much." He'd already made the reservation. When Brody was growing up, his dad had never done anything special for his mom for Valentine's Day, unless you counted not using her as a punching bag that one day of the year.

"Can't. That's why I called." His mother hesitated. "I already have a date."

As a lawyer, he'd had very few things render him speechless. This news was in the top-ten category.

"Since when do you date, Mom?"

"Since a nice man asked me."

"Who is it? Where did you meet him? What does he do?" He'd have a friend run the guy's background. No way would he let his mom get hurt again. She was too trusting. Too tenderhearted, always looking for the good in people, and it nearly cost her her life.

"Baby, it's just dinner." After several long seconds of silence from Brody, she went on. "His name is Kevin Stewart. He's widowed, with two grown kids—Kelly and KJ—originally from Chicago and is a chiropractor. We met when he attended my cooking classes at the community center."

"How'd the wife die?" Brody scribbled the man's info on a notepad.

A deep sigh met his question. "Really, Brody . . ."

"Fine. Rain check, but I'm calling you at nine." He hung up and stared at the note. He was happy for his mom. She'd spent way too many years with the bastard known as his father, then several more learning to be her own person again. If anyone deserved to find love it was his mom. And, well, his two best friends. It seemed as if in the last year everyone Brody knew had been given a second chance. Except him. Not that he wanted the complication of a love life or cared.

His office door clicked open and his secretary, Angie, walked in with a stack of mail. "Did your mom tell you her new beau is taking her to the White Horse Tavern over in Newport Sunday? They want to see if the place is haunted, like the rumors say."

He took the bundle and set it on his desk, ignoring it. "Nope. We didn't get that far."

She cocked her hip and rested her hand. Great; he knew that pose and look. Time for round two of his weekly lecture.

"Probably because you were giving her a hard time, and don't try to deny it. She's right, you know. If you found a nice girl to settle down with, you wouldn't work so much."

"Were you listening in again, Angie? You know, you could have pulled up a chair, it would have been easier."

"Don't get fresh with me. There's not another administrative assistant in the state who'd put up with your moodiness and you know it. Besides, we had a little chat before I transferred her call. She's very excited about her date."

"It's Valentine's Day. No one should be alone." He thumbed through the correspondence, separating them into piles based on priority.

"Including you, Brody."

"What are you saying? Are you finally ready to ditch your husband for me? Thirty years is a long time to be with one person. We can sail around the world and see the Seven Wonders. Just say the word."

His secretary, who was around his mother's age and more like a second mom to him than an assistant on most days, turned several shades of red as she smacked him on the arm with her tablet.

"You're going to have to wait a bit longer. His insurance doesn't pay out the big bucks for a few more years. Until then, don't forget to call Mr. Padgett back about the case. He has some questions for you." She stopped as she headed toward the door. "Oh, almost forgot. You've got a new client showing up at six. I'm leaving now to prepare for my trip to Boston with the hubby, so don't forget to listen for the door. Name is Sanders but didn't want to discuss any details other than to say it was a consult."

"Thanks, Ang. Have a good time."

He knew she would too, for Angie was the type who never let life get her down, always found the positive side of everything, and was still madly in love with her husband after all these years. It probably didn't hurt that her husband worshipped her, treated her like a queen. Maybe this Kevin guy would be the one for his mom, the man to see the wonderful, loving woman who'd raised him, defended him, and made sure he and his two buddies stayed out of trouble. His mom was the sweetest woman he knew, and the fear of bringing any more pain into her life had kept him on the straight and narrow growing up. Not that it had stopped him from a few scrapes here and there.

Kind of hard to avoid with a friend like Dave.

Not that Brody or Jase were angels either. Not by a long shot, but at least the two of them knew when to keep their mouths shut.

Brody pulled up his e-mail and shot off a note to another friend who worked at the Bureau and could run a quick check on one Kevin Stewart for him. Trust in his mom's judgment had nothing to do with it. Some people were too important to take risks with. He'd do anything to keep his mom safe and happy.

The outer door clicked shut and heavy footsteps made their way to his office door. Must be his new client. He'd stood to meet him at the door when a familiar laugh had him dropping back in his seat. He sat back and waited.

"See, I told you he'd still be working." Dave "Fubar" Farber walked through the door first and plopped into the visitor chair across from him.

"And, as usual, you're not," Brody fired back. He turned to his other best friend, Jason "Cupid" Valentine. "What brings you two by?"

"Yeah, well, I bet when we deposit the final payment on the job we just completed you won't be complaining, Bro." Dave propped his foot up on the edge of the desk and dared Brody to complain.

Instead, Brody ignored him. "You finished the Downing job early?" he asked of Jason.

"What can I say? The stars were in alignment and Mr. and Mrs. Downing are very satisfied with their new kitchen and master suite, which means Monday we can contact Dr. Cherko to see if he wouldn't mind us starting early on his expansion." Jason sat on the edge of the low-rise bookcase next to the desk.

"You should take a long weekend and celebrate with your ladies." Brody glanced at his wristwatch, noting his new client was late.

"Cherry's got homework," Jason said.

"Work for Tawny," David added.

"Business has really picked up in the last six months. Looks like the work on the rec center paid off. You two ready to buy me out yet?"

"Never," both guys responded in unison.

"Cherry wants you to come over Sunday for a barbeque to celebrate finishing the job." Jason tapped his fingers in a steady rhythm against his legs as he looked out the window.

"Are you sure you deserve the nickname Cupid? You know Sunday is Valentine's Day, right? Plus, it's the middle of winter in New England. Your grill is three feet deep in snow." Brody shook his head in disbelief.

"Of course I know what day it is. The women have something planned. A surprise. And it includes you," Jason said.

"Don't look at me. You're the last person I want to spend the evening with," Dave groused.

Brody had a feeling he knew what the women were up to—a setup with one of their friends. Nice gesture. Not happening. "Tell them thanks, but I've got other plans."

"Breaking out the blow-up girlfriend again?" Dave blew him a kiss, smirking because he knew the desk kept Brody from pounding him. He'd always been like that.

Brody flipped his friend off and told him what he could do with his suggestion.

"I know you're not taking your mom out. She's got a real date."

"How do you know about it already?" Brody asked.

"Stopped by earlier to wish her a happy Valentine's and give her flowers and chocolate." Jason continued drumming his fingers against his thigh. A sure sign something was on his mind that bothered him.

"You always were a suck-up, Cupid."

"And you used to have a sense of humor. Want to tell us what really happened at my wedding? Because you've been a prick ever since."

"Nothing happened. Nothing important." Brody turned back to his computer, pulled up a client file, and glared at the screen. No way would either drop the subject, but they could tough it out. He wasn't talking.

"Told you." Dave jumped up out of the chair and headed for the door.

Jason didn't move for several long seconds. When he pushed away from the bookcase he wore an annoying half grin, like he knew Brody's secret.

"You hear that, Fubar?" Jason called after Dave. "Nothing important has knocked the mighty Brody Nichols off his game." Jason stopped long enough to get Brody's attention. "Lacrosse, tomorrow at noon. Prepare to have your ass handed to you."

Brody ignored the two of them as they left. He had more imperative things to focus on, like work. He also knew if he felt like talking about his feelings—which he didn't—the guys would be there for him. Shoving unwanted thoughts and memories away, he picked up the phone to call his client back to let him know the defendant settled out of court. At least Padgett and his wife would have a good weekend. The outside door opened again. Figuring the guys had forgotten to razz him about something, he held off hitting the last number.

"Go away. I'm working," he called out.

"Is that how you greet all of your appointments?"

His head jerked up, the receiver dropped back to the base, and for the second time that day, Brody Nichols had the surprise of his life. He looked at the woman standing in the open doorway and his gaze dropped to her stomach.

"Are you pregnant?" he asked.

Credit: Julia Gerace

Gail Chianese's love of reading began at the tender age of three, when she'd make her grandpa read *Fourteen Country Rabbits* over and over and over again (and correct him when he skipped parts). While she's branched out over the years by reading mystery, women's fiction, and urban fantasy, she always circles back to romance in the end. That's probably because she's married to her reallife hero. Her wonderful hubby has served in the US Navy for the past twentytwo years and he's done things he can't tell her about. But it doesn't stop her from being extremely proud of him and the sacrifices he makes for her, his family, and his country. He's also ubersupportive of her dreams and of their three children. Living in Mystic, CT and a member of Connecticut Romance Writers of America, Gail loves to hear from readers. Visit her online at GailChianese.com, follow her on Twitter @ Gail_Chianese, or send her an email at gail.chianese@yahoo.com.

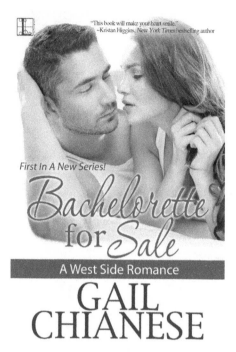

"This book will make your heart smile."
~Kristan Higgins, *New York Times* bestselling author

First In A New Series!

Bachelorette for Sale

A West Side Romance

GAIL CHIANESE

*This sparkling debut dives right in to everything funny,
flirty, and fiery about modern dating with the tale of a sexy
singles auction that comes with the prize of a lifetime...*

As far as Cherry Ryan is concerned, the bright lights of Hollywood
are nothing but glare after her heart is broken on a reality show
for millions to see. Instead she's throwing herself into fundraising
for the local community center that was a priceless lifeline to
her as a kid. But when a volunteer for the singles auction bails at
the last minute, Cherry finds herself on the block—and sold to
Jason Valentine, a handsome contractor with a gorgeous body—
and a really bad attitude about her days in the limelight...

Cherry soon finds that Jason's more than eye candy, and not
entirely sweet—especially his quest to win the bid for the center's
renovation. Mixing business with pleasure doesn't seem like
such a good idea—until Jason has a chance to reveal the big heart
beneath his surly exterior. Cherry's falling for him hard, but trust
isn't easy when you've been burned. To conquer her fears will
take a giant leap of faith—straight into the spotlight again...

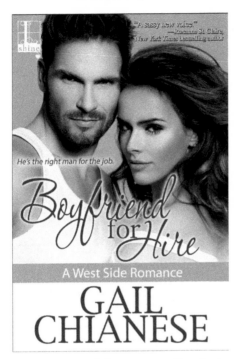

"A sassy new voice."
—Roxanne St. Claire,
New York Times bestselling author

He's the right man for the job.

Boyfriend for *Hire*

A West Side Romance

GAIL CHIANESE

**"Engaging and down-to-earth...features
characters readers can root for."**
--*Library Journal*

*In this sexy series, author Gail Chianese celebrates the
heart—and the heat—of modern dating. This time, a temporary
boyfriend may be the right man for a permanent position...*

The only girl in a family of three brothers, Tawny Torres
has had enough of waiting on men. She has her life and her
career all mapped out, and neither includes an apron, an iron,
or a husband—yet. But when a new job emphasizes a healthy
balance of work *and* play, she needs a guy to stand in as her love
interest at a company picnic. Gorgeous charmer David "King of
Pleasure" Farber fits the bill perfectly—so well that Tawny is
shocked to realize she's having a hard time letting him go...

David's a confirmed bachelor, but he can't get enough
of Tawny's firecracker combination of tough and tender.

Unfortunately, he's overloaded with work at his construction firm
and now definitely isn't the time for distraction—he struggles
enough with that already. Still, he can't ignore his feelings for
Tawny. He'll just have to convince her that he's more than a
boyfriend-for-hire. And she'll have to prove he
can trust her with his biggest secret...

CPSIA information can be obtained
at www.ICGtesting.com
Printed in the USA
FFHW020417190419
51869276-57272FF